Illustrated Children's FACTOpedia

over 550 Entries

Vikas Khatri

PUSTAK MAHAL®

J-3/16 , Daryaganj, New Delhi-110002
☎ 23276539, 23272783, 23272784 • *Fax:* 011-23260518
E-mail: info@pustakmahal.com • *Website:* www.pustakmahal.com

Sales Centre

- 10-B, Netaji Subhash Marg, Daryaganj, New Delhi-110002
  ☎ 23268292, 23268293, 23279900 • *Fax:* 011-23280567
  E-mail: rapidexdelhi@indiatimes.com
- 6686, Khari Baoli, Delhi-110006
  ☎ 23944314, 23911979

Branches

Bengaluru: ☎ 080-22234025 • *Telefax:* 080-22240209
E-mail: pustak@airtelmail.in • pustak@sancharnet.in
Mumbai: ☎ 022-22010941, 022-22053387
E-mail: rapidex@bom5.vsnl.net.in
Patna: ☎ 0612-3294193 • *Telefax:* 0612-2302719
E-mail: rapidexptn@rediffmail.com
Hyderabad: *Telefax:* 040-24737290
E-mail: pustakmahalhyd@yahoo.co.in

ISBN 978-81-223-1264-5

Edition: 2012

Printed at : **Unique Colour Cartoon, Delhi**

INTRODUCTION

We were just having a cosy chat, a few writers and an artist. We had talked for a while about important things, when, suddenly, there came a knock at the door.

'Come in!' we cried.

A boy's head appeared in the doorway. Two large eyes looked at us inquisitively. Behind the boy stood a girl.

'Good morning, gentlemen,' said the boy.

'Good morning,' we replied.

'The fact is,' he began, 'my father has a 12-volume encyclopedia. And my elder brother had a big encyclopedia for young people given to him for his birthday. So we want to say that something's wrong.'

'What's wrong?' we asked in surprise.

'There isn't an encyclopedia for us, for children:

'Aha!'

'Yes. So we have come to ask if you would kindly make us one.'

'An encyclopedia for children?'

'That's right — and full of stories.'

'And lots of coloured pictures,' said our artist quickly.

'Yes, yes, lots of coloured pictures.'

We talked to each other about the idea. The children were quite right. Why shouldn't they have an encyclopedia?

'All right,' we said, 'We shall have an encyclopedia printed for you. But first we must write it and put pictures in it.'

‘Splendid then the first thing you must do is to come along with us.’

‘With you? Why? Where are we going?’

‘To see our friends. They will tell you everything that must go into the encyclopedia.’

‘Oh yes. Of course.’

So we went with them and talked to their friends,

‘What shall we tell you about in our new encyclopedia?’ we asked.

‘All about railways and cars.’

‘About planes and ships.’

‘And how to make things, and all about sport.’

‘And all about animals.’

We wrote down everything that the children said. And we wrote down lots of the words we wanted to explain in the encyclopedia. Of course, not words which every child understands like ‘sleeve’, ‘ball’, ‘nose’. Everyone would laugh at that. We wrote down words that our young friends knew little about, though they probably heard them spoken every day.

At last our children’s encyclopaedia was ready. We were delighted that it had all turned out so well. We should like to thank everyone who has helped us make this fine book, especially the many children who gave their advice. And we should like to thank their teachers, too.

A

Accordion. It is a large musical instrument. It has keys, just like a piano.

Acrobats. Have you ever been to a big circus? Then you must have admired the acrobats who fly high above the arena from one trapeze to another. Perhaps you saw other acrobats, performing on a tightrope or doing somersaults on the ground. It took them many years of practice to become so skilful.

Adam and Eve. At the beginning of the Bible it is written how God created heaven and earth and how He made the first man and woman. God called the man Adam and the woman Eve. The Bible says God created Adam from earth and Eve from one of Adam's ribs. Some people think everyone is descended from Adam and Eve.

Adder. Whenever you go picking blackberries on open commons you should take care not to step on an adder basking in the sun. Sandy heaths and commons are adders' favourite homes.

You can easily recognise one of these snakes by the dark zig-zag pattern which runs down its back. Adders are really useful animals because they catch many mice. But if you get bitten by an adder, poison from its fangs will flow into your bloodstream. What should you do if that happened? Move as little as possible and tie a bandage tightly just above the wound. Then get someone to bring a doctor as soon as possible.

Advertising. Mr. Sharma sat in front of his television set. A picture of a girl appeared on the screen. She was drinking a glass of milk. Then some words appeared. Mr. Sharma read: 'Drink milk! Milk is nourishing: it does you good.'

Then Mr. Sharma went out for a walk. Soon he saw a large poster. When Mr. Sharma got closer to the poster he saw that it showed a picture of a woman. She was holding a bottle of milk. Under the picture was written: 'Every housewife buys milk because she knows that milk is nourishing. It does you good!'

Mr. Sharma went home and listened to the radio. A speaker said: 'Dear listeners, you should drink at least a pint of milk a day. Milk is nourishing! It does you good!'

Then Mr. Sharma said to his wife, 'We really ought to buy more milk. Milk does you good.' And all over the country people were saying and thinking the same. And they bought more milk.

They bought more milk because they had seen and heard advertisements telling them to buy more milk. The advertisements were made by the people who sold milk. They hoped to make more money by selling more milk. People advertise all sorts of things to help sell them.

Air. Something we all need, to breathe. Air is a mixture of many gases. Most of the air around us is made up of colourless, odourless oxygen and nitrogen. Roughly one-fifth of the air is oxygen and four-fifths nitrogen. Warm air is lighter than cold. In high mountains the air is much cleaner and thinner than on lower ground. Clean air acts as a medicine for sick people. When air contains dust, smoke, exhaust gases or the gases of used air which you breathe out, it is not healthy. That's why people air their rooms and why you should often get fresh air yourself.

Alaska. *'A Paradise in the North,'* a writer once called his book about this mountainous land in the far north-west of North America. Alaska is still the home of Indians and Eskimos. They keep and hunt furred animals whose skins make warm winter coats. Vast pine forests cover part of this cold country where people mine gold, silver and lead.

Alcohol. Gin, whisky, beer and wine contain alcohol. Many grown-up people enjoy these drinks and every year people spend whole fortunes just to buy them. They are harmless to grown-ups if they don't drink very much.

But alcohol can be very harmful if people take too much of it. You often read in the papers that a man drunk on alcoholic liquor had an accident or killed someone else by careless driving. Alcohol makes people feel merry but it can make them stupid as well.

But alcohol can be useful. You can dissolve varnish with its aid and people use it as fuel for some sorts of engine. Doctors also use alcohol to treat wounds.

Alder. Beside the banks of streams and on marshy ground you often see alder trees growing. In autumn their leaves fall while they are still green. When they grow beside a stream, alder roots are often under water. But their reddish wood is resistant to the effects of water; it does not rot them. People make toys, cigar-boxes and many other things from alder wood.

Allah. The Mohammedans call their god by this name. Once it was their battle cry.

All Saints' Day. On the first of November Roman Catholics celebrate 'All Saints' Day'. The reason for this is that there are many saints without their own holy day.

Alps. If you look at a physical map of Europe you will see the mountains coloured red-brown. Europe's highest mountains are the Alps. They stretch from south-east France (near the Mediterranean Sea) as far as the low-lying plains of Hungary. These alpine mountains have jagged peaks. Glaciers (rivers of ice) fill the highest valleys, and on lower slopes dark mountain lakes nestle in the hollows. Dense forests grow on the lower slopes except where bright-green meadows cling to the rocks. Waterfalls tumble down many of the steepest valleys. The highest of the Alps is Mont Blanc in France. It is over 15,700 feet high. Other well-known mountains include the Matterhorn and Monte Rosa. Many roads cross the Alps. People have even tunnelled railways through some mountains. From all over the world tourists come to relax in the clear mountain air, to go sightseeing, to climb or to go ski-ing.

Alpine animals. If you climb high enough up in the Alps you will reach the tree line. Above it, no trees grow, for the weather there is too cold and windy.

Take a look at a distant mountain slope through your magnifying field-glasses. Very high on a mountain meadow you can see the shy little marmots sitting in front of their holes. If you are lucky, you may glimpse a golden eagle, the monarch of the skies, gliding in a wide circle around a mountain peak. Some alpine choughs come flying from a nearby rock face. They have yellow beaks and bright-red legs. High above, a chamois leaps over great masses of rock to reach the mountain summit. If you went mountaineering early in the year you would see mountain hares and ptarmigan (birds like big partridges) both in their white winter camouflage. As you walk down through the pine forest a capercaillie, a bird nearly as big as a turkey, may startle you suddenly by flying noisily away. With luck you may also see a rare ibex, and a great griffon vulture soaring overhead.

Alpine plants. People have written many songs about the Alps, especially about the flowers that grow high up among these mountains. The people who live among the Alps often sing these songs. Alpine flowers are often beautifully coloured like Gentian, Alpine carnation, Auricula, Edelweiss, Mountain rhododendron. Many of them grow on almost bare rock. When you climb up among the mountains you should only pick one of each kind of flower. For many alpine flowers are protected just like many of our birds and animals. If everyone picked a lot there would soon be none left.

Aluminium. Take a look at the pots and pans which your mother uses to cook your food. Many of them have a bright, silvery shine. They are probably made of aluminium. This is a very light metal, three times as light as iron. Aluminium is an important building material. People also use it a lot for building strong, lightweight aeroplanes.

Roald **Amundsen.** 'Do put that book away now,' said Amundsen's mother to her 15-year-old son who had been reading a travel adventure story for hours on end.

'Mother,' said Roald, 'wouldn't it be splendid to explore the land of eternal ice!'

It was Roald's dearest wish to become a famous explorer; but his mother did not like the idea.

'You will become a doctor,' she said.

But after she died, Amundsen gave up his studies and went to sea as a simple sailor, in a sailing ship which penetrated icy waters. Roald became a stearsman first and in 1900 became a sea captain. When he had been a boy, Roald took part in many sports, especially ski-ing. And he had studied navigation very carefully. For 22 years Roald Amundsen had prepared himself for his life's great achievement – to conquer the North Pole. Then the shattering news reached him that the American Peary had beaten him to it.

'This was a heavy blow,' wrote Amundsen in his diary. At once he decided to conquer the South Pole which no one had yet reached. But the Norwegian Amundsen had a rival – the British explorer Scott. The two raced each other for a year and a half; for in those days Antarctic travel was a slow affair. Amundsen had more luck than Scott. With only a month's lead he reached the South Pole on 15th December 1911.

In May 1926 Amundsen reached the North Pole too – flying with the Italian explorer Nobile. In 1928 he heard that Nobile had had an accident in the Arctic. Amundsen took off to find him. But Amundsen's plane crashed in the sea and the great explorer lost his life.

Anchor. When a ship is in harbour, or stops off-shore on a harbourless coast, the sailors drop a heavy iron anchor into the water. The

anchor is attached to the ship by a hawser (a thick rope). The anchor's pointed ends dig into the soft sea bed and thus keep the ship from drifting with wind or current. We say that a ship which has dropped anchor is 'at anchor'. When her sailors raise the anchor we say the ship is 'weighing anchor'.

Hans Christian **Andersen.** Who knows the story of the poor tin soldier and the adventures he had in a paper boat? Who has read about the princess who was so sensitive that she could feel a pea through 20 soft eiderdowns? Have you read the story about the ugly duckling that became a beautiful swan; and the story of the red shoes that always wanted to dance? These, and many other tales, were written for you and all children by the Danish poet Hans Andersen. Andersen came from a very poor family. His father was a shoe-mender. Hans Andersen was born in 1805. He died in 1875.

Anemone. The anemone is a spring flower. There are several kinds of anemone; one of the best-known is the wood anemone which grows wild.

Antarctic. The Antarctic Continent is the great frozen mass of land that lies around the South Pole.

Antennae. Perhaps you have seen cockchafers – big insects with long 'feelers'. These feelers are really called antennae. The erect steel rods which you often see swishing about on the outside of cars are also called antennae, or aerials. They 'catch' radio waves and conduct them to a radio inside the car. Radio waves themselves are first 'thrown' into the air by giant antennae, the high steel towers of a radio station. But a better name for these towers is transmitting masts.

Antelope. The swift–footed antelopes and gazelles that live on the great dry pasture lands of Arabia and Africa are relations of the deer that browse in our zoos. Few beasts of prey can outrun the swiftest gazelle.

Anthracite. Anthracite is a special kind of coal. You can recognise it by the way it shines. Anthracite is very good for burning in stoves. But its nice shining coals are expensive.

Ants. Have you ever seen an ants' highway? Ant highways can be as busy as a human city street. Worker ants hurry along with dry pine needles or tiny bits of twig. More ants will be helping one another to move a bigger twig.

Let's look closer. Let's go along with these worker ants and see where they lead. Where are they all travelling? They are moving several yards towards a small hillock about a yard high. That's where they live. How busy it all is. The ants look after their huge nest very well and keep it spotlessly clean. Inside the nest lives a queen ant. She lays many thousands of eggs which workers carry to the many rooms inside the nest. During summer these eggs hatch into larvae which in a few weeks become fully adult ants.

On a fine summer day you will sometimes see hundreds of winged ants streaming from a nest and flying away. Sometimes they meet swarms from other nests, until they join in one huge swarm that darkens the sky, like a cloud of smoke. These ants help to start new nests.

In winter, ants stay shut up inside their nests. Some of them survive the whole winter without food. Then they help to build up their city-home. Often half a million ants may live in one nest. Ants can sting you but they are useful animals – each day a nest of ants may eat 10,000 harmful insects.

Apostle. Jesus Christ always had a number of close followers around Him. From these He chose 12 men whom He called His apostles. They were to preach the doctrine which Jesus taught everywhere and to carry on His work of saving people's souls. The Greek word 'apostle' means messenger.

Apricot. The apricot is a fruit which almost all of us love to eat. Inside its soft yellow skin is the fleshy golden fruit; inside the fruit is a big seed stone.

Aquarium. 'You can have a small aquarium. I'll pay for everything you need to put in it.' This was Uncle Gupta's present to his nephew Harish – a birthday present. You can imagine Harish's delight. He had wanted an aquarium more than anything else. Harish had already learned all about aquaria from his pet shop.

First he bought a glass tank about two feet long, a foot wide and a foot deep. Then he put it on a table near his bedroom window but so that the sun would not shine directly on it. Then Harish began to make ready a home for the fishes he would buy. First he put a layer of sand on the bottom, deeper at the back than at the front. Next, Harish bought some water plants, grass-like vallisneria and lacy water milfoil. He planted them in little clumps towards the back of his tank, leaving plenty of room for the plants to grow and the fishes to swim between them. He left the front of his tank unplanted so that he could easily see his swimming friends. Now he put a layer of coarse sand on top of the fine sand, washing it first to get rid of any particles of mud that might cloud the water.

When Harish filled the tank with water he did not want to stir the sand about so he laid a sheet of newspaper on the sand and poured his water on that. Then he carefully took away the paper. Harish had to leave his aquarium empty for a couple of days. The plants had to get properly rooted and the water had to become quite clear. Harish's fishes would not want to swim in dirty water and he was patient enough to wait a while.

At last the great day came. Harish went to his pet shop and bought some fishes and some fish food. Carefully he put the fish into the aquarium. When they had settled down he gave them their first meal. Harish did not give them too much. He knew that uneaten food rots and makes water cloudy, which is bad for fishes' health. Harish wanted to show his aquarium to his friends with pride.

From time to time he cleaned the aquarium with the help of a glass siphon. And two good friends helped Harish to keep the glass sides clean. Do you know who these friends were? They were two ramshorn snails.

Arabs. These people will be familiar to you from the tales of *The Thousand and One Nights.* Their homeland is a peninsula between the Red Sea and the Persian Gulf, but they also live in North Africa and Asia. In cities many work as merchants or tradesmen.

The Arabs who live in villages are farmers and are called 'fellahs'. But most of the Arabs are cattle-farmers who travel with their herds from one grassland to another. These are the Bedouins. They wear long white garments to protect themselves against the hot sun, the cold nights and the sand-storms. The head of a Bedouin tribe is called a 'sheik'. Most Arabs are Mohammedans. They believe that Mohammed was the chief prophet of God whom they call 'Allah'. In Arabia there is a town called Mecca which is a holy city to the Mohammedan Arabs.

Architect. If you want to have a house specially built, you go to an architect. He will draw a plan for your house. An interior designer is a person who plans the inside layout of a house. Landscape gardeners lay out gardens and parks.

Arctic. The Arctic is the region around the North Pole. The North Pole is in the middle of a sea that is forever frozen.

Ark. The Bible tells how God once sent a flood to devastate the earth. But first God told Noah to build an ark, a large kind of ship. Noah took one pair of each kind of animal on board. Then he and his family lived safely on the ark while floods drowned everyone else. When the waters went down, Noah's ark stood high and dry on a mountain.

Aroma. Aunty says, 'What a nice aroma this curry has.' When she says this she simply means that the curry has a nice smell.

Asbestos. Father has bought a new fire-guard. But it is not made of a thin sheet of iron like the old one. It is asbestos, a material made of fibres which don't let heat through. Now the furniture that stands near the fire is properly protected against its heat. When Mother has been ironing, she puts her hot iron on a small sheet of asbestos. Firemen often wear asbestos suits. Then they can even walk quickly through a blazing fire and be unharmed.

Atoms. Nowadays you often read about atomic power and atom bombs. But what is an atom? All substances and gases, iron and oxygen – even you and I – are made up of atoms. They are tiny particles that you cannot even see with the strongest microscope. When scientists first discovered atoms they thought that these tiny particles could not be split up into even smaller ones. But 50 years ago scientists discovered that even a minute atom consists of still smaller parts a nucleus and tiny particles that circle around it.

Today scientists can even split this nucleus. When they do this, enormous powers are released. When they are released inside an atomic bomb these powers become the fear of mankind. But scientists have succeeded in using atomic power for peaceful purposes. Soon, perhaps, atomic power will make life more pleasant for everyone. Atomic energy might drive trains, planes, ships and cars. Atomic energy could provide heat and light for factories and great cities.

Automatic machine. An automatic machine is a machine which has to have a little push and then does the rest of the work itself. It is a kind of 'magic box'. You put a coin in the slot at the top, and a bar of chocolate appears at the bottom.

In factories one automatic machine can often do the same amount of work as many people. Some automatic sales machines have a record inside them. It is a record of a voice which says, 'Thank you very much. Please buy here again.'

Axe. Hand tool used for chopping, splitting, chipping, and piercing.

Stone Age hand axes originated in simple stone implements that acquired wooden hafts, or handles, about 30,000 BC. Copper-bladed axes appeared in Egypt about 4000 BC and were followed by axes with blades of bronze and eventually iron. The development of the iron-bladed felling axe in the Middle Ages made possible the vast forest clearances of Europe, North and South America, and elsewhere. Though the axe has lost much of its historic role to powered saws and other machinery, it remains a widely used tool with many uses.

B

Johann Sebastian **Bach**. He is one of the most famous of all composers. He lived from 1685 to 1750. He was very good at playing the organ and harpsichord too. For many years he was leader of the church choir in the famous church of the St. Thomas at Leipzig in Germany. Bach wrote many pieces of music specially for choirs, and for organs and harpsichords. He also wrote simple pieces of music for children.

Bacilli. These are the cause of many illnesses, especially the infectious ones. Bacilli are rod shaped bacteria. You cannot see them with your naked eye, but you can see them through a powerful microscope.

Bacteria. Don't go near anyone who has whooping cough! Infectious illnesses like that can be carried from one person to another by very small living plants and animals called bacteria and viruses.

You cannot see bacteria with your naked eye. If you put 25,000 bacteria in a row they would only form a line one inch long. Where do these tiny living things thrive? They live in dusty air, on dirty hands and on dirty floors. How easy it is for them to get from dirty hands into your mouth. Don't ever forget to wash your hands before you eat a meal.

Luckily not all bacteria are dangerous. Some are very useful to us. Without these bacteria we could never turn milk into cheese, or make vinegar from wine.

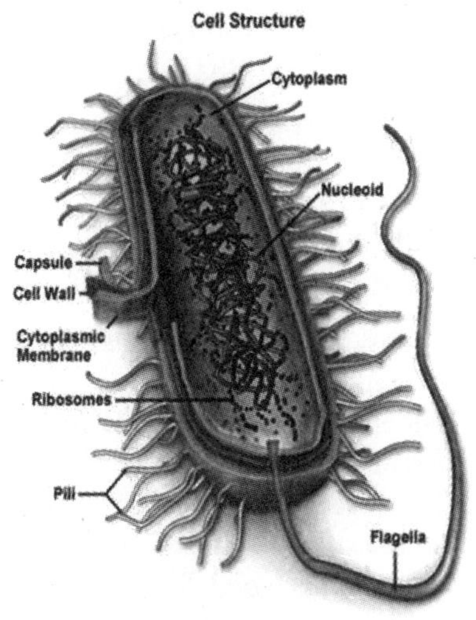

Badger. 'Master Grumblebeard'– that's the badger's name in one fairy tale. Real badgers live in big holes that they have dug for themselves. The long nails on their claws make fine digging tools. Badgers usually leave their holes as evening draws on. They spend the night looking for food. When snow covers the ground in winter, badgers sleep cosily in their underground homes. People use badgers' hair in European countries for making shaving brushes.

Bagpipes. Ancient musical instrument of Scotland. When someone plays the bagpipes he blows into a leather bag. He presses this bag under his arm, and squeezes all the air out through three pipes. Two pipes make a steady droning sound. The bagpiper plays a tune on the other pipe by covering up different holes along it with his fingers.

Ball games. Ball games are games that are usually played with the help of ball. Football, Basketball, Table tennis, Lawn tennis, Hand-ball, Volley-ball, etc.

Balloons. Wood is lighter than water. When you hold a piece of wood under water it rises to the surface again as soon as you release it. Balloons filled with lighter-than-air gas float upwards in the sky just as the wood floats upwards in water. If you don't hold your balloon string tightly in your hand you may lose your balloon for ever.

The people who forecast weather also fly balloons. Attached to their balloons are several measuring instruments. These instruments record weather high up in the atmosphere.

The first person to fly did so by means of a balloon. If you want to know more about that look up '**Flying**'.

Bamboo. Have you ever seen a meadow where the grass grew over two feet high? Maybe you think that this is impossible. But it is possible. For there are places where bamboo grass grows to this height. Bamboo grows in the hot climate of parts of America, Africa and Asia. There, bamboo thickets become as dense as forests. Bamboo grows very fast. Though woody bamboo stems are light they are very strong. People use them to build rafts, huts and bridges. With thinner bamboo stems people make fishing rods, alpenstocks, and furniture.

Bananas. 'I think I'll buy apples instead,' says Mother. 'Bananas are too expensive in the shops this week.' Bananas often do cost more than apples because they have to be brought from far across the sea in the specially cooled holds of ships. Bananas grow best in the hot lands of Central and South America and Africa. There, they hang in large bunches from tall plants which have great broad leaves. People pick bananas and send them to Europe while they are still green. Then the bananas are stored in warehouses where they turn yellow.

Africans often make a sort of flour from dried bananas. And they eat young banana shoots as vegetables. People make use of big banana leaves to thatch the roofs of their homes. Even the plant fibres come in useful for making string.

Barber. An old word which means the same as 'hair dresser'. Barbers used to prepare their shaving soap in a flat metal saucer. They would hang one of these saucers above the door of their shop as an advertisement.

Barometer. 'Let's hope that we shall have fine weather for our trip,' said Father.

'The barometer has risen, so that means it should be fine,' said Ritu.

Is this magic? No, it is very simple, really. When it is going to rain the air pressure gets low. When it is going to be fine the air pressure rises. We don't notice these slight changes in pressure but a barometer does. Of course the barometer can't be always right. Sometimes the pressure gets low and we sit indoors expecting it to rain, afraid to go out and have a picnic. Then perhaps the sky grows overcast but nothing else happens. Does this mean our barometer is wrong? No. The indicator on a barometer can only show the pressure of the air, it can't really make magic weather forecasts.

Barrel. A cylindrical container with a flat top and bottom, used to store liquids.

Bat. You may sometimes see a bat flying about on a warm summer evening. He is on the hunt for small insects, flies, beetles and moths. The bat's wings are really thin skin stretched between its body and limbs and between its very long fingers. Its skin wings make a bat one of the world's cleverest flying animals. In the coldest weather bats go to sleep in a hollow tree or an attic or a cave. They hang with their head downwards, supported by their feet. Let's creep away and leave them to their winter sleep.

Bathing. Bathing is the activity of swimming in an area of open water, for example, the sea or a river.

Battery. Have you ever taken the battery of an electric torch to pieces? It is made up of several parts. These separate parts – there are usually three of them – are called elements. Each element creates a weak electric current. Together, the three elements are strong enough to make a little bulb glow brightly.

Bears. Have you ever seen a brown bear? This thick-set animal, covered with dark-brown fur, is not at all as sweet as he looks. And he is quicker moving and more agil than you might guess. He can climb very well. For an animal which lives in woods this can be very important.

Baby bears are delightful, woolly little creatures. They are born in midwinter. When summer comes, their mother teaches them how to find food for themselves. Of course they must learn to climb trees too.

When the young bears are a couple of years old their mother does not look after them any more. But the young bears may go on wandering about together for a while. At last they separate and each goes off alone to explore the forests. Brown bears were plentiful in India but now there are very few left. But there are many brown bears in the great pine forests of Russia. In the Rocky Mountains of North America lives a bigger cousin of the brown bear. This is the great, grey, grizzly bear. Farther north, among the snowy arctic wastes, live white-coated polar bears.

Beasts of prey. Cats, dogs, hyenas, lions, tigers, bears and even seals are in a sense all beasts of prey. They all have sharp teeth to help them get their food – and their food is other animals.

Beavers. The beavers lives mostly in North America, though there are still a few in parts of Europe, and you can usually see one at the zoo. Beavers have a wide, flat tail and webbed feet which help them swim about in the streams and lakes that are their homes. In Canadian forests, beavers build themselves a kind of castle in the water, several feet high. Beavers use these buildings as food stores and as homes. The entrance to their castle is hidden under water. Beavers ensure this by building reed, mud and stick dams across their stream to make it deeper. A beaver's strong teeth can cut through a three-inch-thick willow tree in five minutes! Beavers eat bark, leaves and young shoots. People turn their fur into fur coats.

Bed. Piece of furniture on which a person may recline or sleep.

Beds of simple construction appear in medieval manuscripts, as do more decorative beds with carving and inlay, embroidered coverlets, and elaborate hangings. The canopy, or tester, was introduced in the 15th century. In the 1820s the development of coiled springs fitted into mattresses revolutionized the bed. In the Middle East beds consisted of rugs piled up on the floor. In China raised and canopied beds were used 2,000 years ago. The traditional Japanese bed (futon) consists of quilted padding and a coverlet arranged on the floor.

Beech tree. Take a walk through a beech-wood. Look how the smooth, grey tree trunks rise straight up into the sky. The ground beneath them is covered with beech-mast, the fruit husks of the beech trees. People use beech-mast to make an oil. In past centuries people gave beech-mast to their pigs to eat. Beech-wood is very hard and is used for making furniture, vats and railway sleepers.

Bees. Let's pay a visit to a bee-keeper. He is waiting for us beside his beehives. Small yellow and blue openings in them help every bee to find the way back to its own hive. Come along, let's take a look inside a hive with the bee-keeper.

Through the glass window let into the side of the hive we can clearly see the big drones, with their large heads. These drones do not work at all. You can recognise the queen at once by her long body. Some worker bees are flying in and out, looking for honey. The young worker bees are climbing about on the honeycombs. These 'housekeeper' workers are cleaning the hive, collecting up pollen and honey, or keeping guard at the entrance.

In some cells of the honeycomb you can see the eggs. In other cells there are young white grubs the bee larvae. They hatch from the eggs a few days after the queen has laid them. Many cells are closed up with a lid of wax. Inside these closed cells are larvae which have turned into pupae. After three weeks in their wax prison, the pupae come out – as fully formed bees, The young bees break open the wax lids and crawl out unaided. In the specially large, acorn-shaped cells the future queen bees are growing up. Worker bees have fed them with special foods.

Let's have another look outside, with the bee-keeper. Great activity is going on all the time. The worker bees never seem to stop bringing in honey and pollen. They must make sure that there is always enough in store, for bees must live on honey during the cold winter months.

The bee-keeper will tell us how bees move house. Did you know they did that? One fine day in midsummer, a queen bee leaves her hive at about noon. The hive has become too small for its growing family. A long string of worker bees follows the queen as she flies away. But the bee-keeper is always on the watch. Wearing a protective mask, he catches the swarm of bees and puts them in an empty hive. This will become their new home.

A few weeks later begins the battle against the drones. The workers drive all the drones away from their hive, for now they only eat up valuable food without gathering any themselves. Workers even kill some of the drones. In a single year our bee-keeper collects 20-30 pounds of honey from his bees! Bees also supply him with wax. And in their flights they carry pollen from flower to flower. This helps the flowers to turn into fruits, so we have good reason to thank the bees. There are many hundred kinds of bee. Most of them are wild. The smallest bee of all lives in the Far East, in Indonesia. Its hives are only as big as a man's hand; the cells of its honeycomb are each the size of a pinhead.

Beethoven. Ludwig van Beethoven was a famous composer. He was born in 1770 at Bonn in Germany. When Beethoven was only a six-year-old boy he played in concerts as a piano soloist. He wrote his first compositions when he was 11 years old. In 1792 he went to Vienna in Austria. There he wrote many famous pieces of music, including the splendid opera *Fidelio.*

When Beethoven was only 30, something began to go wrong with his hearing. In time he became quite deaf. He could not hear his own music or anybody else's. So Beethoven became a lonely man. But he went on composing fine music. Somewhere in the world someone plays his music every day. Beethoven died in 1827 at Vienna.

Beetle. Scientists have found that there are 300,000 different kinds of beetle! Beetles belong to the huge insect family. There are running beetles, swimming and diving beetles, carrion beetles, snapping beetles, long-nosed beetles and many others. Most of them have wings and can fly.

Bellows. A pair of bellows makes the smithy fire burn more brightly. Bellows produce the stream of air which blows through organ pipes and helps them to make music. Once, all organ bellows had to be worked by hand. Nowadays, electric machinery can make them work.

Benjamin. 'I have got a big brother and a little sister,' said Vinisha. 'My sister is only four years old. She is our Benjamin.'

Vinisha meant that her sister was the youngest of the three. For in the Bible story about Jacob, Benjamin was his youngest son.

Berries. In the summer and autumn months, many kinds of juicy berries get ripe. There are black and red currants, gooseberries and bilberries. Inside each berry are many seeds. Every single blackberry and strawberry is really many separate berry fruits joined together. Thus plant experts say that these fruits do not belong to the same family as the true berries. But plant experts say that oranges, tomatoes, cucumbers, melons and the huge pumpkins do belong to the berry family. Who would have thought it?

Bethlehem. It is the birthplace of Jesus Christ. It is a town in Israel. About 1600 years ago someone built a church in Bethlehem, on the spot where it was thought Jesus was born. That church still stands.

Bible. It is a book of holy writings. The Old Testament tells us the history of the Jewish people before Jesus was born. The New Testament tells us about the life of Jesus Christ and the work of His apostles after Jesus had died on the Cross.

Bicycle. Everyone knows what a bicycle is. But have a close look at the picture. Do you know all the parts of a bicycle? You can travel far on a bicycle; some people go for long cycling holidays, and even ride through several countries. Many modern bicycles have a three-speed gear. This makes it much easier to cycle up a steep hill or against the wind. Every cycle must have good brakes. When you cycle in the dark, your front and rear lights must shine brightly. How funny the bicycles of long ago looked! Do you think you could have ridden them?

Birch. The birch is a woodland tree with lacy twigs and delicate, light-green leaves. Its bark is silvery white and black. You can easily peel off strips of its white outer skin. In spring, when the first young leaves appear, some people make cuts in a birch trunk. Out runs a sugary liquid. Some people use this as a medicine. Cabinet makers often use birch wood for making furniture.

Birds. What a lot of birds there are! Chickens have blunt strong claws which help them scratch in soil for food. Chickens can just lift themselves off the ground with their wings. They can't fly properly. But swallows are birds that can fly very fast through the air. As they fly, their beaks are snapping at tiny insects. The great ostrich can run as fast as a racehorse through the African veldt. Yet its wings are stubby. It can't fly at all. High above the ostrich circle the birds of prey whose sharp eyes help them to see food many miles away.

All these birds are very different from each other, yet all have something in common. All birds have feathers and a horny beak. Beaks are very different in shape. The shape of a bird's beak may tell you if it eats seeds, insects and caterpillars, or if it is a bird of prey. All birds lay eggs with a hard shell. Most birds hatch their eggs by the warmth of their body. Many of the birds we see do not go to warmer countries in winter, but stay with us. But migratory birds fly to the warm south when days grow short and cold.

Birds of Paradise. You would be astonished by these wonderfully coloured birds if you could see them. But they live in the dense jungles of New Guinea, many thousand miles away. There, the male birds do a strange dance and unfold their immensely long feathers, to show off. They hope that the female birds of paradise will admire them.

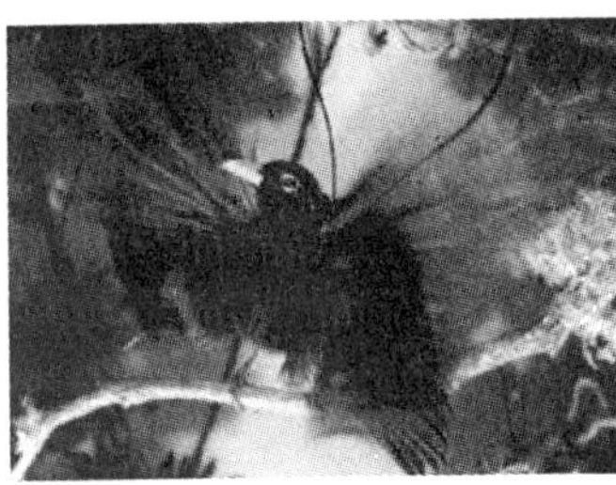

Black bird. At the very beginning of spring you will hear the blackbird singing his lovely song from morning to evening. But only the male birds sing. You can easily recognise a male blackbird by its glossy black feathers and bright yellow beak. The female blackbird is dusky brown and does not have a bright yellow beak.

Blood-poisoning. People often get blood-poisoning after an injury. If you cut your finger, tiny living things called bacteria may get into your blood. In your blood are millions of white blood cells. They swarm around the bacteria and eat them up. Their job is to get rid of all harmful things which enter your body. If they succeed, your wound should heal up quickly. But the white blood cells are not always successful. Sometimes bacteria go on infecting your wound. Then you may get blood-poisoning. Then your parents would have to call the doctor. So if you should cut yourself, try to keep the cut clean, and get someone to bind it up.

Blossom. You can sometimes hear the buzzing of hundreds of bees among the branches of a flowering tree. They are collecting nectar, the sweet juice which lies inside each blossom. At the same time their legs are dusty with pollen brought from another flowering plant. This is terribly important for the flowering tree. If the pollen from one flower falls on a special part of another, it makes that flower begin to turn into a fruit. Inside the fruit is its seed, and from that seed a new plant may spring up.

Boats. Types and construction of any small, waterborne vessel that displaces and excludes the water surrounding it. Traditionally, boats were distinguished from ships by size—any vessel small enough to be carried aboard a ship was considered a boat. Today, the boundary between boats and ships is no longer defined with precision. Some larger vessels are called boats, although they are longer than some ships.

Body. Your body and how to look after it. Can you see Rohit? He is watching while Mother puts his little brother in the bath. 'That's funny,' he says. 'When you put little Dinesh in the bath he stops crying. Why's that?'

'It's because he likes being bathed,' says Mother. 'He isn't afraid of water, like you.' Mother soaps the little boy and washes him with a sponge. Dinesh laughs for joy and kicks his legs. Then Mother puts Dinesh on the bath towel and dries him. She puts some talcum powder on his skin, especially upon his armpits and in the hollows of his thighs.

'What a lot of time you spend on such a little child,' says Rohit contemptuously.

'It is worth while spending some time taking care of your body,' says Mother. 'There's a proverb which says "good health is one-half cleanliness"'

'What has being clean got to do with being well?' asks Rohit.

'A great deal,' says his mother.

Yes, Rohit, your mother is right. Good health is one-half cleanliness, and we'll tell you why. In your skin there are countless tiny openings called pores. Through these pores perspiration escapes. If the pores are blocked up by dirt you may get rashes and very bad illnesses because poisonous matter cannot escape in perspiration and stays in your body. So you should wash your body once a day, even when it doesn't look dirty. Another reason for this is that dangerous disease germs can collect on your skin. You should clean your finger nails with a nail-brush too.

'You don't really want to be ill, do you, Rohit?' asks his mother. 'And you don't like having horrible toothache? I know you don't like going to the dentist. You can help to keep away from him by cleaning your teeth regularly every morning and night.

'There's dust and dirt everywhere in the air. If you blow your nose you often see black specks in your handkerchief. They are the dust that has got into your nose when you breathe. So you should always try to breathe through your nose. It stops dust getting down your throat. If you breathe through your mouth you may get soot and dust in your lungs.

'When you eat fruit you should wash it first. Remember, Rohit, that fresh fruit before you eat a meal is very good for your digestion. And another rule – properly chewed food is already half digested. Saliva in your mouth also helps to break down food so that your stomach juices can turn it into nourishment that you can use.

'You don't really think that looking after your body is a waste of time, do you, Rohit? No one need feel silly about looking after himself properly. It's the sensible people who look after themselves, and the silly ones who don't. There are lots of sensible ways you can protect yourself against illnesses – cold, for example. Coughing and head-colds are passed on by disease germs. Always take care that other people don't cough or sneeze in your face. And when you cough or sneeze, put your hand or your handkerchief in front of your mouth or nose.

Some boys are proud of a grazed knee. But what happens if dirt gets into their wound? They might easily get blood poisoning from it. So everybody should learn how to bandage up an injury, and how to give first aid, and, first of all, how to keep fit.

Sometimes in the newspaper you read of other kinds of accident. You may have read about children who played with fire or explosives. Often, they or their friends got killed playing these dangerous games. If you ever find a dangerous object don't touch it. Go to the police straight away and tell them where it is.

'Health is the greatest of all treasures,' says Mother. 'You will learn what this means if you really get ill. But you can help to keep well simply by being careful just as I have described. And if you do get ill, Rohit, tell your mother and father where it hurts. We shall call the doctor and he will help you. That's what the dentist is for too. You ought to go to the dentist twice a year to let him have a look at your mouth, even when you don't have toothache.'

Books. You probably get a lot of enjoyment from reading books and looking at their pictures. But do you know how a book is made and printed? It has to go a long way before it reaches your hands.

First the book is written. This writing is done by an author; sometimes he is a poet. What he writes is called a manuscript. The writer gives his manuscript to a publisher and the publisher begins to turn it into a book. The publisher's editors correct mistakes in the author's manuscript. Then the publisher pays an artist to draw or paint pictures to illustrate the book. At last the book goes to a printer to be printed and bound.

At the printer's are type-setters who type out the text of the book on a type setting machine. First of all they print the text on long sheets of paper called 'galleys'. The printer's readers and the publisher's editors correct these galleys. Then they may be made up on huge sheets, each one containing 16 or 32 pages of the book.

Then the printers fold the sheets by hand or with a machine. Another machine cuts and fastens the pages together in their proper order. Then a bookbinder puts a cover on the book and it is ready. Millions of books are made in this way every year.

When they have been printed, the books go back to their publishers who send them to bookshops all over the country.

Now you know what a lot of work goes into making a book. Well-made books are worth taking care of!

Once there were no printing machines. All books had to be slowly copied out by hand. Many centuries ago there was no paper. People scratched their words on soft clay tablets. Then they baked these pieces of clay like bricks. Long ago, Egyptians made sheets to write on from the leaves of the riverside papyrus plant. Our word 'paper' comes from the word 'papyrus'. The Egyptians stuck their papyrus together to make long scrolls. They wrote on a long scroll, then wound it on to a wooden roll. Actors still say they are learning their 'role'.

Later, people wrote on the dried skins of sheep or goats. They called this skin parchment. People learned to fold their parchment sheets. In time they became the shape of a book like the books we know.

In the Middle Ages a book was a valuable possession, so valuable that people chained up their books. Books were scarce because people still had to write every copy by hand. The words were written on parchment, with very beautiful letters. The capital letters were especially beautifully decorated. People usually had a leather cover on their books. Sometimes it was decorated with precious stones.

Over 500 years ago, the German, Gutenberg, discovered how to print books with mcvable type. Then it became possible to make many copies of a book much more quickly and cheaply. Soon, almost everyone could afford to own a book. Today many of us have quite big libraries of them, thanks to the marvellous invention of printing.

Boomerang. It is a sickle-shaped piece of wood. Australian natives use boomerangs as weapons. They are very skilful with a boomerang. They can throw it to hit a bird or animal. If they miss, the boomerang curves through the air and flies back to their hand.

Bottles. Container for holding liquids and other substances that can be poured through an opening at the top of the container. Bottles have traditionally been made of glass, but they may also be made of clay, metal, or plastic. The mouths of bottles vary in size from wide to narrow, and they are normally sealed with corks, glass stoppers, or metal or plastic caps.

Various industries use bottles to package their products. The food industry has replaced glass bottles in many cases with aluminum cans, cartons, and plastic bottles, but wine, beer, and occasionally soda are still sold in glass bottles. Medications such as cough syrup and liquid antacid are sold in glass or plastic bottles. Cleaning solvents and many beauty supplies are usually sold in plastic bottles. Perfume companies often package their products in bottles with unique designs so that consumers associate the bottle's shape with a particular scent.

Brass. When soft copper is melted and mixed with molten zinc (a brittle metal), the result is hard brass. People use brass for many things for the fittings of electric-light bulbs, door-knobs and reading and table-lamps.

Bread. 'Please, Mother, may I have another sandwich?' Pooja asked, while she was still eating her first.

A day never goes by without you eating bread in one form or another. Yet there was a time when nobody had ever heard of bread. 'What did people eat then?' I can hear you asking. They had a hard time to find enough food. Their biggest worry in life was how to find enough food to keep alive.

In those days people lived in pits or caves. Father would go out every day, hoping to kill a roebuck, a horse or a wild pig. Meanwhile Mother was out searching for berries, mushrooms and edible roots. Of course in those days no one expected his meals at regular hours. People probably ate their food as soon as they found anything fit to eat. Probably no one grew fat from over-eating as people can – and some do – today. What happened when these early people were unable to find anything to eat? They simply chewed leaves or grass.

Of all the many kinds of grass, the seeds of wild wheat and wild rye probably tasted the best. If only their grains were not so small! But anyway you could keep these grains throughout a cold winter as a food supply.

Perhaps someone once left a grain store on damp earth. After some weeks the grain sent up shoots which sprouted into new wheat stems each with its own seed-head. Soon, people found out for themselves how to grow these cereals. When this happened, they became farmers and no longer had to go out hunting to collect food.

But people still did not know how to bake bread from these whole grains. They did not know that you have to dry them and crush them into flour. At first they simply crushed their grain between two stones to make a floury powder. This was very laborious work. Other people tried crushing their grain in a pot by pounding it with a thick stick.. Some people still do this with rice and maize. The early farmers learned to separate the coarse husks from their finely ground flour with a sieve.

With time, people built big mills where they could quickly turn great amounts of grain into flour. At one time, slaves and prisoners turned these enormous mill-wheels. Later, people used a fast-running river or the wind to turn the waterwheels of a mill or the sails of a windmill.

Yet many people still did not make bread. They only made a kind of porridge from their flour. For many centuries this porridge was the most important food that many people ate. Our ancestors ate porridge made from barley and oats. Today, Italians are still very fond of a porridge called 'polenta' which they make from maize.

Several thousand years ago, people made their thick porridge into chunks which they put on a hot plate over a fire. In this way they cooked small, flat cakes which looked like our tarts. You could keep these 'tarts' for several days without them going bad. With porridge this was not possible. Porridge turned sour after a few days. But even the tarts made in those days would not seem very tasty to us. There was something missing from them, something which makes our bread puff up and which helps to flavour it: yeast.

Yeast is really millions of tiny living plants which make dough ferment and swell up when it is baked. How did people discover this? Yeast plants are too tiny to be seen. Perhaps a woman once mixed some old dough with fresh dough. The dough mixture started to rise when she heated it. It became full of little air bubbles and when it was baked it had a very pleasant taste. That woman had made the first loaf of bread!

Do you like to eat pastries and biscuits? It's true they taste nicer than bread as a treat. But you would soon get tired of them. Yet you can always eat bread without getting fed-up with it.

Breathing. You cannot live on air alone, but without air you can't live at all. Every minute you have to draw breath about 15 times. Every day you are pumping at least 2,000 gallons in and out of your lungs. When you are lying or sitting down you breathe in about a pint of air at each breath. When you walk, jump, or bend your knees you breathe much deeper. Then, nearly a gallon of air goes into your lungs in a single breath.

Bridge. A bridge is a structure designed to carry pedestrians or vehicles across such obstacles as ravines, rivers, or other roads or railroads. The earliest bridges may well have consisted of tree trunks or flat stones thrown across a stream – like the "clam" bridges of southeastern Cornwall or the "clapper" bridges of Dartmoor, which were the first beam bridges. Alternatively, the earliest types may have been primitive suspension spans formed of twisted bamboo or creepers hung across a stream, with their ends tied to tree trunks on either side; such bridges can still be seen in Africa and Asia.

Little doubt exists that these were built long before the first masonry arch, even though both types were preceded by natural rock arches such as those at Ardeche in France or in Lexington, Va. In all three types of bridge – beam, arch, and suspension – the foundations must carry the full weight of the bridge and the traffic on it. The vital differences, however, are that arched bridges, by virtue of their shape, are in compression and thrust outward on their end supports or bearings, whereas the cables of a suspension bridge are in tension and exert a continual pull on their end anchorages.

Broad-leaved trees. They have wide, flat leaves. Most of the broad-leaved trees which grow in our country – the beech, lime, oak, chestnut and many others – have paper-thin leaves. In autumn these leaves fall from the trees and leave them bare. In countries near the Mediterranean Sea, many kinds of broad-leaved tree produce thick, leathery leaves. They include the olive tree, the laurel and many others. The leaves on some of these trees remain on their branches for several years. When they fall, they do so one by one, not all together. So these trees are always green and never seem to shed their leaves.

Bronze. Copper was the first metal from which people made tools and weapons, long ago, at the end of an age we call the New Stone Age, Copper alone was a soft metal. People learned to harden it by mixing it, when molten, with molten tin. This mixture hardened into a tough metal called bronze, ideal for weapons, tools and ornaments. We call the time during which people made these bronze articles the Bronze Age. The Bronze Age began many centuries before the birth of Christ. Today people still make bronze bells and statues.

Broom. When you go for a walk on a dry, sunny common in the summer, you may see some low-growing shrubs full of golden yellow flowers. The plant on which these flowers grow is called broom. Some people mix it up with gorse which also has yellow flowers. But gorse flowers all the year round and its leaves are prickly spikes.

Bulbs. Imagine that you had to spend a whole winter all by yourself in a wood or on the top of a mountain. Of course you would first lay in a big store of food. Many plants do the same. They keep a well-filled store underground.

We call the plants' store a bulb or tuber. In the winter a snowdrop can draw on its underground store to produce beautiful white flowers – even among snow and ice. Tulips, daffodils and hyacinths all have similar underground stores.

In Holland, people grow many thousands of these flower bulbs every year and send them to flower gardens all over the world. A tulip field in bloom is a beautiful, colourful sight.

But not all bulbs produce bright-coloured or sweet-scented flowers. Strong-smelling onions and garlic also grow from bulbs.

Bullfinch. This is a beautiful bird which lives in our woods. In the winter, bullfinches do not fly away to warmer countries. They stay with us all the year round. Bullfinches have thick, strong beaks. They eat berries and the buds of trees. Farmers say bullfinches are a nuisance because they eat so many fruit buds. It is a pity that such beautiful birds can be harmful to our crops.

Bumble-bee. It looks very much like a honey-bee, but a bumble-bee is fatter and bigger. You can see bumble-bees best when they alight on a flower. Bumble-bees probe flowers with their long proboscis and sip the nectar. These bees build an underground nest. Each year, a queen bee that has survived the winter starts a new nest.

Butterfly. You will see many of our butterflies in the summer months. They flutter about from flower to flower and from the blossom of one tree to the next. At twilight, moths start flying. They are often attracted by blossoms whose scent is strongest in the evening. On the leaves of fruit trees you can often see the threads spun by caterpillars which live among the branches.

All butterflies have four wings, covered in a coloured powder. Their food is nectar, the sweet juice they find inside flowers. Butterflies suck it out with their proboscis.

'I love butterflies, but I hate clothes moths,' says Mother. Clothes moths are the little drab brown moths that get under carpets and inside wardrobes. Their caterpillars eat holes in carpets and woollen clothes.

Buzzard. The buzzard soars high above the fields and wooded hillsides in a wide circle. It cries just like a cat mewing, and looks rather like an eagle. But a buzzard is much smaller than an eagle – its body is about as big as a chicken's. Buzzards eat many mice. You can easily recognise them by their long wings, short tail, soaring flight and mewing cries.

C

Cable. 'Our street is being repaired,' said Dinesh when he came home from school. 'I have just seen workmen unloading some huge reels. They were reels of wire as thick as your arm!'

'Those are really cables for carrying strong electric currents,' explained Harish.

A cable is not made up of just one wire, but of many. Wrapped round the wires is a layer of rubber or some other insulating material. This insulation is a waterproof layer wrapped round a cable to stop its electricity escaping. The biggest cables carry electric current from power stations. They take this current to all parts of the country; that's why Dinesh saw them in our street. There are telephone and telegraph cables too. People even lay them across the bottom of the sea to join one continent with another. If you want, you can even telephone someone in America from your home in India.

Camel. The camel lives in hot deserts and he feels most at home there. Camels can endure much hunger because they carry a store of fat in their hump. They can turn this fat into food. When a camel has a drink it is days before he really needs another. So camels are well suited for long desert treks.

Dromedaries are one-humped camels which live in many eastern countries and in North Africa. People use them as beasts of burden. In Asia lives a two-humped camel.

People used to call the camel the 'ship of the desert'. But today people use cars much more than camels. Nowadays few camel caravans still cross the deserts. But there are still desert police who travel about the sandy wastes on the backs of camels. Camels have cousins which live in South America. These are the llama and alpaca, animals which live high in the Andes mountains.

Camping. It means living in a tent for some time. Many people on holiday in the country live in this way. As evening draws on, country ramblers will put up their canvas tents in some pleasant meadow. Then they will sleep as snugly as if they were at home. Many fields in the country are specially set aside for camping ramblers.

Canary. Do you know how this yellow song-bird got its name? It is called after the Canaries, a group of islands west of North Africa, in the Atlantic Ocean. Look up these islands in your atlas. Canaries still live wild in the Canary Islands. But people breed them in our country and keep them in cages because they sing so beautifully. It is very nice to have such fine singing birds right inside your living-room.

Canoe. There are several sorts of boat called 'canoe'. A dugout canoe is a hollowed tree trunk. It is one of the oldest and simplest of all kinds of boat. Some people who live in far-away forests still use canoes for travelling up and down the rivers.

Capercailzie. This is a bird related to our farmyard chickens but bigger than them. It lives in Scottish pine woods. In the spring a cock capercailzie bird attracts hen birds by making the strangest noises. While he makes these sounds he does not seem to see or hear anything. You would think he was mad. In some countries people hunt these birds.

Car. Brrrm!! We speed smoothly along the broad highway in our up-to-date car. It does not jolt us at all and its engine only makes a quiet purring sound. But things were not always like this. The first cars, built about 75 years ago, shook their passengers about like peas in a pod. These cars made such a noise that people on the streets took to their heels with fright. Some say the Austrian, Siegried Marcus, made the first car.

Today, if you want to drive a car you must first pass a test. An examiner will ask you many questions. You must know how to stop and start and steer a car. You must know what road signs mean. And of course you must show that you really can drive. Don't think it is enough to be able to answer questions. You must show that you keep a careful watch for people who might stray into the road. And when you yourself are walking, watch the traffic carefully

– especially before you cross a road. You should look right, look left, look right again. Then, if the road is clear, cross over. This way, you will always get home safe and sound.

Carp. In a pet-shop you sometimes see a tank full of silver-grey fish, swimming up and down. They are carp. Very long ago, people brought these fish from China to our ponds and rivers. In the Middle Ages, monks kept carp in fish ponds, and ate them. Nowadays we don't eat carp: we prefer watching them in an aquarium. Our colourful goldfish are the descendants of the plain silver-grey carp.

Castle. Medieval European stronghold, generally the fortified dwelling of the king or lord of the territory in which it stood.

The castle developed rapidly in western Europe from the 9th century. In form it was somewhat sprawling compared to later fortified buildings. The castle's enceinte (outer wall) was surrounded by one or more moats, which were crossed by drawbridges that could be raised from the inner side. The gateway itself was heavily protected and often defended by a barbican, or watchtower. One or more baileys, or walled courtyards, surrounded the donjon. The age of the medieval castle came to an end with the increasing use of firearms in the 15th–16th centuries.

Carrier-pigeon. If you take a carrier-pigeon miles away from its home, it will often find its way back again. People knew about this centuries ago, before telephones were invented. In those days, people took pigeons with them when they travelled. When they were far from home, they let the pigeons fly home with a short note.

Today, people still breed these pigeons and race them. Now people can send long messages by pigeon-post. First they photograph the message very small, then they attach it to a pigeon's leg in a rubber cover. A good carrier-pigeon can fly 100 miles as fast as many cars can travel.

Cat. 'Puss, Puss,' Vinisha calls to her cat. And here comes her cat, running along. Just see how she rubs her head against Vinisha's dress. And how she purrs. Vinisha likes it. But Vinisha is not so pleased when her cat catches a bird or a mouse. But there is nothing Vinisha can do about it, for all cats are – and always will be – beasts of prey. Our small tame cats belong to the same family as the lion, tiger, jaguar and leopard. Luckily for us, a cat is not nearly so big or dangerous as a tiger. Just imagine keeping that for a pet!

Caterpillar. Many caterpillars are prettily coloured; they are pale green, or perhaps covered with red and blue spots, with fine hairs on their backs. One day, when a caterpillar has eaten itself plump, it starts to take a long rest. The caterpillar turns into a stiff-shelled chrysalis. After some days or weeks, a beautiful butterfly comes out of this chrysalis.

Cedar. This needle-leaved tree grows in the mountains of Asia and North Africa. But you can also see it growing in our parks. Just like the needles on a larch tree, the cedar's needles grow together in small bunches. People use cedar wood for making pencils.

Celsius. 'Isn't it hot today?' said John, as he looked at the thermometer. The thermometer showed 25 degrees Centigrade in the shade. For John was a Dutch boy, living in Holland, where thermometers measure in degrees Centigrade not degrees Fahrenheit, as our thermometers do. John's 25 degrees was equal to more than 77 degrees Fahrenheit. The Centigrade thermometer was invented by Celsius, a Swedish physicist, who divided the distance between the freezing point and boiling point of water into 100 parts which we call 'degrees'. People also call Centigrade thermometers 'Celsius thermometers'.

Cereals. Cereals are amongst the most important of all plants that people grow. Every day we eat wheat in our Rotis, Parantha, breads or cakes. Every day farmers somewhere are feeding oats and barley to their farm animals. The fruits, the parts of cereals that we eat, are tiny grains. These grains grow together on an ear. Each ear grows from the end of a stalk.

From **Cave to Skyscraper.** 'I'm jolly glad to be home again,' said Sunil. Outside it was a cold, rainy day. Sunil took his favourite book from the bookcase, sat down in an easy chair and began to read. He was sitting in a snug, warm room.

Many thousand years ago, no one could protect himself properly against the weather. And people had much worse enemies than weather to fear – they dreaded the many fierce, wild beasts.

'Look out, wolves are coming!' cried a Stone Age father to his family. 'Quick, into that tree!' His family had no secure house to hide in. Each evening, they simply made a kind of nest of branches and twigs and slept there, in a tree. They probably covered the nest with moss to make it softer. A tree-top bedroom was a poor refuge but it may have been man's first home.

Some people learned to live in caves. There, they were safe from weather, but sometimes bears came on the prowl and the people might be driven out. Some caves were high up on rock-faces. 'No bear can climb here,' said the Stone Age hunter who had discovered such a cave.

'What does a mammoth look like?' Uma asked his father. Father took a sharp flint and made a drawing of a mammoth on the wall of the cave. People had learned to use flints and other stones as tools. Where there were no caves, people dug pits with pickaxes of stone and bone. People covered the pits with branches and twigs. Sometimes they built a wicker-work hut on top of the pit. Then they lived inside it.

When the ground was too rocky to dig pits but not rocky enough for caves, people gathered stones and piled them up into two walls. They learned to prop a roof of thin tree trunks covered with grass on top of their walls. This kept out the worst weather. But the people who dwelt in this primitive hut had to keep their fire outside. They feared it might set alight their low, wooden roof.

'If only we didn't have to go inside on 'our hands and knees,' sighed the people who lived in these huts. They learned to dig a hole and build their low walls and roof over that. Now it became safer to bring their fire into the hut, for the roof was much higher. During winter, people had some light and warmth in their homes.

You can make all kinds of things from clay even a whole house. People did make clay huts but they were not content. 'Our house just melts away,' they said, after a heavy rainstorm. But when they made their walls of branches and spread clay over them, they found their houses were much stronger.

Other people built their homes on poles. 'I built my house in a lake,' said the fisherman Hano. At one time there were villages built on poles in many parts of Europe.

People who lived in forested mountains made their homes of wood. They cut down trees and piled up the trunks to make a log cabin.

In the times of the Crusades, people built farms and manor houses of wood and loam. Farmers and their animals lived together under a single great straw roof.

In the Middle Ages, people started to build houses as we know them. They set up a large frame of beams and filled the spaces between them with willow branches plastered with clay. People in towns preferred to live in houses which stood on stone foundations.

Anyone who had enough money could pay to have tiles put on his roof.

People came to the towns from all directions. Often, there was a great stone wall running round a city. Soon, there was no spot in that city that had not been built on, because everyone wanted to live within its safe walls. To hold all these people, houses had to be built higher, and they had balconies outside their upstairs windows.

Outside the towns stood the knights' castles, on hilltops, great rocks, or on islands in lakes and rivers. The knights built high walls and towers with battlements and loop-holes – all made of heavy chunks of stone.

Our present-day towns look quite different from the towns of the Middle Ages. Then, all houses were built with many bricks and much mortar to cement them together. People roofed these houses with hundreds of separate tiles or slates. 'If only we could make a liquid stone that we could pour into a huge mould,' the people probably said. 'Then we would let it set like jelly and make a solid stone house in no time at all.' Today concrete has come to fulfil this wish.

In a modern concrete house, the liquid cement is poured into a mould round a metal frame. Soon, the concrete sets and turns as hard as natural stone. America's towering skyscrapers are made of metal and concrete in much this way. But people are making more experiments. Already there are houses made of glass and aluminium. You can build them in a single day.

Chaffinch. In early February you will hear the chaffinches begin to sing. But if you frighten a chaffinch at any time of the year you will hear it cry: 'Pink, pink!' This is its alarm call. The beautifully coloured little chaffinch builds a neat round nest and covers it with moss. You may easily pass it by without spotting it.

Chalk. Of course you all know what chalk looks like. But did you know that chalk is a kind of limestone? It is a limestone built up from the shells of tiny sea animals that lived many million years ago. In time their shells formed layers of chalk, hundreds of feet thick.

Chameleon. Chameleons belong to the same family as lizards. They are not much bigger than our own lizards. Chameleons mainly in the hot countries of Africa and India. When a chameleon is frightened or hungry or thirsty, it changes colour. It usually changes from its natural colour (which is often green) to orange or flesh colour, sometimes to rusty brown or grey-blue.

Chameleons have a tongue which they can shoot out a very long way. This tongue looks just like an elastic catapult, as it flashes out to catch a fly. The tongue has sticky tip – and it brings many an insect to a sticky end.

Charity. It nowadays often means giving money to poor people. But it really means more than that. The Bible says that 'Faith, Hope and Charity' are all good for anyone to have. But best of all is Charity. That sort of charity means loving everyone and doing good to everyone, not just to those without much money.

Chickens. What a terrible noise farmyard hens make when they cackle! Our farm chickens are fowls whose wild ancestors were tamed by man thousands of years ago. Today they spend most of their time scratching in the farmyard with their long claws, which are just made for such work. The cock has splendid feathers and a brighter comb than the hens. But they lay the eggs. After a hen has sat on a clutch of eggs for about three weeks, the eggs hatch into fluffy chicks, like little balls of wool.

In the same family as our chickens are guinea-fowl, pheasants and peacocks.

Chief. A chief can be the head man of a tribe of Indians, or he may be the head man in a factory, office or shop. Policemen and gangs of thieves both have chiefs to organise them.

Choir. When children at school sing a song together you can say that they are singing in a choir.

'Last night I went to a concert,' said Father. 'The choir sang some beautiful folk-songs.'

In a church, the choir stands in the choir-stalls next to the organ.

Christianity. This is the religion which was founded by Jesus Christ. His apostles preached Christianity in many countries. Now, in the twentieth century, Christianity has spread all over the world. Millions of people are Christians, though not all Christians belong to the same sort of Christian church.

Church. A church is a building. But it can also mean the people who worship in that building. You can call a group of people who believe in the same religion a 'church'.

In our country, towns and villages are grouped as parishes. Each parish has a vicar who holds services in a church. In the Roman Catholic church a priest holds services, administers sacraments and often gives religious education to children. In large parishes he is helped by an assistant priest. The priests and their assistants in each country work under the leadership of a bishop. They are really the helpers of the bishop. In all parts of the world there are Catholic Christians. The head of the whole Catholic church is the bishop of

Rome, the Pope. All the bishops and priests and believers in the Catholic faith are under the Pope's leadership. Catholics believe the Pope is Jesus Christ's chief representative on earth. Pope, bishops, priests and Catholic Christians together make up the Catholic church.

But in the Protestant churches people believe they should follow the Bible's teachings without so much help and direction from priests. The first Protestant church was founded over 400 years ago through the work of several people including Martin Luther, Calvin and Zwingli.

In many Protestant churches, the preacher is chosen by the church parish. He preaches according to the Holy Scriptures, christens, and teaches children. At a certain age these children become members of the church. The preacher also administers the sacraments, baptism and Holy Communion. Marriages are blessed in Protestant churches. The various parishes keep in touch with one another

The church itself is the building where services are held. Usually you can see from the outside of a building whether it is a church. Many old churches have tall spires or square towers. Smaller buildings where services are held are called chapels. There are even mobile chapels built in motor-coaches. There are floating chapels too, for the passengers and crews who travel on large steamships.

Circus. 'Ladies and gentlemen, boys and girls, roll up! Roll up! The Roselli circus has come to town. Here is music! Here are horses, bears, elephants, lions and tigers. Roll up and see the conjurers, the bareback riders, the acrobats, the animals – and of course the clowns, big and small! Roll up!!'

Behind the band which leads the circus parade comes the circus chief's own carriage, pulled by two lovely white horses with flowing manes. Look, the chief has jumped down from his carriage. He is walking beside it, waving his broad-brimmed stetson hat to the cheering crowd.

Look closely, children. Behind the chief's carriage come Bruin and Bimbo, two of the cleverest bears in the whole world. They can run on their hind legs, pedal a bicycle and throw balls – all inside the circus. Have you ever seen bears do that before?

Ah, can you hear that roaring? It's the lions in the van behind Bruin and Bimbo. They are called

Leo and Caesar. The lion-tamer raised them from little cubs, and he has taught them all sorts of unbelievable tricks.

Now here comes Jumbo the elephant. He was born in India, and has made a very long journey to come here. The Indian who sits on his back came all the way from India with him. The Indian who rides on Jumbo's back is a fakir. Many fakirs can sleep on planks with nails in them; they can swallow knives and forks too.

The men and women who follow Jumbo are the other circus artists. Some do difficult tricks, balancing on ropes or swinging from a trapeze. They even turn somersaults in mid-air. The man in the black hat and black suit is the best magician in the world. He is called Magicus because of his 'magic' tricks.

Last in the procession come the clowns and other funny men. They are always making funny jokes. They can also caper about, do somersaults, walk on stilts and dance on a rope. They pretend that they can do everything as well as the real acrobats, though they can't really do acrobatics at all. Ha! Ha! How they make us laugh.

Soon the circus procession winds its way back to the big top (the big circus tent) to get ready for its first performance. Let's hope the circus soon comes to your town.

Clock. Harish went to the clock museum on Sunday morning. His friend Rohit had already told him about it and Father said, 'Go and have a look. You'll learn a lot at that museum.'

Now Harish found himself standing between all kinds of strange clocks and instruments. Many of them did not look like clocks at all.

'How boring,' thought Harish. 'It makes me yawn.'

'How bored you look,' said a voice behind him suddenly. An old gentleman stood watching Harish. He was the curator of the museum. 'Could you please tell me the time?' asked the curator. Harish looked at his new wrist watch. 'Ten o'clock,' he said. The old gentleman took an old-fashioned pocket watch from his own pocket. Then he looked over his glasses at the large electric clock which was standing on a table. 'That's right.' he said. Then, 'Imagine that your watch and my watch and all the clocks in town suddenly stopped. How would you find out what time it was?' Harish thought for a bit. Then he said, 'I'd look at the sun.' 'Right!' said the curator. 'People did that thousands of years ago, before anyone had made any clocks. Some farmers still sometimes do it.

'The Greeks were very clever people. They built columns and by the length of a column's shadow they could tell what time it was.

'Look. On the wall over there hangs a sun-dial. You can still sometimes see them on the walls of very old houses. But what do you think people used as a clock when the sun wasn't shining? They had an answer to that problem. They used hour-glasses, half full of sand. There's one over there. But as soon as it emptied you had to turn it upside down to keep good time.

'The watchmaker Peter Henlein of Nuremberg invented the first pocket watch. Instead of heavy weights he used a spring. His watch looked like an egg. So it earned itself the name of the "Nuremberg egg". A Dutch inventor called Christian Huygens invented a pendulum clock about 300 years.

Suddenly a loud 'ping' sounded in Harish's ear. Harish spun round. The sound had made him jump. But the old gentleman just laughed. Beside them, on a table, stood a beautiful clock. A small statue had just struck a metal shield on the clock with a hammer. It was half-past eleven.

'What a pity,' said Harish. 'I must go home now. Thank you very much. It's been very interesting. May I come again next Sunday?' Harish had to ask this because he had not nearly seen everything. And he had just realised how interesting it all was.

There was a water-clock. It worked by a drop of water falling from one tin into another. As the water rose in that tin it lifted a little float. An indicator on this float pointed to the time with surprising accuracy.

And then there were candle-clocks! They consisted of a candle which melted a thread as it burned. A ball was attached to the thread. When all the candle had melted, the ball fell on to a bell. In this way the candle-clock told the time every hour.

Nowadays we can buy clocks which only need winding once every eight days. There are even clocks which only have to be wound once a year. Or perhaps you have an electric clock which never needs winding at all.

Cloister. A cloister is a monastery or a nunnery. A monastery is a place where religious men called monks spend their lives. A nunnery is a place where religious women called nuns spend their lives. Both serve God by praying and working. The men and women who live cloistered lives do a lot of good work. They teach children in schools, look after poor and sick children in orphanages and other homes. And they nurse sick people in hospitals.

Each monastery and nunnery has its own church, and of course it has a house where the monks or nuns live. Some monasteries have large stables, barns and workshops. In a few old monasteries there are large libraries full, of valuable old books. Some of these were written by monks over 1000 years ago, before the art of printing was invented.

Some cloisters send their monks or nuns to far-off countries to work in missions. There, they teach people, ignorant of Christ, about the Christian religion.

Clover. When superstitious people find a four-leaved clover in a meadow they are delighted. 'Look,' they say. 'This is sure to bring us luck!'

Four-leaved clover is rare because clover usually has only three leaves. There are several kinds of clover. When clover is in bloom its flowers may be red, white or mauve. Farmers feed clover to animals and its roots enrich their farm soil.

Clown. Clowns are the funny men in a circus.

Coal. Coal began forming many million years ago. It is hard for us to imagine such a long span of time. There were no people at all living in those forgotten centuries. There were only strange animals which died out long ago. For many thousand years the coal forests were growing and their trees were dying and falling into the waters of a huge swamp. The trees fell on top of each other and sank deeper and deeper into the swampy water.

Then it all began. The trees slowly started to change into coal. They did not just rot; they were covered under layers of mud and more dead plants. More and more layers of mud pressed on the tree trunks. They pressed very heavily. Slowly the pressure began to crush the bottom layers into a solid, hard mass. The sunken forests had begun to turn into brown-coloured coal.

How long was it before black coal was formed? Don't be surprised. It took about 280 million years!

Today, miners with pickaxes and air-pressure drills help to ensure that coal buried deep underground can be raised to the surface. A miner works in coal mines sometimes miles beneath the surface of the earth. His work is very hard. By the light of his miner's lamp he often stands bent double in a hot, low-roofed tunnel. He hacks or drills the coal loose and throws it into little wagons.

Then the coal is lifted to the surface. After a long train journey it reaches towns all over the country. What a long time it may take for coal to reach you, before you can put some lumps on the fire to heat your home.

People don't use coal only for heating houses. When people invented steam engines two centuries ago, they began using coal to heat the boilers in their factories and railway engines. Nowadays, people heat boilers in power stations with coal as well. Burning coal turns water into steam. Steam spins the great turbines which help to make the electricity we use at home.

People have discovered that you can make many useful things from coal. When you heat coal you get coke, coal-gas and tar. Coke is a good fuel and gives even more heat than coal. Coal-gas has many uses as a fuel. People make many things from tar, including paints, medicines, plastics, perfumes and many other objects. In all large towns there is a gas-works. A gas-works is a factory where people make coal-gas, coke and tar from coal. Clever people have succeeded in making various motor fuels from coal – even petrol and diesel oil.

Who would have thought that tree trunks which died 280 million years ago would mean so much to you and me today?

Coal-gas. Mother turned on the gas-tap and lit the coal-gas. Then she put a cake into the oven. Now Mother only had to wait for the cake to become nice and brown. Just then, Chetan came home from school.

'Teacher taught us something about coal-gas today,' he said. 'It is made from coal. From the gas-works it travels through pipes under the streets to our homes. A hundred years ago there were gas lamps to light our city streets. Today there are still a few towns lit by gas instead of electricity.'

'Very good,' said his mother. 'But did your teacher also tell you that coal-gas is very poisonous? When I have cooked my cake I must make sure to turn the gas-tap off properly.'

Cockchafer. In May, Harish and Ritu take a walk in the orchard every morning. They shake the trees and watch the cockchafers drop out of them. These animals are still sleepy from the cold night air.

Cockchafers are harmful insects. They eat the leaves of fruit trees. A mother cockchafer lays 70-80 eggs in loose soil. From these eggs hatch tiny grubs. They are the larvae of the cockchafer. For two or three years they will live in the ground, eating the roots of plants. Then a cockchafer grub turns into a pupa. After its body has passed through several changes it becomes a beetle. But cockchafer grubs have many enemies, including moles, hedgehogs and foxes.

Cocoa. Mother will make a nice cup of cocoa for you. She will make it with milk and sugar. It tastes very good and it is very nourishing at the same time. Where does the cocoa powder come from? From cocoa beans. These are the seeds which come from the fruit of the cacao tree. People grow cacao trees in West Africa and in the warm parts of America and Asia. People also use cocoa beans to make chocolate.

Coconut. 'What a treat, we are going to have coconut biscuits again today!' Nisha just loves them. Teacher told her all about the coconut palm tree and coconuts at school.

Coconut palms grow along the beaches of some tropical countries where they may reach 100 feet high. So you see that a ripe coconut must often fall a long way before it reaches the ground. But its very tough shell can easily stand up to the shock. The shell is completely covered in fibres, and they protect the nut when it falls.

Natives open the fruit and drink its refreshing juice, which is called coconut milk. The dried inside of the coconut is called copra. From this copra people make the liquid we call coconut oil.

Coffee. Many hundreds of years ago a shepherd in Africa saw that his goats were eating red berries from a shrub. The goats suddenly became happy and frisked playfully around. The shepherd himself tasted the berries and felt fitter and more full of energy.

The shepherd told the people of his village and so the strange shrub suddenly became well-known. It was the coffee plant.

Coffee beans are the seeds of its berries. They look like little cherries. Coffee beans are grey-green in colour and only become brown when roasted. Almost everyone loves his cup of coffee. What a delicious scent it has – even when you only smell it as you pass by a coffee shop. But do not drink too much of it, for too much coffee may be bad for your heart and nerves.

Collapsible boat. It can mean tremendous fun for young people. You can make it to pieces and put it in your rucksack. When you arrive at a river, you can quickly put it together again. Its waterproof material is stretched over a wooden or metal frame. It is great fun to glide downstream in a collapsible boat. But make sure you can swim before you try it out!

Colorado beetle. This beetle is the potato's greatest enemy. If you ever find a Colorado beetle, you should report it immediately to the pest control officer. We'll tell you just what it looks like. It is half an inch long or slightly less. It has 10 long black stripes running down its yellow wing-cases. The Colorado beetle lays eggs on the underside of the leaves of a potato plant. In time each egg hatches into a reddish larva with a black head and two rows of black dots down its side. These larvae bury themselves in the earth and turn into pupae. The pupae are orange-red in colour.

What can gardeners and farmers do to protect their potatoes from these dangerous insects? They search their potato fields carefully and spray their plants with a liquid, poisonous to the Colorado beetles. But farmers burn all those plants that they find already affected.

Colour. There are very many colours. In the rainbow you can see red, orange, yellow, green, blue, indigo and violet. When we mix pure colours with each other we obtain new colours. For example, if you mix red and blue you get the colour mauve.

People say that white is the colour of innocence and peace. Black is the colour of mourning and sadness. Red means love and joy. Blue stands for faithfulness, yellow means hate and jealousy, green is the colour of hope and purple is the symbol of royal dignity.

Christopher **Columbus.** About 500 years ago many people thought the earth was a great flat disc. They thought it became more dangerous the farther you sailed across the Atlantic Ocean. Sooner or later (they believed) you were bound to fall off the edge of the earth. These people knew no better.

But a few people thought otherwise. 'No,' they said, 'the earth is round. If you sail into the west, you will travel right round the earth.'

The Italian sailor Columbus believed what these people said. And he set out westward, partly to prove it for himself. He sailed with three Spanish ships into the unknown Atlantic Ocean. The crews of these ships had to endure many hardships. They had little drinking water and much of their food went bad. But after 70 days, a sailor in the crow's nest of one ship shouted, 'Land! Land ahoy!'

The next day, Columbus and his sailors landed on an island. This was on October 12th, 1492. Out of gratitude for his safe journey, Columbus called the island 'San Salvador'. It means 'Holy Redeemer'.

Columbus believed that this island was part of India or one of the eastern spice islands. But he was wrong, for it was an island off the coast of America. Columbus did not know that he had discovered the outpost of a new continent.

After this voyage, Columbus sailed across the Atlantic three more times. He even landed in South America. In 1506 this famous, brave explorer died. By then he was very poor and many people had forgotten him. Seven years after his death, other sea-men proved that Columbus's islands were part of a great new continent.

Commerce. 'May I have a banana, please?'

'Yes,' said the shopkeeper. 'You can have the biggest one I've got. They have just come from West Africa. They have had a very long journey over land and sea.'

There are many sorts of goods which come from countries far away. We get coffee from Brazil, Coco from Africa, oranges from Italy. The jeweller may get his diamonds from South Africa and the silk merchant gets his silk from France and maybe even China.

These goods go through many hands before we get them. Our grocer round the corner cannot go to South America himself to buy his coffee. This is done by special buyers who are sent to all countries by wholesale merchants. The buyers buy up vast amounts of coffee which they find, stored ready for them, in huge warehouses. These warehouses are built in the ports of the foreign countries. Dock workers carry the coffee in large sacks to ships which are sailing to India. When these ships arrive at a Indian port (for example, Mumbai) more dockers unload the coffee and it is stored in more warehouses. Then the wholesalers who deal in coffee make sure that it arrives safely at its destination – shops all over the country.

Each shopkeeper orders from the wholesaler as many sacks of coffee as he wants. He also orders crates of oranges and sacks of flour, semolina, sugar, and many other things. When the shopkeeper opens his crates and sacks he has to stack up his goods so as to display them on shelves and in the window. And he has to measure out bulky goods into smaller bags.

When we go into a shop it doesn't take a minute to pop tea, sugar, coffee and rice into our shopping bags. Yet all these goods have taken many weeks and the work of many people before they reached us. Farmers, pickers, buyers, warehousemen, dockers, wholesalers, retail shopkeepers in our own town – all have worked together to help make our cup of tea or coffee. And we should not forget the clerks who write and type the necessary letters and invoices. It is largely thanks to their work that we are able to buy the many goods we see in the shops today.

Composer. 'Mother, I am a composer!' shouted Dinesh, and he danced around the room. 'You told me yourself that a composer is someone who can make up songs and pieces of music. And now I have made up a song.' And Dinesh really did sing a new song.

'Very good,' said Mother. 'But a real composer must also know how to write down his songs in musical notation. And not only the music for the singer but for his accompaniment on a piano or a flute or some other instrument. Composing is very difficult. It is an art. Just think about a big orchestra. In an orchestra every instrument plays something different, but at the same time all the instruments together sound good. Do you know the names of any famous composers?'

'Oh, yes, Mother,' said Dinesh. 'There's Bach, Haydn, Mozart, Beethoven, Elgar, Schubert, Brahms, and Benjamin Britten.'

Concert. Many people are sitting together in a large hall. They are all wearing evening dress. The platform or stage in front of them is full of musicians. There are ladies and gentlemen with violins, trumpets, trombones, flutes and many other instruments. These musicians make up an orchestra. Suddenly another man walks on to the platform. He is the conductor. In concerts given by military bands he is called the bandmaster. The people in the concert hall clap their hands. The conductor bows and then he turns to the orchestra. Everyone in the concert hall becomes very silent. The conductor lifts his baton, and, as soon as he gives a sign, the orchestra begins to play. After each piece of music, the people in the hall applaud. Sometimes the orchestra plays all together in a symphony. Sometimes the orchestra accompanies a piano or violin in a concerto. When the concert has finished, the whole orchestra stands up and bows while everyone claps.

Conductor. A conductor directs a choir or an orchestra. If he conducts a military band he is called a bandmaster. (See **'Concert'**)

Copper. Copper is a soft, reddish metal. It is about nine times as heavy as wood and even heavier than iron. In past centuries people made their kitchen utensils of copper and how they glittered and shone when they were polished. Nowadays we use copper wires to conduct electricity. Have you ever seen a green roof on a church? Such roofs are made of copper and the green is called 'verdigris'. Verdigris on copper is rather like the rust which forms on iron. Some of the world's greatest copper mines are those of North and South America, Russia and Africa.

Coral. In the jeweller's shop-window you may often see necklaces made of small pieces of round or pointed polished coral. Coral is found in the warm, clear waters of tropical oceans, especially in the Pacific Ocean. There are many kinds of beautifully coloured corals – some pink, others red and orange. Coral can build up underwater reefs. The reefs grow upwards, for coral is really the shells of tiny living sea creatures.

Cork. Anita cannot swim yet, but her mother and father let her play in water.

'Nothing can happen to me!' she shouts. 'I'm wearing a life-belt made of cork.'

Cork float on water. It is very light and can't get waterlogged. Cork comes from the bark of the cork oak tree which grows in Spain and other countries near the Mediterranean Sea.

Cornflowers. When you walk Beside a yellow cornfield in late summer, you can often pick a lovely bunch of bright-blue cornflowers. (But take care not to tread on the growing corn.) Farmers do not like to see cornflowers in their fields.

'Cornflowers may be pretty,' they say. But a cornflower is a weed. It takes up rowing space that our corn needs and robs the corn of valuable foods in the soil.

Cotton. Does cotton grow on trees? No, cotton does not grow on trees. Where does it come from then? It grows on low bushes. Cotton plants grow best in warm countries, like ours. The white hairs which grow on the seeds of the plants are cotton which pickers (and nowadays often machines) gather.

People spin these hairs into threads which they weave into cotton materials. Under-clothes, for instance, are often made of cotton. So are shirts. As its name suggest even soft, fluffy cotton-wool is made of cotton.

Cowboy. Ranchers graze great herds of cattle on the vast prairies of North America. One herd often holds several thousand beasts. The cowboys who are the shepherds of these herds are splendid horsemen. Expertly, they can drive a great herd of cattle into a small corral. There, they will count the animals and brand them. By looking at the brand mark on a cow you can see at a glance whose it is.

Cowboys move with the times. As well as horses, they use tough cars, suitable for driving across the bumpy surface of the prairies.

With horses and modern vehicles, cowboys keep their herds together. But even with cars to help them, cowboys find their life often dangerous, and their work is seldom easy.

Craftsmen. Several craftsmen live in our street. They work in their work-shops. They are the shoe-mender, the tailor, and the cabinet-maker. They have assistants to help them. And working under the assistants are young apprentices. In these work-shops there are only small, simple machines. For most of these craftsmen still do their work by hand.

Crane. A crane is a machine which can lift heavy loads and move them a little way. Where do you usually see cranes? In stations, on construction sites, beside harbours and inside factories.

Crayfish. Once upon a time, someone found a crayfish crawling about on dry land. He showed his friends. None of them knew what the strange animal was. It rather frightened them because it could walk backwards as well as forwards, and it pinched the man who found it with one of its claws. The ignorant, terrified people condemned the creature to be drowned. Of course when they dropped the crayfish in a river it felt much more at home, for it is a water animal. The crayfish crept happily away over the shallow stony bottom of the river.

'Look!' said the stupid people. 'It is wild with fear,'

Though a crayfish has powerful claws and looks like a little lobster it is not really a dangerous animal. It lives on worms, snails and small fishes. Its true home is in rivers and lakes. Its hiding-places are under stones or in holes in the banks.

Cricket. On a summer night you can sometimes hear a cricket singing somewhere, often under some old paving stones. Do you know how he makes his noise? He does it by rubbing his legs together. If you are very quiet and careful, you may see this dark insect sitting in front of his hole. But as soon as you move, he will dive underground.

Crocodile. Our harmless little lizards belong to the reptile family. This family includes some creatures which are very dangerous indeed. These are the crocodiles and alligators of distant, hot countries. In Africa, the Nile crocodile may grow to 20 feet long; it has a tough, leathery skin and its mouth bristles with very sharp teeth. But a crocodile's most dangerous weapon can be his powerful tail.

Crocodiles are meat-eaters. Some only eat fish. Others will attack a man if he enters the water where they swim. A crocodile lays eggs on a mudbank and leaves them for the sun to hatch. There are crocodiles or alligators in many of the rivers of South America, India and Australia and in parts of North America too.

Cross-bow. The cross-bow developed from the ordinary 'bow-and-arrow' bow. With a cross-bow, people could aim better and their arrows went much farther.

Crow. 'The crow is a singing bird,' said Vinit. Other people may laugh at him, but Vinit is right. In fact he would be right to say that almost any bird sings. We think singing means making pleasant sounds. But to birds, singing is a way of telling other birds to keep off your home ground.

In our country live several kinds of crow – each with a different sort of croaking or screeching 'song'. Besides the carrion crow, there are the hooded crow, the rook, the raven, jackdaw, magpie, jay and the rare red-legged, red-billed chough.

Cuckoo. Sometimes in May and June you hear 'Cuckoo!' echoing through a wood. When you first hear the cuckoo's piping call you know that spring has really come. The cuckoo is a lazy bird. It does not build a nest for itself. Mother cuckoo lays an egg in the nest of some other, smaller bird. When the young cuckoo hatches, its little foster mother has to bring it up.

D

Dachshund. The dachshund is a funny little dog with a long, low body, long ears and bowed legs. Once, people used dachshunds as hunting dogs. A dachshund would dive into a fox's earth or a badger's hole and chase out the fox or badger. But nowadays most people just keep dachshunds as pets.

Dahlia. In the late summer and early autumn the great yellow, pink and deep-red flowers of dahlia plants make a blaze of colour in many gardens. They look just like stars. Our dahlias are descended from the much smaller flowers of a wild dahlia which grows in Mexico.

Dandelion. At the beginning of summer, the meadow behind our house is completely covered with yellow dandelions. The village children make long chains of dandelions, threading them together by their hollow stems. When the flowers finish blooming, they turn into fluffy white balls. These are the many grains of seed. Each grain of seed has its own little parachute. The wind blows the seeds away. Where a seed comes to earth it may put out roots. Next year there will be a new dandelion plant on that spot.

Date. 'What is the date today?' asked Sunita, who wanted to write a letter.

'It's the 9th of August, 2011,' replied Chetan. Sunita wrote that date at the top right-hand corner of her notepaper.

Dates. The camel caravan has madc a long journey through the scorching, treeless desert. But its travellers know they will soon reach an oasis. Already they can see the fronds of date-palms waving above the horizon. The fruits of the date-palm are an important food for people who live in the desert. We like to eat these sweet, honey yellow fruits too. Unlike the desert-dwellers, we don't pluck our own dates; we buy them ready packed in boxes in a shop. In a desert without shops or even date-palms, for many hundred miles, the Arabs sew dried dates sheepskins. Thus they can keep a store of dates for years, in case of sudden need.

Decorations. Someone has placed garlands of flowers and evergreen branches around branches around neighbour's front door. And above the door, someone has hung a beautifully lettered notice. It says 'Welcome Home!'

'Harish is coming back from Australia to visit his mother and father,' says woman.

'I haven't seen such fine decorations for a long time,' says a man.

When it was your birthday, your mother probably decorated the table at tea-time. Perhaps there was a birthday cake with candles on it. I expect you received some birthday presents wrapped in beautifully decorated paper.

'Decoration' is a hard word because it means several things.

You sometimes hear on the news that a king or queen has 'decorated' a man. This means they have awarded him some sort of medal. A man may be decorated because he has performed some great service for his country.

Democracy. Every country is governed in one way or another. The people can govern their country themselves. But they can't all govern at once. They choose representatives to rule for them. In our country people choose their representatives at elections where everyone over 18 years old has a right to vote.

When a country is governed in this way we say it is a democracy. The Greek word 'demos' means people. 'Democracy' means government by the people. Representatives chosen by the people make laws to benefit everyone, not just themselves. In a democratic country all the people have the same rights. India, Britain, the United States of America, France, Holland and many other countries are ruled by democratic governments.

Diamonds. They are the hardest and most valuable of all precious stones. They glitter brilliantly and reflect all the colours of the rainbow from a single ray of light. Because diamonds are so hard, people use them for cutting glass and for making drilling machines.

Diet. Sometimes you get stomach ache – especially if you eat too much unripe fruit. Then you may be told not to eat many of the things you usually eat. Mother, or the doctor, may say that you must go on a diet. This simply means that you may not eat some things which are not good for your health.

Dike. People build dikes along the beaches of low shores and the low-lying banks of broad rivers. Dikes protect towns and villages against floods and storms. In Holland, where much of the country is actually below sea level, dikes keep the sea out all the time. Sometimes, great waves, whipped up by a storm, force their way through a dike. Then many farms will be flooded and many people may have to leave their homes.

Disinfectant. When, someone has had an infectious illness, you should carefully clean and disinfect everything with which the patient has come in contact. Usually people do this with special disinfectant liquids. These can free everything from germs, even the room where the sick person was in bed. Then other people can live in that room, safe from infectious illness.

When a surgeon has to do an operation, he first makes sure his knives have been sterilized. If they have been placed in boiling water for about 10 minutes, the surgeon knows they are free from any harmful germs. He has his linen clothes sterilised too, to free them from germs.

Divers. 'Divers are working underwater, trying to save the valuable cargo of the sunken ship.' You may often hear news like this on the radio, or you may read about it in a newspaper.

Some men become divers to earn their living. Wearing a special diving suit, they can stay underwater for quite a long time.

A diver's suit consists of airtight, waterproof material and a round headpiece with glass portholes to see out of. The soles of the diver's shoes are made of lead, so that the diver will be heavy enough to sink to the sea bed. An air tube and a telephone wire link the diver with his companions on the ship above.

Take a glass, turn it upside down and stand it in water over a floating cork. You will see that the water around the upside-down glass does not get inside it. A 'diving bell' works in the same way. Diving bells may be shaped like a box and lowered into the water with the open side downwards. Men can work safely underwater in a diving bell.

Document. Do you possess a birth certificate? This is a document. A document is an official paper. 'Document' is also the name given to a paper or notes which have survived many centuries. From documents of this kind we can learn how people lived, almost ever since writing was invented.

Dog. Dogs were the first animals that man tamed. In fact they probably tamed themselves. Wild dogs learned to follow man because they knew that where he hunted here might be leftover scraps for them. In time they learned to help man in the hunt. Ever since, they have been his friends. Man has bred many kinds of dog from the first few wild sorts.

Dolphin. The dolphin belongs to the same family as the whales. It breathes air and so is not a fish at all – it is a mammal. Sometimes, dolphins swim after ocean steamers for days on end. They are fine, fast swimmers.

Domesticated animals. A farmyard is like a big, mixed, animal family.

Chickens scratch about in the earth and fight for the choicest worms, watched by their proud cockerel from his perch on a cart-wheel.

There goes the farmer's wife. She is carrying a basket of eggs into the farmhouse.

Here comes mother duck, waddling along with her children. She has just come out of the farmyard pond. And a little farther on you can see the geese. If you walk near them they will flap their wings and make an awful din. People use their soft, white down feathers to fill pillows.

Can you hear the pigs snorting? How sweet the little piglets look, jumping about, full of the joy of living. The farmer gets meat and fat from pigs, and people use their skin to make soft leather.

A white billy goat pokes his head round a corner of the milking shed. Inside the milking shed you can hear the cattle rattling their chains, for it is milking time. In lots of ways, cattle are the most useful animals of all. Just think of the milk we get from them. And from their hides, shoemenders make strong leather soles to repair our shoes.

In our country, oxen pull heavy farm wagons and plough the fields.

Oh, we nearly forgot to mention the sheep. They are just running, bleating, through the farmyard, on their way to their pasture. It won't be long before the farmer shears their long woolly coats. People use their wool for weaving into all kinds of warm materials. In the winter you probably wear a warm knitted pullover and knitted gloves - thanks to the wool that the farmer will shear from his sheep.

Over there a black-and-white cat was just walking sedately through the farmyard. Whoosh! Suddenly she leapt inside the cow-shed. I expect she saw a mouse scuttle inside it. Rover, the watch-dog, barks loudly at the cat. He is a fine watch-dog. It is his task to guard the farm, day and night.

All the domesticated animals that we have described are man's friends and helpers. And we still haven't mentioned one of the best. Here he comes now. The farmer is walking into the yard leading a faithful cart-horse who is pulling a big wagon.

It looks as though the farmer has guessed our thoughts.

'Aren't all domesticated animals really our, servants?' he says. 'This horse pulls my wagons, and ploughs my fields, and if someone wants a ride, he will take them on his back. But he can't lay eggs. The chickens do that. But chickens can't give milk. I get that from my cows.'

The farmer is right. We can't do without any of his domesticated animals. They give us food, clothing and their labour. And often they can be real friends. Intelligent dogs and horses can often understand what we say to them.

In foreign countries, people keep other kinds of domesticated animals. Laplanders, in the far north of Scandinavia, keep reindeer instead of horses, sheep or cows.

In the hot deserts of Asia and Africa, the camel is the chief beast of burden. In our country, people have tamed elephants which can haul great logs weighing several tons.

People have also tamed water buffalo, and the long-haired yaks, and turned them into useful draught animals, riding-animals and pack-animals. Llamas and donkeys can sturdily carry heavy loads across rocky mountain trails.

Donkey. There goes a donkey, trudging patiently along. He does not seem to mind the heavy load he has to carry or the glaring heat of the sun-dried mountain road. Donkeys are well-known as pack-animals and riding-animals. They are hard-working and patient.

Sometimes people say, 'He is as stupid as a donkey.' But donkeys are not specially stupid. Do you know the story of the donkey that lay down in a brook?

One day a donkey was walking over a bridge. He was heavily laden with bags of salt. Because he was thirsty, he lay down in the brook. The water dissolved all the salt in the bags and washed it away. The donkey felt his heavy load become much lighter. Contentedly he trotted on. He remembered the same trick the next time he came that way. But this time he was carrying sponges on his back. Again the donkey lay down in the brook – and drowned. Of course he did not know that sponges soak up water and get heavier. This donkey had learned something from his first experience. But he had not learned enough.

Dragon. Windy autumn weather is just right for flying kites. Perhaps you have flown one yourself. But have you ever seen a kite that looked like a dragon? The Chinese people fly 'dragon kites'.

The Chinese have many legends and fairy tales which describe dragons. The stories say they are ugly, fire-spitting monsters which kill people and burn their homes. Luckily there are no dragons in real life. You will only 'see' them in puppet shows or at the zoo. There, you may see a big lizard called the Komodo Dragon. It really does look a bit like a fairy-tale dragon.

Dragon-fly. On warm summer days you will often see these brilliant-coloured insects dancing and buzzing about above a brook. A dragon-fly's long, thin body flashes green and blue. Its transparent wings have very fine veins.

Dredging machine. This is an enormous machine made of steel. It swallows sand and stones inside its great metal mouth and spits them out again somewhere else – into a lorry for example. You can see these machines at work on building Sites.

There are also dredging machines for cleaning mud, sand and stones from river beds and canals. People do this to keep these waterways clear for ships that pass through.

Dromedary. It is a camel with one hump. It lives in Africa.

Dry-dock. To repair the bottom of a ship, or its propeller, people have to put it in a dry place. Sometimes divers can do this difficult work underwater, but this is not always possible. That is why some harbours have a dry-dock. A dry-dock is a huge tank. A ship sails into the tank. Then all its water is pumped out. The ship rests on huge wooden supports. Some dry-docks are huge floating tanks.

Ducks. Ducks are birds which can swim. You can guess that, even when they are on dry land. Have a look at a duck's webbed feet. What fine paddles they must make. On land, duck waddle clumsily. But in the water they become skilful swimmers. Many ducks can tip up and search for insects on the bottom of a pond with their head and neck submerged. Some ducks can dive and swim underwater. Our big white farmyard ducks are descended from smaller wild ducks.

Dung-beetle. It feeds on the droppings left by various animals. Some beetles collect droppings into a big ball which they roll front of them.

Dynamite. It is a powerful explosive. People use dynamite to break up rocks in mines and quarries. AlManish Nobel, a Swede, who was born over 160 years ago and died in 1896 was the inventor of dynamite.

Dynamo. Harish has got a new dynamo for his bicycle. A dynamo is a small machine which is driven by the bicycle wheel as it spins round. The dynamo produces an electric current which makes the bicycle headlamp and its red rear light burn. People have also invented enormous dynamos which produce enough electricity to light a town.

E

Eagle. The Eagle is a huge bird with a very sharp, curved beak. Eagles are strong enough to push lambs over the edge of a precipice with their wings. An eagle's wingspan may be over seven feet. An eagle's nest is called an eyrie. It is usually built against a steep rock-face. Because eagles are strong and brave, kings and brave knights often put the picture of an eagle on their coat-of-arms.

Ear. 'Bang! Bang! Boom! Boom!' A band was going past the window. Chetan looked at his father in surprise.

'Father,' he said, 'why are the windows vibrating so much?'

'Because the bandsmen are playing so loudly. The sound of their music is enough to make our windows vibrate.'

Glass windows only vibrate when there are very loud sounds.

Inside our ears there is a thin piece of skin, a membrane called the tympanum. Even when there is a very quiet sound, our tympanum vibrates. Behind the tympanum lies our inner ear. This is very sensitive. It conducts the sound vibrations to special nerves which tell our brain what we are hearing.

Ear of corn. Have you ever looked carefully at an ear of corn? Its grains, the fruits of the plant, grow very close, to its stalk. There are other plants where flowers and fruits also grow in 'ears'. Look up **'cereals'**.

Earth. If you hold an orange in your hand you will see that countless tiny ridges and furrows wrinkle the surface of its skin. If you were a giant who could take the earth in his hand, its surface would seem much like that of an orange. Mountains would appear as tiny ridges, valleys would seem little furrows.

The shape of the earth is like a ball, flattened slightly at the North and South Poles. About two-thirds of the earth are covered by water. One-third is land.

The earth moves around the sun. This takes a year. The earth also spins on its own axis like a top. It spins once every 24 hours. The earth is surrounded by an atmosphere. It is impossible for people, animals or plants to breathe without the air in the atmosphere.

The sun gives the earth light and warmth. A ray of sunlight travels about 186,000 miles a sccond. Yet the sun is so far from the earth that it takes about eight minutes before a ray of sunlight reaches us. The sun does not give the same amount of warmth and light everywhere on earth. At the North and South Poles it is always winter. At the Equator it is always summer.

Earthquake. We are always hearing about an earthquake or an earth tremor somewhere in the world. Even a slight earth tremor may be enough to make pictures and lamps move about. If the shock is stronger, furniture may slide about. In a severe earthquake, walls crack, chimneys fall, and houses often collapse. Deep chasms appear in the ground, great lumps of rock crash down hillsides and destroy all the buildings in their way. Undersea earthquakes send vast tidal waves crashing against coastlines.

Earthquakes are caused by large masses of rock which shift beneath the earth's surface Sometimes they cause the rock roof of some huge underground cavern to collapse. Earthquakes also happen during volcanic eruptions. In 1908, an earthquake killed 200,000 people living beside the Straits of Messina (between Italy and Sicily).

Earthworm. Have a really close look at a lawn. Between its grass blades you may notice tiny holes in the earth. These holes are the homes of earthworms. After a warm shower or a damp night, they come to the surface, sometimes wriggling up holes which are yards deep.

Earthworms do not like warm sunshine. The sun dries up their moist skin and makes it difficult for them to breathe.

Did you know that earthworms are really very important little animals? They burrow in the soil and loosen it, keeping it well 'aired'. They also drag leaves into their holes to eat. These leaves help to manure the soil. Yes, even a tiny worm can be a help to the farmer. When a farmer ploughs a field he must often cut a worm in two. But that does not mean the worm always dies. From its two halves may grow two new earthworms!

Ebony. 'White as snow, red as blood and black as ebony,' says a fairy-tale. Ebony wood may be coloured black or very dark brown. It is very valuable and very hard. Ebony grows in India and Africa. The black keys on a piano are made of ebony. People also use it for mosaic work or for furniture, especially for making patterns with different coloured inlaid woods.

Echo. 'Hello!' we shout loudly through the woods. 'Hello!' we hear a voice call back to us. Is someone making fun of us? No, it is only the echo of our own voices. Tree trunks or rocks have reflected them back to us. Some animals which move about at night use echoes to help them find their way. Listening to its own squeaks, reflected from trees, a bat can fly through a wood at night without once touching a twig.

Thomas Alva **Edison** was a famous American inventor who created many important things. He invented electric-light bulbs, a microphone and a record-player, beside many other things that we take for granted. When Edison was about your age, he sold newspapers. Later, he became a telegraph operator and himself manufactured telegraphic apparatus. Edison made his first invention when he was 17 years old. And during the years that followed he made 800 more! Edison built the world's first electric power station, in New York. He lived from 1847 to 1931.

Eel. An eel looks like a snake, but it is a fish. Male eels grow up to nearly two feet long. Females sometimes reach five feet. Eels live in our rivers. But once in their lifetime they make a long journey. They may travel thousand of miles, swimming far into the Atlantic Ocean. There, they lay their eggs and die. When young eels (called elvers) hatch, they swim back to the rivers of the countries where their parents lived.

An eel has a slippery, slimy skin which makes it hard to grasp. Often you hear someone say, 'He is as slippery as an eel.' This means that a person is always making excuses for himself. Like the slippery eels, he always manages to find some way of saving himself by crafty means.

Eiderdown. Do you know the fairy-tale of the princess and the pea? In this tale there was a princess with such sensitive skin that she could feel a pea through twenty eiderdown mattresses. 'Eiderdown' is the name of the very soft, small feathers which grow on the breast of the eider duck. People collect eiderdown from the ducks' nests and use it to fill pillows and to make eider-downs for beds.

Electricity. No one yet fully knows what electricity is. Yet almost everyone uses its mysterious power. Electricity makes a light-bulb glow, heats an electric iron, drives the motor of a vacuum cleaner and makes a radio or television work.

People have invented great machines in power stations which make electricity go to work for us. These machines make tiny particles of electricity (called electrons) move along thick high-tension cables to the thinner wires in our homes. Electrons make the thin wires in a light-bulb glow and heat electric irons and hot-plates. They cause the spark in the sparking plug of a petrol engine; without it the engine would not work. Electrons make iron magnetic and because of them a doorbell rings, the loudspeaker in a radio works and teleprinters write. Electrons also make it possible for you to speak to someone many miles away through a telephone. Electrons make it possible for the motors of trolleybuses and electric trains to run.

Electricity is a good servant. But, like fire, it can be a bad master. Always be careful not to touch bare wires when you use any sort of electrical apparatus.

Elk. Elks are at home in the swampy forests of North America, Northern Asia and parts of Europe. Elks are really a sort of very big deer. They are much bigger than any of the deer which you may see wandering about parks in our country. These are mostly fallow deer and red deer. Elks are fine strong swimmers. When they are fully grown, male elks have great flat antlers and look very impressive. It is a pity that elks are getting more and more rare.

Elephant. Leela and Anita had been to the circus. They specially liked the elephants. They began worrying their father to take them to the zoo. He soon gave in.

There were two elephants at the zoo.

'Look,' said Father, 'the elephant with the big ears is an African elephant. The one with smaller ears is an Indian elephant. All elephants belong to a special family of thick-skinned mammals. They can brush through dense forests in their homelands without feeling the thorns scratch them

'Wild elephants travel in herds. Their leader is the most cunning of all. They feed by pulling down leaves from quite high trees, helped by their long trunks. These huge animals have huge appetites, so they must be always on the move looking for more food.

'Elephants have a formidable weapon – their long, ivory tusks. People carve valuable ornaments from ivory.

'In India men tame elephants to work for them. They make patient and obedient helpers. An elephant can shift huge loads and can lift a ton weight. But nowadays machines do most of the heavy work.

'Guess how old an elephant can live. Some live for more than 65 years!'

Epidemic. Throughout the past, until about 100 years ago, outbreaks of terrible disease killed people by the thousand. Two of the most terrible diseases were cholera and the plague. Many people died when an epidemic of plague struck a city. For this sort of disease is contagious – people can catch it by touching other people who have it. Sometimes a whole town died in an epidemic.

Even today epidemics can happen, and in parts of the world they do. Such diseases happen when people eat food which has gone bad, or drink water which is polluted.

But modern doctors can quickly check an epidemic. They find out where the epidemic started and make sure that more people cannot catch the disease from that source. Doctors keep sick people away from every one else so that fit people do not catch the disease. Doctors can often cure the sick people with the help of up-to-date medicines.

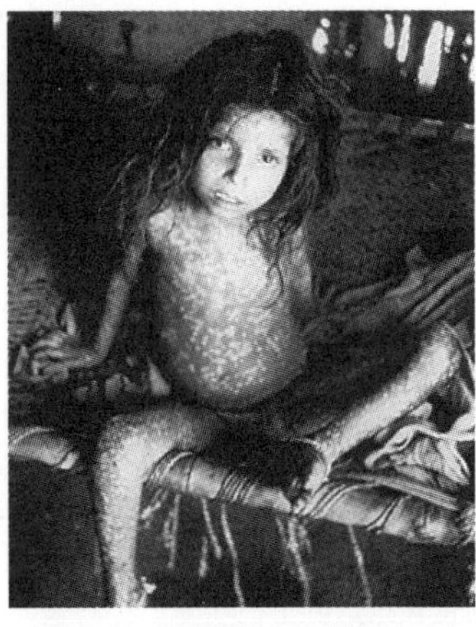

Equator. The earth is round. You can think of it as an apple. The place here the apple's stalk joins the apple corresponds to the North Pole on the earth. Opposite the North Pole is the South Pole. Of course these poles are only imaginary – you can't see them like the stalk of an apple. Around the poles the earth spins.

Cut through your apple from the side, where it is fattest. You have made a line in its skin which is a circle. The earth also has a circle round its middle: the equator. The equator divides the earth into a Northern and a Southern Hemisphere (half-sphere). Like the poles, the equator is imaginary. You can't actually see it.

If you went round the equator by express train, you would take 21 days to reach the place you started from.

Escalator. In some large stores, and on our underground railways, there are very strange staircases. One by one, their steps rise out of the floor and travel slowly up to the floor above. You just stand on one of these steps and let it take you up. What a pity we don't have an escalator at home!

Eskimos. Eskimos are small people with yellow-brown skin and sleek black hair. They live in Greenland and North America, along the frozen Arctic coasts. The word 'Eskimo' means 'eater of raw meat'.

Eskimo men hunt seals and walruses. The women prepare oil for burning as candles from seal-fat (or 'blubber'). They clean and tan skins and make clothes from them. These clothes are called 'anoraks'. An anorak is a kind of blouse without buttons and with a hood attached. The high boots of the Eskimos are called 'kamikkers'.

Eskimos use seal-skins to waterproof their 'kayaks', the speedy, slender, covered-in canoes in which they do their hunting.

In the months of June and July, when the weak sun melts much of the Arctic snow and ice, Eskimos live in tents made of animal-skins. In the long, dark winter they build huts of snow called 'igloos'. The Eskimos are a peaceful people. In their language the word for 'war' does not exist.

Extinct animals. Many thousand years ago, enormous mammoths roamed our woods. They were like giant woolly elephants with enormous, curving tusks. Cave-bears and sabre-toothed tigers lived about that time, too.

Maybe you have heard of the giant lizards called dinosaurs. They lived 150 million years ago. In museums you will still find the fossil skeletons of these enormous animals – some much longer than a bus.

These animals lived and died out many centuries before there were any people. Today, people are helping to wipe out some of the modern animals. Man helped to hunt some sorts of wild ox and horse out of existence. Today, European bison, Mongolian wild horses, the Indian rhinoceros, Indian Tiger and several kinds of whale are in danger dying out. Man, hunting for food and sport has killed so many of them.

F

Fable. Once upon a time a lion was having his mid-day nap. Suddenly a mouse came running by, and scuttled over the lion's nose. The lion woke up.

'Hey!' he called. 'What are you doing?' In one bound, the lion caught up with the mouse and pinned it beneath a huge paw.

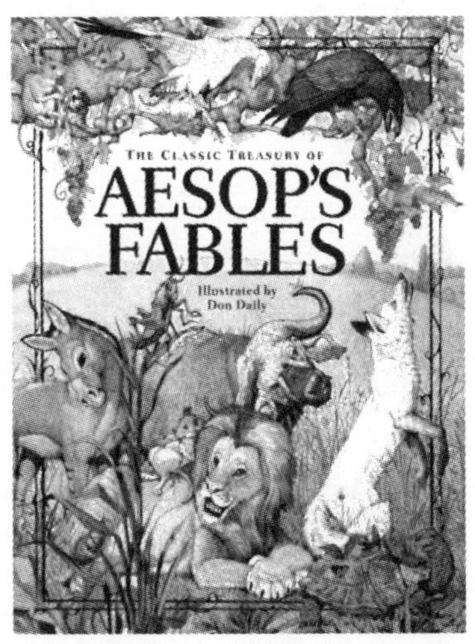

'Please let me go,' pleaded the mouse.

'All right, then, just this once,' said the lion. And he let the mouse run off.

Some time later, the lion got entangled in an unbreakable net. A hunter had set it as a trap to catch the lion. No matter how he struggled, the lion could not free himself. Suddenly the mouse came scurrying into sight.

'Please help me,' roared the lion.

The mouse wasted no time. He began gnawing at the ropes of the net. Soon he gnawed right through them and the lion was free.

'You see,' said the mouse, 'one good deserves another.'

This short story is a fable. In fables animals can speak. Fables are entertaining stories which also teach us something.

Fabulous characters. In fairy-fables you read a lot about 'living' creatures. But many of these creatures do not exist. They include Dragons, Nymphs, Giants, Imps, Mermaids, Unicorn and many other strange beings.

Fairy-tale. 'Once upon a time'... Look, here come Hansel and Gretel, holding hands and walking through a wood. What is that flapping sound? It is the seven ravens flying toward the glass mountain. A light is shining between the tree trunks of the forest. It is coining from Snow White's hut. What is that noise? It can only be the music of a fairy band.

Come along, give me your hand. Let's go together to fairyland. We shall find lots of fairy-tales that we did not know.

Fakirs. A Hindu beggar in India is often known as a 'fakir'. Fakirs wander all over the country. Many of them inflict injuries on themselves and they are able to bear much pain. Some of them lie on planks studded with nails. Others spend their lives as hermits, shut away from everyone else. Some of these people fast for many days. They think it makes them better people. Fakirs are greatly honoured by most Indians.

Farmer. In olden days, farmers had to work terribly hard for terribly long hours each day. They only had bulls to pull their ploughs and hoes, and to haul their farm wagons about. Cart-horses were willing and obedient workers. But they were slow-moving and they got tired, just like a man gets tired.

Nowadays things are very different on most farms. Nowadays, farmers have sowing machines, mowing machines and tractors to pull them. One tractor may be driven by a small engine a yard long, which is as powerful as 40 horses all pulling together.

But farmers don't only work in their fields. There is plenty of work for them to do with the cattle in their cowsheds. They have to gather their sheep and dip them in a special bath to keep them free from disease. They have to feed and clean the pigs in their sties. Many farmers keep pigs and sheep as well as cattle.

In many farmyards, close by the farmhouse, you will see chickens, ducks and geese. The farmer fattens them up to eat or keeps them for the eggs they lay. But most farmers only eat a little of what they produce. They sell many eggs as well as their corn, cattle, butter, milk and fruit, in nearby towns. Without farmers we could not live, for they supply our food.

There are farmers all over the world. The farmers in Africa and America grow different plants from the ones our farmers grow. Strawberries and oats and pineapples – many of the foods we eat come from abroad. They need a cooler climate than ours in which to grow.

Ferns. They are beautiful plants, though they never grow attractive blossoms. Their leaves make up the most lovely patterns. Ferns mostly grow in cool, shady woods. There are hundreds of different kinds of fern. They grow all over the world.

Ferry. A ferry carries people, animals and vehicles across a river. Small ferry boats are sometimes worked by oars and sometimes by a motor. A cable ferry is a ferry boat or very big raft which hangs from a cable. A train ferry is a ferry which can carry a trainload of people. There are train ferries between England and Belgium and between Germany and Denmark.

Fever. Chetan feels terribly tired. His head and hands are very cold.

'Perhaps you have a temperature,' says Mother. She puts a thermometer under his arm to take his temperature. The thermometer shows 102 degrees Fahrenheit. To bed with you, Chetan! Your temperature is (usually it is 98.4 degrees). It is a warning you have a fever coming on.

Fig. Figs are the juicy fruits of the fig tree which grows in North Africa, South America and in the south of Europe. Unripe figs are bright green; ripe ones are deep purple. Sometimes your mother buys dried figs in a shop. They are brown.

Fir tree. There are many kinds of fir tree. Most of them contain a lot of sticky resin inside their trunks. Some fir trees, grow best on low ground. But others grow high up among mountains, even at an altitude of 9,000 feet. To protect itself from the searching, icy, mountain winds, it does not grow upright but sprawls along the ground.

Fire. Fire is man's friend and foe. 'Fire! Fire!' People dread to hear that cry ringing through a great building. For fire can be one of man's most terrible enemies.

Yet imagine that someone had put out all the fires everywhere on earth. All the flames in all the stoves and all the fires that heat boilers – all would go out. There would be no heat to melt iron out of iron ore. We would have no metal tools. Without fire to keep them warm and without tools to help them get their food and cook it, most people would probably die.

Long ago, before people knew about the use of fire, they managed to scrape a living. They had to eat their food raw. They had to grope their way around their cave-dwelling in the dark. When it was cold, they simply huddled together in some sheltered spot.

It is true that fire can destroy people and their buildings, but people have learned to capture fire and to use it well. How did man get to know about fire? He saw it when lightning struck a tree trunk. The first men who saw this happen were probably frightened and ran away. But when the fire began to die down and was no longer dangerous, they crept back and started to experiment with it.

People found that fire would roast the animals they had caught in the hunt, and roast meat tasted nicer than raw flesh. In winter, fire gave man welcome warmth. A family would sit together around the open fireplace in their cave.

'Fire is our friend,' said the cave-dwellers, and their women folk guarded it so that it should not go out. Some people even worshipped fire as a god.

But sometimes it did happen that their fire went out. Then they had to try to bring it alive again. People rubbed two bits of dry wood together, and in time someone invented the idea of a fire-drill. Today shepherds in remote lands and the Eskimos in the Arctic still make fire in these simple ways.

When someone found that two stones struck together made a spark he had invented the first simple 'lighter'. People found that they got the biggest sparks by hitting a piece of iron against a piece of flint. If they held a little bit of sawdust (or some other dry woody material) close to the flint, the sawdust soon began to burn. It caught alight from the sparks.

In time people found that the concentrated rays of the sun could set a fire alight. They concentrated the sun's rays through a burning glass. But people could not always wait for the sun when they wanted a fire. So they preferred to use their flint lighters. Today, people use petrol lighters instead. The flints in a modern lighter are made artificially. A small wheel, which rubs against the flint, produces sparks. The sparks ignite the wick which is soaked in petrol - a fuel that burns very easily.

In the kitchen your mother may use a gas lighter. In a gas lighter the part that makes the sparks is made of metal. Not everyone uses lighters but almost everyone uses matches. For only a few paise you can buy a whole boxful of them. There is a lot of fire locked up in a little matchbox. With one movement of your hand you can make a match burn.

What a great help to us fire can be. But many accidents have happened when people have used it carelessly. They often happen when children play about with matches. So remember that though man has captured fire, he has not tamed it. Don't let the wild beast get loose in your home!

Films. Vikram has got a strange toy. It is a small book full of pictures. When you look at the pictures you think at first that the same one is drawn on every page. Each picture shows a runner jumping over a hurdle. But when you look more carefully, you see that the runner has moved forward a little bit in each picture.

Vikram flips through the pages very quickly, and what do you think happens? The runner seems to move and jump over the hurdle. It is just like watching a film at the cinema. And that's hardly surprising, for cinema films work in the same way.

A camera-man aims his film-camera at a runner and takes a film of him. A film-camera is a special sort of camera. It takes many pictures very quickly, one after another, about 24 in a single second! In this way, it photographs a runner's movements one at a time on a reel of film. Each picture is a continuation of the one before. When the reel is complete and its film has been developed it is unrolled on to a projector.

The strong light of the projector shines through the film and the pictures on the film are projected on to a white screen in your cinema. As the reel unwinds, the separate pictures flash by very quickly. And look – you seem to be watching a runner moving in real life!

The first films were a marvelous invention. And skilful inventors have made them better still. They have found how to link voices with pictures and how to show pictures in colour. You have probably also heard of '3D' stereoscopic films. In these films the people and animals on the screen seem to step out of it.

Of course making any kind of film means a great deal of work before the finished film is ready to show. People make films in large halls. These are called film studios. But people often film some parts of a picture out-of-doors. Film-stars – the most famous film-actors – and the other actors have to stand in the bright light of spotlights. Then a film-camera can clearly record their movements.

A big film will consist of lots of separate pieces. Each piece is called a 'scene'. When all the scenes have been made they are put together to make one big film.

Fire-brigade. The night watchman had just cried out, 'Twelve o'clock and all's well,' as he stumped through the slumbering city streets. Holding his stick firmly, he passed on. Not a light to be seen anywhere. But wait! What was that? A candle flickering? Perhaps someone was ill. Then the light glowed much stronger. Could it be a house on fire?

The night watchman ran towards the light. Then, 'Fire! Fire!' he cried. His shouts rang through every street, every house. People woke up and jumped from their beds.

Ding dong! Ding dong! A great bell began to toll its summons. Men and women rushed into the street, grasping buckets filled with water. Quick, there's the fire! In no time people had formed a long line which ran from the burning house to the nearest well.

They passed their buckets down the line – full from the well to the fire, then empty, back to the well for more water. They all worked at top speed. Firemen flung each bucketful of water against the high, roaring flames.

Fire-fighting was like this in many of our towns and villages two centuries ago. Today, it is very different. Today, the telephone number of the fire service is printed on the first page of every telephone directory. In case important buildings catch fire, they have electric alarm bells which give instant warning to a fire-station a few streets away. And you will see fire-alarms in the streets of our bigger towns and cities.'

When someone reports a fire, an alarm rings a loud bell in the fire-station. People at once open its gates, and within seconds fire-engine after another is speeding to scene of the fire. Ding-a-ling! Ding-a-ling! Their bells echo through the streets. A policeman controlling traffic at a cross-roads holds everything up to let the fire-engines through. Buses and cars pull in to the roadside. The fire-engines must always go first.

Soon, the engines turn into a side street. A little farther on is the fire. What a lot of smoke! Great crowds of people are standing watching it. Policemen nearby see that they keep a safe distance away from the blaze.

Suddenly brakes scream and before the fire-engines have even stopped, firemen are jumping down. Their chief gives his instructions and his men begin pulling great drums from their engines. The men unwind fire-hoses, rolled round the drums. Swiftly they link one end of a hose to the nearest river or hydrant. But the hoses are too short! In a flash the firemen join up extra lengths. They turn a great ladder towards the burning house.

Sssssh! A hose directs a powerful jet of into the smoke. Then there is another jet of water. Soon there are three, four, five! One jet is so powerful that it lifts the tiles off roof and begins squirting water straight through the rafters. An enormous cloud of smoke rises in the air.

On the second floor stands a frightened man, waving from the window. Behind him the room is on fire – he cannot get downstairs. Twelve firemen run beneath the window, carrying a safety-blanket.

'Jump down!' they shout. Will the man dare to jump? Yes! He climbs out on the window-ledge. Crash! He leaps and falls exactly in the middle of the blanket. Luckily he is unharmed.

Now firemen protected by fireproof asbestos suits are making their way into the house. Slowly the fire is getting feebler. At last it is put out. The tired firemen reel up their hoses and load them on to their fire-engines. They drive off, but one fire-engine stays behind. This is a safeguard.

Fire-fighting is still very dangerous, and very hard work. Many people can still lose their lives or get burnt during a big fire. Some people start fires deliberately. But many cause fires through carelessness.

Our fire-service does more than put out fires. Wherever help is needed, the fire-service plays an important part. In floods or after storm damage it may help to pump water from flooded homes. Firemen rescue children who get wedged in iron railings. They even climb trees to rescue frightened cats which can't get down unaided. The brave and helpful men of our fire-service do all these things. Don't you think they are splendid people?

Fireworks. Vinit and Ritu were watching a fireworks display. Rockets were shooting into the sky. High above, they burst and a beautiful shower of sparks cascaded down. In a few seconds it was all over.

'What are rocket fireworks made of?' Vinit asked his father.

'Rockets are made of gunpowder packed inside a cardboard tube,' his father replied.

'You light a tube and the gunpowder burns and explodes, to push the rocket hundreds of feet up into the air.'

First aid. Rohit, Deepak and Jassi were playing in the garden. Rohit almost caught his friend Deepak. But suddenly, Rohit slipped on the loose gravel path and fell full length on the ground. He was badly hurt. He had cut hands, cut knees and a bleeding nose. Jassi was frightened and just stood looking on, not knowing what to do. Deepak was frightened too, when he saw all that blood. But Deepak was brave.

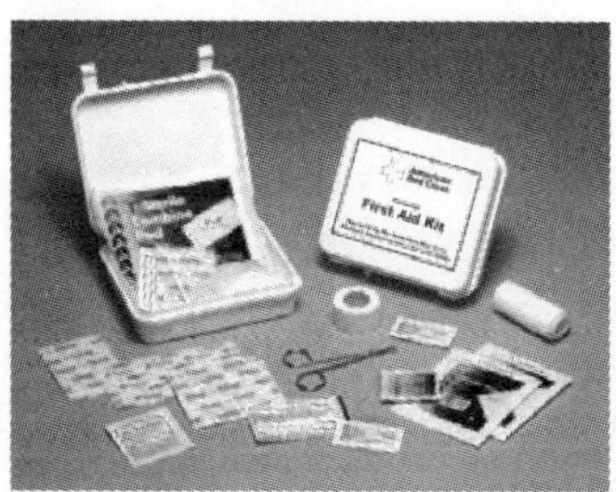

He went to Rohit and pinched his nose with his handkerchief. The bleeding became less.

'Jassi,' said Deepak, 'run quickly and fetch Mother.' A few moments later, Mother came hurrying down the path.

Rohit's nose had already stopped bleeding. Mother said, 'Come along with me.' Rohit hobbled a bit but Deepak helped to support him. Mother put Rohit to bed while Deepak ran to the chemist to buy bandages. Then he helped his mother to clean Rohit's wounds and bandage them up.

Which of Rohit's friends was the bravest? Jassi, who stood and did nothing, or Deepak, who helped his friend? Deepak, of course! When someone has an accident and you see it, you should give them first aid. It isn't a pleasant duty, but brave people don't shrink from it.

Yogesh sprained his ankle playing football on the sports ground. Ritu burned her hand at the kitchen stove. Harish capsized his boat and nearly got drowned. Nisha was knocked down by a bicycle. Don't forget that anywhere, at any time, you may see someone have an accident.

But though you may want to give them first aid, it's not so easy. First aid is something you have to learn. If you do it wrong you may only make an injured person worse. But there are special first-aid courses where-people can learn how to care for anyone who has just had an accident. First-aid courses teach you how to bandage up an injured arm, how to put a splint on a broken leg, how to give artificial respiration to someone who has almost drowned, what to do with someone who is unconscious or who has fainted.

If you are near an accident when it happens and you know some first aid, give all the help you can. But if there are grown-ups helping, or if the police, ambulance-men or doctors are already there, just walk on. Children should give all the help they can; but when people already have all they need, extra helpers may only get in the way. And the poor injured person won't want a crowd fussing round him.

Fish. If you have a good look at a fish you will understand how it is so well suited to living underwater. Its smoothly curve slippery body glides easily through waters. Strong muscles move its tail fin from side to side. It works like an oar to thrust the fish through the water. A fish's other fins help it to change direction, and a swimming bladder inside the fish fills with liquid and empties, to help the fish go up and down. Gills make it possible for a fish to breathe the air dissolved in water.

Because its scales do not protect it again the cold, its body changes temperature with the changing temperature of the around it. So a fish never feels the cold we do.

Flags. In some countries, everyone decorates his house with flags when there is a national holiday.

When young people go hiking, they often carry a small flag. This is called a pennant. Pennants which bear the colours of their country are called flags too.

Every country has its own flag with its national colours. India has the colours saffron, white and green, with an Ashok Chakra in the middle. Great Britain has the colours red, white and blue. Belgium has red, yellow and black. Germany has black, red and gold. Austria has red, white and red. Switzerland has a white cross on a red background.

Flat feet. Bhanu often complains of pain in his feet when he walks.

'Your arches have dropped,' the doctor told him. 'You must wear supports in your shoes or you will get flat feet.'

Flowers. We all enjoy the bright colours and sweet scent of flowers as we ramble through meadows and woods or take a walk through a flower garden. The scents and colours of many flowers attract honey-bees, bumble-bees, butterflies and, other little insects. Inside the flowers they find food – nectar and pollen. The insects accidentally carry pollen from plant to plant. This helps their blossoms to develop into fruits with seeds.

Do you sometimes put cut flowers in a vase? Don't forget to give them enough water.

And plants in pots need fresh water regularly to replace what they drink. Many nutritious substances are dissolved in water and plant roots can suck them up by drinking water. If you put rooted plants in pots you should take care to see that you plant them in the right sort of soil. In time they will use up all its nutritious substances. But you can replace them by adding several sorts of fertiliser to your soil.

Many plants do not like bright sunlight or dark corners. Put these flowers on a table, fairly near a window. Cut off those leaves which wither. And don't forget once a month to clean the healthy leaves with a sponge to remove the dust that has collected on them.

Fly agaric. It is perhaps the most beautiful fungus which grows in our woods. It is dark red, covered with vivid white spots. But be careful not to eat it, for it is poisonous. People used to fly agaric to get rid of flies. They put it in milk which the flies drank. Then the flies died.

Flying. 'I have been sitting in a train and a, ship for 14 hours to get from London to Dublin,' sighed a traveler. 'Now I have to go to an important meeting and I am tired out.'

'Then I am better off than you,' laughed another man. 'Two hours ago I was still in London, and I am not tired at all. I flew to Dublin by 'plane'.

Flying is a wonderful invention. It was not so very long ago when no one believed a man could ever fly as high or fast as a bird. Probably when your grandparents were born there were still no aeroplanes. At that time there were only railways and steamships. Sometimes a car would drive through the streets of a village and everyone would flock to see it. For; even cars were scarce in those days. And they made a great deal of noise.

Then some brave men tried to copy the birds and fly through the air. People had already invented balloons that flew and were big enough to carry people. They had been making these balloons for over 100 years. But people were not content with this kind of air travel. A balloon always travels with the wind. The people in a great basket hung beneath the balloon could not steer it.

They could only throw out bags full of sand, called ballast. Then the balloon would rise. Or they would let some gas escape from the balloon. Then it would sink downwards. No, just going up and down in a balloon did not satisfy people.

People wanted to go somewhere, and somewhere they had chosen to go to. So they made experiments with airships which they could steer. Balloons had been round; airships were often shaped like a huge cigar. Their silk, gas-filled skin was supported by a strong framework. They were just a huge, rigid balloon, but a balloon with engines.

Airships had several engines with propellers and steering gear. An airship pilot could direct his aircraft more or less at will. The passengers sat in a large cabin, slung beneath the huge balloon. Many airships earned themselves the name 'zeppelins' after Count Zeppelin, a great airship inventor.

Today, people no longer travel in airships, but in much faster aeroplanes. Engineers started building aeroplanes soon after airships came into use. Before people built the first heavier-than-air plane they had already made heavier-than-air gliders. A German, Lilienthal, flew in a glider whose wings were made like those of a great soaring bird. But soon 'planes were to fly under their own power. Several people tried fitting engines in gliders. But all failed to make a 'plane that flew. All except the Wright brothers - in America. In 1903, their 'plane called *The Flyer* took off for the first time and flew for 12 seconds.

Our modern planes don't look at all like the Wrights' biplane, which carried one man. Some modern air-liners can carry 200 people! Today there are flying boats that can land on water. There are helicopters – a very strange kind of 'plane. A helicopter has no wings. But above its fuselage is a huge propeller which whirls around. Its blades look a bit like the sails of a windmill. These blades screw a helicopter straight up into the air and it can easily land on a small, flat roof. People use helicopters to save shipwrecked sailors, to carry letters between islands, and for many other things. In times of flood, avalanche and other accidents, helicopters can be a great help. They can reach people cut off from any other sort of rescue.

For about 15 years, jet planes have been whistling through our skies. Their fuel burns with air, and the burning mixture of fuel and air makes hot gases which rush from the back of the engine. As they rush out, they kick backwards and so push the plane forwards. A jet plane can fly faster than the speed of sound, which is about 750 miles an hour at sea level. Do you know how fast the Wright brothers flew? Only 36 miles an hour. Since their first flight, nearly 100 years ago, people have flown 50 times as fast!

Football. Or soccer, Game in which two 11-member teams try to propel a ball into the opposing team's goal, using any part of the body except the hands and arms. Only the goalkeeper, when positioned within the penalty area in front of the goal, may use hands and arms. The game's first uniform set of rules was put in place in 1863, when England's Football Association was created. Professional leagues began appearing in the late 1880s, first in England and then in other countries. The Federation Internationale de Football Association (FIFA) was founded in 1904, and has hosted the World Cup every four years since 1930. Football has been included in the Olympic Games since 1908. Now played on all continents in over 150 nations, with over 40 million registered players, it is the world's most popular ball game.

Fox. Reynard the fox is a crafty animal. He lives in the woods. There he feels safe and at home. The rabbits and pheasants who also live in the woods don't stand much chance of escaping a fox on the prowl. But foxes are often content to eat field-mice and insects.

Sometimes foxes dig their own hole, called an 'earth'. But they may enlarge a rabbit burrow or make a home in a badger's hole. A mother fox (called a vixen) brings back live mice and birds to her cubs in the earth. While they play, the young foxes are learning to catch and kill their prey. People make furs from the fox's long winter coat.

Fungi. 'Mushrooms for sale! Fresh mushrooms! Delicious mushrooms!' They are very good to eat and in no time the man has sold his basket of mushrooms. The last few days, the weather has been ideal for growing mushrooms. Some warm rain fell. When the sun began to shine, the woods steamed. Then the mushrooms began to grow.

Mushrooms are only one of several kinds of fungi that you can eat. Some fungi are poisonous. People have died because they ate the wrong sort. If you go picking mushrooms, make sure they *are* mushrooms.

Frogs. Of course you all know about frogs. They live in ponds and ditches and in the long, damp grass close by. But you often find toads far from water. They live in, meadows and gardens. There are some frogs in foreign countries that grow much bigger than our frogs. Others, like the little tree-frogs, grow much smaller than our common frog.

It takes about five years for some frogs to grow up properly. They begin life as an egg in a mass of frogspawn laid in a pond. The egg becomes a tadpole. Gradually it grows fore-legs and hind-legs and its tail is absorbed into its body. Then it has become a tiny frog.

Fur-bearing animals. How warm a fur collar or a fur hat can be in winter. Fur collars and hats are often made from the skins of rabbits or lambs. People breed and hunt many kinds of animals for their fur alone. With this fur people make not only collars but whole fur coats – often they are very beautiful and very costly – they can cost thousands of Rupees each!

Animals with valuable furs include foxes, martens, ermine, raccoons, beavers, hamsters and mink. People prize the skins of some Asian sheep as well.

G

Galanty show. Uncle Khatri is a magician. He can move his hands about in such a way that their shadows make all kinds of strange shapes appear on a wall. Vinit tried to copy his uncle. He found he could do it quite well, too.

In past centuries, people used to perform shows with shadow puppets in this way. You can make a galanty show for yourself, if you want. You and your friends could be the actors.

Hang a linen cloth across an open door and light it with a lamp from behind. Then collect an audience of friends and let them sit in front of the cloth where they can watch it. Then two actors should stand between the cloth and the lamp. Their shadows start moving about on the cloth. The audience will hear their voices saying, 'Oh, doctor, I feel so ill. I have eaten too many sweets.' 'Ah, well, we'll have a look, old boy. Just sit down on this chair. Open your mouth wide.'

The shadow doctor seems to reach down inside his patient's mouth. Then he draws out spoons, fork and knives. If you can make this look real on the shadow screen, the audience will laugh a lot and they will be puzzled to know how you did it.

Garage. The doctor visits his patients by car. In the evening he drives his car into a garage. In garage, people clean the car and refill its tank with petrol. Above the entrance of the garage are the words, 'No Smoking'. Do you know why?

In the big cities of a few countries there are garages which consist of several floors. In these garages your car may go up in a lift. There are other garages where cars can drive to the top floor up a long, gradual slope.

Garden. 'Isn't the bus coming yet?' asked Rahul, impatiently.

'I can't see it,' said Ritu.

Father and Mother smiled. How impatient the children were. They were just off to see their Uncle Vinit who kept a wonderful garden. At last the bus came in sight and soon the children were on their way.

Uncle Vinit walked to the garden gate to meet them as soon as he heard their eager footsteps. Rahul and Ritu ran straight into the garden and began to explore. What a lot of fruit trees there were. And there was a big concrete tank full of water.

'May we bathe in that?' asked Rahul.

'As far as I'm concerned, you may,' said Uncle.'Usually I use it for watering my young plants. I let the sun take the chill off before I use it, for young plants are tender things.

'As you can see, I grow my flowers, ornamental shrubs and lilacs near the house. I keep my fruit trees farther away, on the lawn. Those young trees have sticks to support them. Opposite the trees you see my vegetable plots with a gardening shed and a compost heap.'

Ritu looked at all the lovely flowers, but Rahul was soon busy in the shed. There, he found some garden tools: a spade, a shovel, a rake, a scythe, a sickle, a hoe and a garden fork. And a strange pointed stick. What could that be? Rahul's uncle soon told him. It was a dibbing stick to make holes in the ground for young plants. Rahul explored further and found more spades, watering-cans and a wheel-barrow.

'What a lot of tools you have, Uncle,' said Rahul admiringly.

'You must come with me and have a look at the nursery at the bottom of my garden,' said Uncle Vinit.

'That's where I buy my young plants and fruit trees, and where I get a lot of good advice.'

At the nursery, some vegetable plots seemed as big as a whole field. Many of the small beds were covered with glass. Under the glass, tender green shoots were just appearing above the black earth. Ritu and Rahul thought the young nursery fruit trees looked like soldiers. For they were planted in very straight rows. Each trunk had a label fixed to it with wire. The label bore its name.

The nurseryman walked over to the fence where the three stood, and chatted with them. He said he had been lucky that there were not so many insect pests this year. But of course he daren't neglect spraying his trees with insect poison, in case. And he still had to prune trees, insects or no insects.

'Yes,' agreed Uncle. 'And I'm sure you have to protect the nests of the song-birds that help to eat harmful insects.'

Anyone who looks after his garden really well reaps a worth-while reward – juicy fruits, tasty vegetables and beautiful flowers.

Garden spider. The garden spider is a real artist. She only takes an hour or so to weave a beautiful web. When it is finished, she sits in a corner and waits for her prey. When a fly comes along and gets stuck in the web, the garden spider bites it, kills it, and wraps it up into a silken larder. You can easily recognise a garden spider. It has a big white cross on its back.

Gas. 'Oh, I know all about that,' I can hear you saying. 'Mother cooks on a gas-cooker.' True enough, and she probably does. The gas that burns in her gas-cooker is called coal-gas.

But there are many other sorts of gas. Did you know that you are always breathing gases in and out? These gases are mixed up to make air. We cannot live without the oxygen gas in air. Air is mostly a mixture of oxygen and nitrogen.

Gazelle. Imagine that you are a real explorer. You are plodding across a boundless plain, deep inside the huge continent of Africa. Suddenly a herd of gazelles runs past you. They are so quick that you just have time to notice that they look like little antelopes but have extra-long legs. They are related to the deer in our parks, but much more graceful and much faster.

Gem. It is another word for an artistic and valuable piece of jewellery.

Geometrical figures. 'Oh,' you will be saying. 'This sounds hard.' But it isn't at all. Just take a sheet of paper from an exercise book. A sheet of paper is a geometrical figure in shape. It is a rectangle. When you cut the sheet so that all four sides are equal in length you have made a square. Rectangles and squares are both quadrilaterals – each has four sides.

Now fold your paper like a serviette. It has became a triangle. An oblong box is called a parallelepiped. When its sides are all equal in length it is called a cube. Even a simple ball is a geometrical figure. It is a globe. And of course there are lots more geometrical figures.

Giant snakes. There really are giant snakes. Some grow to a length of 18 feet. Some people say that the anaconda – a giant water-snake that lives in South America – sometimes grows 30 feet long. But many naturalists believe that the pythons which live in India and Malaya sometimes grow even longer than that.

These giant snakes kill their victim by wrapping their coils around its body and squeezing its breath out of it. People kill some South American snakes and make their skins into elegant handbags.

Gills. Man and the other mammals, birds, reptiles and amphibious creatures – all breathe through their lungs. But fishes breathe through gills. Their gills can take air out of the water as our lungs simply breathe it from the atmosphere.

Giraffe. Giraffes live in small herds among the tall grass and thorn bushes of the African veldt. A giraffe may grow 20 feet tall. He can easily eat the leaves that grow high on an acacia tree. The Arabs call this animal 'serafe' which means 'lovable'. From the word 'serafe' came our word 'giraffe'.

Glacier. High up in the mountains it may be so cold that even in summer the snow never melts. Snow and ice gather in the high valleys and may gradually form a glacier.

A glacier is a thick layer of ice – sometimes 300 feet through. It is really a frozen river. Slowly it flows downhill, perhaps only moving a few feet each year. A glacier is shaped like a long tongue, which carries with it great lumps of rock torn from the sides of its valley. These lumps of rock form a wall at the foot of the glacier called an end moraine, and other moraines where two glaciers meet.

Crevasses – cracks in a glacier – can be very dangerous for climbers. Sometimes crevasses are covered in a thin layer of snow so that you can't see them at all.

Underneath the glacier, at its bottom end, runs a stream of icy, melt-water. It rushes from a cavern of ice. Glaciers form not only in high mountains but on lower ground in the polar regions.

Glass. You may not believe it, but the most beautiful transparent glasses are made from very ordinary substances. Glass is made from quartz sand, chalk and soda. People mix these substances and melt them in the great heat of a special oven until they become liquid. Then people can mould them into glass plates, bottles, saucers and glasses which harden as they cool.

People can shape glass bottles by putting them in a mould or by blowing on half-molten glass through a long tube. Of all the different sorts of glass, rock-crystal glass is perhaps the loveliest to look at.

Glow-worm. Have you ever seen a blue-green point of light shining from a hedge on a warm summer night? It is a glow-worm. If you catch it, its light may go out.

Gnats. You must have heard of 'plagues of gnats'. These are the tiny insects that buzz round your ears on summer nights. What is worse, they can sting you and inflict a little wound which itches and irritates for days.

Gold. The rings on your mother's fingers are made from a shiny metal. They are probably made of gold. Because this metal is so valuable, because it is tough and never gets rusty, it is called a 'precious' metal. Goldsmiths make the most beautiful bracelets, watches and ornaments out of gold.

People mine gold or wash it from the silt in rivers. Most of the world's gold comes from South Africa.

People say of someone who is very good, 'He has a heart of gold.' A husband and wife celebrate their Golden Anniversary when they have been married 50 years. In history, a 'golden age' was a time when, country was wealthy. It might have been rich in money or in something else. In England, the reign of Queen Elizabeth I was a 'golden age of drama'. That was the time when Shakespeare wrote his plays.

Goldfinch. Any of several species of songbirds that have a shot, notched tail and much yellow in the plumage. All have a bill that is more delicate and sharply pointed than that of most finches. They live in flocks, feeding on weeds in fields and gardens. They have high, lisping calls. Various species live in western Eurasia and North and South America and have been introduced into New Zealand and Australia. They are typically 4–5.5 inch. long. The male of the American goldfinch (or wild canary), found across North America, is bright yellow, with black cap, wings, and tail.

Good Friday. This is the name given to the Friday in Holy Week. Holy Week is the week before Easter. During that time, Christians think a great deal about the suffering of Christ. Good Friday is the day held as the anniversary of Christ's death on the Cross.

Gramophone record. Records are discs – shaped like a thin slice through the middle of an apple. Most modern records are made of plastic. If you put a record on a record-player you will hear music or people's voices.

Grasshopper. When you walk over a newly mown field, the grasshoppers jump away from under your feet with a buzzing sound. In the evening you can hear the chirruping of the males. They make this music with their wings or with their wings and legs together. You have probably heard of the giant swarms of flying grasshoppers called locusts. When locusts cannot find enough food, they leave their homeland and sometimes fly for hundreds of miles. Wherever they alight they eat every leaf on, every growing plant and tree. They make animals and farmers suffer great hardships.

Grass snake. You may have seen this animal near ponds and slowly running brooks or in damp woods. You can easily recognise it by its yellow 'collar'. Its back is olive-green but its stomach is like black-and-white marble.

Grass snakes grow more than three feet long. They are very fond of eating frogs. Isn't it incredible that a snake's small mouth can catch a frog and swallow it, though the frog is so much bigger than the snake's mouth? This can happen because a snake's jaws are attached to each other by elastic muscles which stretch as it swallows.

Snakes don't blink their eyes like many animals. They have no eyelids to blink with, as we do. How terrible a snake's unblinking stare must seem if you are a frog!

In winter, grass snakes hibernate in underground holes. They wake up in March or April. Grass snakes lay soft-shelled eggs, often in some warm compost heap. The heat of the compost hatches the eggs.

Great Dane. It is a powerful animal. It makes a fine watch-dog. There are yellow, black and spotted Great Danes.

Grimm. Every child knows this name. There are many fairy-tales and most of them were written by the Grimm brothers. They were called Jacob and William Grimm and they lived about 150 years ago. They traveled through Germany and wrote down the fairy-tales which people told them. Don't you think *Hansel and Gretel* is a fine story? They wrote that.

Gross, net, tare. Goods are unloaded from a railway wagon. Amongst them is a case of apples. It is a stout wooden case, nailed together. It weighs 50 pounds gross. Inside the case are 40 pounds of apples. That is the net weight. Can you quickly work out the weight of the empty case? The weight of the case without its apples is called the tare weight.

Groundnut. I expect you have sometime or the other bought yourself a bag of peanuts. The proper name for these nuts is 'groundnuts'. Inside each yellow shell sit one, or usually two, brown-skinned nuts. These nuts contain an oil. People use it to make margarine and cooking oil. Groundnuts grow best in hot countries. Most of them come from India and Africa. How did they earn their name? Because the nuts themselves grow beneath the surface of the ground.

Guilds. Many hundreds of years ago, almost every craftsman was a member of a guild. A guild was an association of people who all did the same kind of skilled work. These guilds had to do many things. They had to see that apprentices (the pupil-craftsmen) learned properly, that the craftsmen themselves worked well and carefully, and that they did not overcharge for the goods they sold.

H

Hair. Ritu is letting her hair grow long so that she can plait it. At the moment she has very short hair, but soon it will be much longer. Do you know how fast your hair grows? About half an inch a month.

Hair consists of horn, as do the nails on your fingers and toes. How many hairs do you have on your head? Have a guess. Now we shall tell you: there are about 110,000. In television or at the cinema you may have noticed that negroes have frizzy hair. The Chinese and Eskimos have sleek, straight hair.

Most mammals have a layer of hair to help protect their body against cold and rain. Close to their skin, the hair is soft and woolly. Outside the soft layer grow hairs that are longer and tougher.

Hammer. Tool for pounding or delivering repeated blows.

Hand hammers have a handle and striking head. Surfaces of hammerheads vary in size, angle of orientation to the handle (parallel or inclined), and type of face (flat or convex). Carpenters' hammers often have a claw on the head for extracting nails. Weights range from a few ounces or grams up to 15 lbs (7 kg) for hammers used in breaking stones. Steam hammers often use, in addition to gravity, a downward thrust from a steam-activated piston. Pneumatic (air-driven) hammers include the hammer drill, for rock and concrete, and the riveting hammer, for construction operations involving steel girders and plate.

Handicrafts. When the door creaks, or the kitchen table wobbles, when the window will not close properly or the coffee mill does not grind fine enough, you can put things right. Any really handy person can do all these things. But he must learn how – he must learn handicrafts.

'Wait till Uncle Yogesh comes,' says Mother. 'He likes doing small jobs. He will fix it.'

It is fun to do odd jobs like these. When you can do them you are always happily busy. When Father makes something, you can help him. You can get the tools ready and hand him the nails. And watch carefully how Father does it, because, of course, you will want to be as handy as he is.

Many children can make things for themselves. With only a pocket-knife, Rohit makes lots of toys and useful objects for his brothers and sisters. He can cut an ordinary potato into such funny figures. He can even shape it into the letters of the alphabet. Then he puts paint on them and presses them on paper. In this way he makes his own simple printing blocks. Rohit also uses corks, nutshells, acorns, fir-cones and horse-chestnuts to make baskets and toy animals.

Uncle Yogesh is even better than Rohit at making things. He has a small tool-box with hammers, several pairs of pliers, chisels, files, saws, drills and screw-drivers. Uncle Yogesh once even made a box of bricks for the children.

There are many handymen even cleverer than Uncle Yogesh. Some can even make their own radio sets and repair them if they go wrong. Some of these handymen have even made important inventions. There should be at least one handyman in every family. Usually it's Father or one of the boys. But why not girls as well?

Do you want to be good at doing small jobs yourself? Have a try. Perhaps you can buy a book that tells you all about them.

Harbour. In the harbour, things are always very busy. Ships just completing a long voyage are steaming in. And there is always a ship leaving the harbour and making for the open sea. What a whistling and a hooting! What a lot of shouting and rattling of chains! Over there, dockers are loading a big cargo-vessel. A tall crane lifts the cargo and delivers it neatly into the holds.

A lot of people are going aboard another ship. They are passengers. They are going to make a long sea-voyage. Their friends stand on the harbour wall, waving to the passengers and shouting, 'Goodbye! Have a good trip!'

In this harbour there are some big work shops too. There, new ships are built and old ones repaired. These workshops are called 'ship-yards'. At the entrance to the harbour stands a lighthouse to help ships, find their way in and out at night.

Hardiness. Do you know any children who are always wrapped up in warm clothes, even in the hottest weather? Some children nearly always wear thick, woollen scarves and even then they always seem to be catching colds. Those children are not hardy, which means they cannot resist cold weather like normal children. Some cannot stand pain. You are not a 'mother's baby' like them, are you?

Strong boys and girls get lots of fresh air. And they take lots of showers – sometimes in cold water. Rambles, gymnastics, swimming, ski-ing, skating all keep your body healthy. But don't overdo it! Too much of a good thing can be bad for anyone. So don't try to prove how hardy you are by walking for hours in bitter winter weather.

Hare. How many enemies the hare has! People hunt him, foxes stalk him, eagles search for him, weasels, cats and dogs, every beast of prey big enough to tackle him thinks the hare would make a tasty meal.

No wonder hares are timid animals. When anyone is frightened we say he is 'as timid as a hare'. Luckily for them, hares can hear and see other creatures coming while they are still far off. And hares are splendid runners. When a hare runs from an enemy he moves in zig-zag fashion. He does this to trick his enemy.

If you walk very quietly through the fields you may see a hare. If you are lucky he will hop across the path ahead, sit bolt upright and raise his long ears. Hares spend all their lives above ground. Their babies (called leverets) are born in a little hollow, not in a like burrow baby rabbits.

Harpoon. It is a weapon used by seamen who catch whales, dolphins and other big sea-creatures. A harpoon is usually an iron spear. There are barbed hooks at its tip. A strong rope is joined to its other end. Sailors sometimes pull a harpooned sea-creature aboard with this rope. Whalers in some ships shoot harpoons at their targets by means of a small gun.

Hawk. 'Eagle Eye' is a Red Indian name for a hunter who can see better than his fellow braves. Indians sometimes call him 'Hawk Eye' instead. No living things have such good eyesight as hawks and eagles.

Hawks are birds of prey. Have a look at a kestrel. See how he circles in the sky, watching the earth far below. He can hover in the air by flapping his wings rapidly up and down. Sometimes he suddenly closes his wings and drops onto his prey below.

In the Middle Ages people kept hawks for hunting cranes and herons. Nobles trained hawks especially for this sport. Peregrine falcons are powerful hunters. In our country peregrines are scarce, but they kill many pigeons, and sometimes poultry.

Hazel nut. This is the fruit of the hazel tree. Have you ever eaten these nuts? They taste very nice. Squirrels are very fond of them too. Ripe nuts just fall from their nut tree. But you have to break open their hard, brown shells before you can reach the nuts inside. You will often see hazel nuts used to decorate fancy cakes.

Heart. When you have been walking very fast, or when you have had a fright, you can feel your heart beating. Your heart is really a muscle as big as your fist. This muscle pumps blood through your arteries and veins. In healthy people you can count 60-80 heart-beats a minute. If you want to keep your heart healthy you should avoid smoking lots of cigarettes when you grow up, and never drink many alcoholic drinks.

Heather. Have you seen whole mountainsides clad in purple, flowering heather? Have you ever wandered on such a mountain slope? Heather-clad slopes are very beautiful in late summer. And their scent is everywhere around you. The air is full of buzzing bees, attracted to the nectar and the pollen inside the heather blooms.

Yet the ground that heather grows on is often rocky or sandy. Only low shrubs and a few grasses grow beside the heather.

Heating. 'I think it feels very cold indoors today,' said Mother. 'Let's have the stove on.' A bucketful of coke stood beside the stove. A bundle of firewood rested on top of the coke bucket.

'I have already collected the coke and the wood from the cellar,' said Mother. 'Will you collect some paper so that we can light the stove?' Vinisha ran to fetch an old newspaper and crumpled it up. Then she opened the door of the stove and put the paper on the grate. Mother put some pieces of wood on the paper, then coal on top, then she lit the paper.

'This coal burns better than coke to begin with,' she said. After a few minutes, she carefully opened the door of the stove.

'Ah, the coal is alight already,' said Vinisha, who also took a peep inside the stove. 'How the wood crackles!'

'There's a good draught,' said Mother. 'Shut the door of the ash-pit and close the flap in the pipe. If you don't, all the heat will escape up the chimney.' Vinisha's mother opened the tiny holes in the door of the stove so that the fire should have some air. Otherwise the stove would go out.

'What would happen if we closed all the doors in the stove?' asked Vinisha.

'The fire would go out,' said. Mother.

'But isn't there enough air inside the stove already?' Vinisha wanted to know.

Mother lit a candle and said, 'Imagine that this is the fire in the stove. See what happens when I put a glass over the candle so that fresh air cannot reach its flame.' To her great surprise, Vinisha saw that the flame of the candle became smaller and smaller, and at last it went out.

'Now all the oxygen which was in the glass has been used up,' said Mother. 'The same would happen to the stove if no fresh air could get in through the holes in the door.'

'It's already becoming lovely and warm in the room,' said Vinisha.

Stoves are certainly good friends in winter. With enough fuel, some stay alight until the lowing spring.

Hedgehogs. Hedgehogs are the gardener's friends, for they will eat all sorts of harmful insects as well as mice and snails. Hedgehogs even dare to attack snakes.

You don't often see a hedgehog in daytime for these animals come out at night in search of prey. A hedgehog has a splendid suit of armour to protect him from his enemies. His armour is the dense, sharp coat of quills which cover his body. When there is any danger, a hedgehog rolls himself up into a prickly ball so that you can't even see his head. Sometimes, hedgehogs accidentally pick up bits of leaves on their quills and carry them around. In winter they go to sleep for months right inside a pile of dry leaves.

Heredity. Anita looks very much like her father. She has fair hair and blue eyes, just as her father. Anita's mother has a nice voice, and Anita can sing very well too. Her looks and her voice are both things she has inherited from her parents. What a pity that her mother is short-sighted. Anita has inherited short-sightedness from her mother and she has to wear glasses.

Herring. The herring is about a foot long. This fish lives in the North Sea. From time to time, herrings join to form enormous shoals which swim into shallow waters to lay their spawn. Then fishermen set out in many ships to catch herrings in huge nets. Herrings taste delicious and they are cheap fish to buy. You can buy them smoked (as kippers), salted, pickled or as roll-mops, or as fresh herrings for frying.

Hieroglyphics. They are the letter signs used by the ancient Egyptians. They do not look like our letters at all. They are all kinds of shapes. Egyptians cut them out in stone.

Hiking and Camping. Harish and Chetan were off hiking! They had been looking forward to it for a long time. They were fully prepared for a long trek. Each had packed his rucksack. There was plenty of room in it for shorts, comb, toothbrush, toothpaste, soap, towels, handkerchiefs, cup, spoon, knife, fork, aluminium plate, torch, sewing things, pencil, shoe-polish and shoe-brush, anti-insect cream, string, safety-pins and, of course, some food.

'Have you got something in case the weather is bad?' asked Harish, laughing.

'Of course,' said Chetan. 'A plastic cape, a warm track-suit and shirts and socks.'

'Be careful, and avoid accidents,' said Mother. 'And take some first-aid dressing with you and talcum-powder for your feet, just in case.'

The boys strapped their woollen blankets to their rucksacks, filled their vacuum flasks with hot tea and pocketed their penknives and road maps. At last they were off!

But just a moment. Mother had a few more words to say: 'Wash your feet with cold water every day. Don't be reckless. Don't try to be heroes. And don't drink too much. The more you drink the thirstier you will get. When you are hot, don't drink at all. Be careful not to drink water that isn't clean. Take care you don't lose the way. Don't be too noisy – think of the animals that live in the woods. Be careful when you make a fire. Never make one in the woods and never throw away a lighted match.'

Soon, Harish and Chetan were out into the country. They were so happy. For three days they hiked; then they came to the banks of a river. They were rather tired and their faces were burnt brown by the sun.

By the river stood a sign. It said: 'To the Camping Grounds'. Harish and Chetan found the camping grounds close by the river.

'What a pity we haven't a tent,' said Chetan.

'Look,' said Harish. 'They have dug little ditches round each tent.' And Harish knew why. When it is rainy you need a moat to drain off the water that runs down your canvas roof. And Harish knew that when it rains you must not touch a tent inside or it begins to leak.

'Come on,' said Chetan, when they had explored the camp. 'Let's go.'

Harish and Chetan walked on to the next Youth Hostel. It was always pleasant and friendly inside a Youth Hostel. And you often met boys from other countries there. Perhaps Harish and Chetan will make a new friend.

Hippopotamus. It is hard to understand how this enormous animal (it's about 10 feet long) can dive and swim about so quickly. As well as having such a great length, the hippo often weighs more than two tons.

Usually hippos are not dangerous to people. They live on plants. But look out if anyone teases a hippo! If it is angry, a hippo can capsize quite big boats.

When a hippopotamus is in the water, you can only see its ears, eyes and nostrils above the surface. Hippos live in herds in and around many African rivers. Sometimes, at night, hippos leave their river and do great damage to farmers' plantations.

History – how people used to live. The first people lived in holes and caves. Their clothes consisted of plaited rushes and animal-skins. One day they saw lightning strike a tree. They overcame their fear of fire and carried off one of the burning branches. Fire became the powerful friend and helper of these people.

In time they learned how to make fire for themselves. They did this with the help of flints.

The women and children spent their days collecting fruits, berries and fungi; and the men went hunting. Stone Age men went hunting in big groups to kill enormous mammoths. When one of these animals fell into a trap, the huntsmen had meat enough to last them many days. But Stone Age people were always wandering in search of food.

After many thousand years some people ceased their wanderings. They settled down in one spot. With the help of heavy branches, the men tore the ground open, making crude furrows a bit like those in a modern ploughed field. On this land the people grew corn. They often kept cattle, pigs, goats and sheep as well.

They made holes in their stone hand-axes and fitted pieces of wood into the holes. Thus they made proper axes with hafts. The women sewed clothes with needles made of stone or bone. They even made materials for clothes on simple weaving frames.

While this was happening in many parts of the world, great cities had already sprung up in Egypt. The kings of Egypt had pyramids built, and enormous stone temples. Over thousands of years, the Egyptians were scratching hieroglyphics letter signs – on slabs of stone.

In most of the world, people still did not know about metal. But Egyptian women wore ornaments of brass, silver and gold. People were making glass beads too.

The Chinese created a great, ancient empire. They wrote by dipping bamboo sticks into a black varnish. They used the sticks as pens and the varnish as ink.

By about 2000 B.C. people in Western Europe had begun to use copper. They mixed it with tin and made bronze. From this tough metal they cast their tools, weapons and ornaments. That's why we call this period of time the 'Bronze Age'.

In a village, one man was sometimes a clever tool-maker. He became the smith making metal tools for the whole village. There were also potters making pots on their potters' wheels. People had already invented feeding-bottles with teats, for tiny children, in time there were special wheelwrights who did nothing but make wheels for carts. Their were shaped as large wooden discs at first. Letter someone invented spokes.

The land now called Iraq was once called 'Land of the Two Rivers' because it lay between the two rivers Tigris and Euphrates. In that country was the ancient city of Babylon, called 'Babel' in the Bible. You probably know the story of the Tower of really Babel. This tower really existed, though it was not one but many towers – one in each around Babylon. They were the tower of temples. In Babylon, clever men could calculate in advance eclipses of the sun. They also kept a week of seven days, and invented many standard sizes and measurements. We owe the beginnings of inventions to the Babylonians. But their city of Babylon no longer exists.

Iron is even harder than bronze. In time, learned to make all kinds of tools is metal. But they went on using gold silver ornaments, and making beautifully painted plates and dishes of clay. Today archaeologists often dig them up when they are exploring ancient tombs.

During the Iron Age, the people who lived in Europe were mostly farmers and they dwelt in villages. The men worked in their fields. They already had ploughs with wheels, like those that some farmers still use today.

In Greece there were many cities by 400 B.C. The finest of all was Athens. Brick and stone houses stood on either side of its broad streets. The citizens of Athens met in the market-square and discussed all sorts of important matters. In the harbour, trading vessels lay at anchor. Above the town gleamed the marble walls of the city-castle. This city-castle was called the Acropolis.

Athens proudly boasted many famous artists. They built fine temples and carved splendid statues out of marble.

In the meantime; the town of Rome was growing up in the land that we now call Italy. First, Rome was just a group of neighbouring villages. Gradually they grew into a big town with city walls and a castle.

Many legends tell how the city of Rome was first founded. Rome's citizens soon took possession of the surrounding countryside. Then they began to conquer the whole of Italy. After several centuries, Roman soldiers conquered all the countries around the Mediterranean Sea.

People built fine roads and towns to link up the whole of the great Roman Empire. It was ruled for much of its history by an emperor, or Caesar, who lived at Rome. The most famous of all emperors was Julius Caesar. He was a great soldier. He even invaded England. England became part of the Roman Empire.

During the time of Augustus Caesar, Jesus Christ was born in the Roman province of Judea in Palestine. After His death, the apostles went abroad, teaching the new doctrines of love for one's neighbour, and of redemption. Very soon, many slaves and poor people were converted to the new religion. The Roman emperors persecuted the Christians. But 300 years after the birth of Christ, the emperor called Constantine said that everyone who wanted could be a Christian.

In eastern and northern Europe, people outside the Roman Empire heard of the rich countries to the south. They were told that 'golden apples' grew on trees in the south. Of course these were really oranges. The northern peoples were multiplying fast. In time, there was not enough land for them. Eager for new land and adventure, thousands of northerners and easterners travelled south with their wives and children. One tribe went to Spain and another reached North Africa. The Huns, savage from Asia, went plundering and murdering through Europe.

Soon, the Roman Empire faded away before the attacks of

plundering tribes. Gradually even these pagan barbarians became Christians. Christian communities now lived in many lands. Beginning from Egypt, Christian monks travelled the world.

These monks founded monasteries wherever they went. Of course each monastery was attached to a church. In a monastery were also workshops, stables and gardens. Different tribes of pagans learned from the monks how to grow new fruits and herbs. At their monastery monks taught children how to read write and calculate.

Meanwhile, nobles and knights had to build themselves strong castles. For these were troubled times. Pilgrims brought messages from the Near East to say Turks had built a mosque – a Mohammedan temple – on Christ's tomb. The Christians could not allow this. So the Crusades to the Holy Land began. Many thousand knights from all over Europe journeyed to a Palestine and tried to capture it from the Turks. When the knights came home, they brought back finely woven cloths and expensive spices.

For centuries, monks had been writing books by hand in their monastery cells. They specially copied the ancient written scrolls by Greeks and Romans. It is thanks largely to these monks that we today know much of those long-dead peoples. But at last two people, Coster from Haarlem in Holland and Gutenberg from Mainz in Germany, discovered how to make printing letters out of lead. They were letters that you could move about. People could rearrange them to make new words, once they printed what they wanted by pressing the inked letters on paper. Soon people were printing many copies of each book and almost everyone could afford to buy one.

Courageous sailors from Portugal and Spain tried to reach India by sea. Some of them found their way around Africa past Cape of Good Hope. That was a great discovery. Columbus sailed westward with threeships and discovered America. Then the Portuguese Magellan undertook the risky task of sailing right round the world. The voyage lasted three years, but Magellan was killed by natives before it ended.

Merchants brought back many treasuresfromthenewly-discovered countries. Unfortunately, merchants also sold many poor negroes from West Africa as slaves to the white settlers in America. That is why there are so many negroes in America today.

In 1683 the Turks wanted to conquer Western Europe. Their Grand Vizier Kara Mustafa led a vast army of 300,000 men into Europe. They got as far as the city of Vienna and besieged it.

Then followed a hard time for the people of Vienna, for the Turks far outnumbered them. The Turks fired on the city day and night. Soon there was hardly any food left in Vienna. But after eight weeks, the Holy Roman Emperor's army arrived from Germany. And from Poland came King John Sobieski with his soldiers. Together with the Viennese they drove the enemy away. There was great rejoicing in Europe.

But the French people were not contented. The French king and nobles lived in great luxury while the poor people suffered hunger. Anyone who said this was wrong was put in a grim prison called the Bastille.

One day the people of France attacked this fortress and a terrible civil war broke out. This kind of war is called a revolution. The king and queen were beheaded. The people of Paris cried: 'Freedom; equality, brotherhood! Nobody shall be oppressed again; everyone shall have equal rights and equal duties.'

In the year 1786, the Scotsman James Watt built his first steam engine. His steam engines were very important inventions. In time, people put steam engines into ships. Steamships traveled much faster than sailing ships.

In England in 1825, George Stephenson built the first passenger railway. People came from far and wide to admire his railway engines. Stephenson's first railway engines moved at only 15 miles an hour. Even that speed seemed high and amazed everyone. Today American express trains travel at more than 100 miles an hour.

A hundred years ago factories began to spring up everywhere, many of them powered by steam. Thousands of people worked at the factory machines.

Nearly every day, nowadays, we read in the paper about new inventions in factories and about record-breaking speeds. We read of rockets and 'planes which fly faster than sound, about submarines that can dive miles beneath the sea's surface, about ships which are driven by atomic power. It is certain that the time will come when people will fly out into space and make a trip to the moon, perhaps to the other planets as well.

But there is a plan much more important than all these inventions and marvels. The plan is to join together all the countries in the world and so to make one enormous nation. In this way, people hope that they could make peace for ever; for there would be no nations left to quarrel with one another. Everyone can help to make this plan come true. You can help. But first, learn how people live in other countries, and try to understand their ways of life, and their customs.

Honey. 'I bet this is one of those things that are good for you but taste awful,' grumbled Rohit.

'It certainly isn't,' said his mother. 'Just you drink it and see. It's honey and hot milk.'

Honey is sweet and wholesome. Rohit soon stopped grumbling because it really did taste delicious. But I don't think he was thinking how honey is made while he was drinking it. Bees make honey. They first collect nectar from flowers. The nectar forms honey in their stomachs. Then they store the honey in the honeycombs of their hive. A bee-keeper comes along, takes away the full honeycombs and puts them in a spinning machine. As the machine spins, the honey is hurled out of the honeycombs.

Horizon. Have a look into the distance – as far as the place where earth and sky seem to meet. This is what we call the horizon. You can see it best when you stand on a high tower or on a beach. At sea you get a clear view of the horizon. On land, the roofs of houses or hills get in the way. At sea, you still can't see beyond the horizon because of the curving earth.

Horse. In America there are children who have never seen a horse. In that part of the world people use hardly any horses to pull carts. Cars, trains and great lorries have pushed the horse to one side. Even in our own towns, horses are getting more and more scare. But in past centuries, these noble animals were man's chief helpmates.

Many farmers still keep horses of all shapes, sizes and colours. The biggest horses are the great cart-horses, the smallest are ponies like the tiny Shetland ponies. Horses come in all colours too. A black-and-white is called a 'piebald'.

Horse-power. 'It is a six-horse-power engine,' said Rohit. The letters 'h.p.' are short for 'horse-power'. What does this mean exactly? One horse-power is the power needed to raise 33,000 pounds weight one foot in one minute. Could you do that? An engine can.

Humming-bird. The humming-bird is a very tiny bird. It is not much bigger than a bumble-bee. Humming-birds live in America. These brilliant coloured little creatures can flap their wings thousands of times a minute. They can hover in the air near a flower and suck its nectar. They can even fly backwards!

I

Ice. When the thermometer indicates 32 degrees Fahrenheit or below, water freezes. It turns into ice. Then you can unpack your skates and go skating. But when the temperature rises above freezing point, this pleasure must come to an end. For the ice melts and turns back into water. Salt seawater freezes at a lower temperature than fresh water.

Food keeps fresh in ice, or when temperatures are below freezing. That's why people keep the temperature in a refrigerator around freezing. People can make their own ice in a refrigerator.

Icebergs. Iceberg are formed from the glaciers of the polar regions. They break from a glacier with a terrific crack and float into the sea. The largest part of an iceberg is under water. Only about an eighth of it shows above. That's why icebergs are so dangerous to ships.

Icebreaker. An icebreaker is a ship with very powerful engines and a bow made of steel. With this bow, the ship can plough a way through the ice of frozen harbours.

Indians (Red). They are the original inhabitants of America. You can read about Red Indian ways of life and customs in many books.

Woods-Indians live in huts which they make from bark. Plains-Indians live in tents in the warm season when they go hunting. In winter they return to their houses, which look very much like the igloos of the Eskimos.

After many long, hard fights, white settlers drove the redskins from their living and hunting-grounds in the Wild West. The

Indians called their European enemies 'palefaces'. Palefaces killed off almost all the huge herds of bison that once roamed the North American prairies.

Today there are still some tribes of Red Indians living in North America in areas specially set aside for them by the government. These areas are called 'reservations'. Indians have become farmers. But on festival days they still wear the feathered headdress and silver jewellery of their war-like ancestors. And Indian women still weave colourful patterned clothes. Today, many Indians have gone to live in the white man's cities. But in South America still live Indian tribes who hunt with bows and arrows and blowpipes.

Infection. Ritu has scarlet fever. Nobody is allowed to visit her, because there is danger of infection. This means that anyone could catch the illness from her. Scarlet fever, measles, diphtheria and many other diseases are infectious. You can catch them just by breathing the same air as a patient. It is specially dangerous to be near a patient when he coughs or sneezes.

Injections. When the doctor wanted to give little Vinisha an injection, she cried a bit first. But the doctor explained to her why he had to vaccinate her.

'When you have been vaccinated against scarlet fever, diphtheria, typhoid, cholera and smallpox you cannot get these illnesses any more,' the doctor said. And when he had finished, Vinisha thought: 'It didn't hurt much after all.'

Insects. Butterflies flutter over the meadow, beetles crawl busily up and down its grass stems, industrious bees search its clover flowers for honey, and irritating flies bite our arms and legs. All these animals belong to the huge insect family. It is a family numbering more than a million different relations.

Insects lay very tiny eggs. They hatch into little animals with big appetites. These animals are called 'larvae'. They look quite unlike their parents. By looking at a larva you cannot guess what its parents were like.

When a larva has eaten so much that it becomes round and fat, it turns into a pupa. Then it takes a long rest. But inside the pupa's shell many changes take place. At last the shell splits and out comes a full-grown insect – a butterfly, a wasp, an ant or a fly. Some insects, like grasshoppers and crickets, do not change from a larva into a pupa.

Many insects carry diseases and are harmful to people. They include the dangerous malaria mosquito and the Colorado beetle – a pest to farmers.

Iron. Hammers, files and many other tools are made of iron. People also use iron to make bridges, railway engines, carriages, cars and machines. Imagine that suddenly there were no such thing as iron. Many things would vanish. A piece of iron is eight times heavier than a piece of wood the same size.

Islam. This is the religion of the Mohammedans. In Arabia in about the year A.D. 600, Mohammed preached a new religion, called 'Islam'. (It comes from an Arabic word meaning, 'submit to God'.) Mohammed's doctrine is written in the holy book of the Mohammedans, the *Koran.*

Ivory. This substance comes from the tusks of elephants. People also use hippopotamus and walrus tusks as a substitute for elephant ivory. From ivory, people, have made many wonderful and valuable carvings. The white keys on a piano are covered with thin ivory plates.

J

Jackdaw. A jackdaw looks rather like a rook though it is smaller. Both these birds belong to the crow family. Jackdaws have grey cheeks and the back of their head is grey. Jackdaws like to build their nests in church towers, in high buildings or hollow trees.

Jaw. Everyone has two jaws, an upper jaw and a lower jaw. These are the two bones in which your teeth grow. You can move your lower jaw but not your upper jaw. Most backboned animals have jaws of this kind.

Jelly-fish. A jelly-fish is a strange sea creature. When it floats its body looks just like an open umbrella. It shuts and inflates its body so that it can float up and down in the sea. The jelly-fish lives on small sea animals which it catches with its long tentacles. When a jelly-fish is thrown upon the beach by waves, it is a delicate pink colour. But on dry land it soon turns into a dirty, slimy mess

Jerusalem. Christians and Jews both make pilgrimages to Jerusalem to visit its holy places. Jesus Christ was crucified there. Jerusalem is the capital of the state of Israel.

Jesus Christ. The Christian religion teaches that Jesus is the Son of God. He became human to deliver the people from sin. Many believe that the name Jesus was given Him by God Himself. Christ means 'anointed' and the word 'messiah' means the same. 'Messiah' was the Jewish name for the deliverer they had long expected. Christians believe that Jesus came to deliver everyone by His life, suffering and death on the Cross. Christians receive grace and salvation through the Church founded by Christ. The life of Jesus is recorded in the New Testament of the Bible. See also '**Church**'.

Jungle. This is thc name of the dense and often swampy forests of the world's hot countries. Jungle trees grow so high and so close together that they often block out the bright sun altogether.

Junior Red Cross. It includes children and young people all over the world. More than 40 million people in 60 countries help to work for the Red Cross. Their motto is, 'I serve'. Their work is to look after their own health and their neighbours and to work for the brotherhood of all people.

The members of the Red Cross know what they must do to keep fit: they know what not to eat and drink because it may be harmful for their body. They know that whole meal bread, butter, cheese and cooked vegetables are good to eat. They know about the things that matter most in looking after your body and taking care of nails, teeth and hair.

Most members of the Red Cross have already taken a course in first aid. They know how to look after sick people at home and how to save a drowning person. They help when other people are in distress. The Junior Red Cross has installed school clinics in many European schools.

Members of the Junior Red Cross think a great deal of the town where they were born. They beautify towns and put seats in quiet spots and places where there is a pleasant view. They even help to keep the streets and squares clean, to decorate schools and class-rooms, and to tend churchyard graves.

How do they serve their neighbours? That is not easy to explain in a few words In the summer they help farmers with their harvest. In the Alps, they help to rebuild villages destroyed by avalanches. The Junior Red Cross people help to clear rubble and plant new trees. And they especially like making new toys for infants' schools. They also sing and play music in old people's homes and in hospitals. They help the old people and collect fruit which they take to hospitals. And special departments of the Junior Red Cross look after blind, deaf or invalid children. Red Cross people visit the schools where these children live and give them small presents and play with them.

The Junior Red Cross wants all the world's children to be friends with one another. So it tries to arrange 'pen friends' – children in different countries who write letters to one another.

K

Kangaroo. The kangaroo seems to us a most peculiar animal. It has four legs yet it cannot walk. A kangaroo jumps. Its fore-legs are short and weak, but its hind-legs are immensely strong and long. They are bent into springs like the legs of other leaping animals such as the hare and the frog.

When a kangaroo sits down it supports itself on its long, thick tail. When it leaps, it pushes itself off the ground by means of its tail. Some kangaroos can jump as far as 30 feet in one bound, and 10 feet high. In her belly, a female kangaroo has a pouch where she carries her baby. Pouched animals like the kangaroo are called 'marsupials'. Where do kangaroos live? In Australia.

Keel. A keel is the underwater 'backbone' of a ship. In earlier days, sailors were often punished by being 'keel-hauled'. They were hauled by ropes beneath a ship, from one side to the other.

Kingfisher. Yogesh saw a kingfisher when he was out for a walk. The bird was perched on a snowy, tree stump overlooking a stream.

'I recognized him at once,' said Yogesh. 'He had a lovely blue green back and his tummy was as red as rust. I stood very still, so as not to frighten him. Suddenly the kingfisher dived into the water and caught a little fish in his long break.'

Knife. A tool, usually with a sharp blade and a handle, used for cutting, slicing, or spreading.

Knights. Knights lived many hundred years ago, in the Dark Ages and the Middle ages. They lived in castles. May be you have seen the remains of some of their castles. Knights were noblemen. They had to help their monarch when there was a war. A knight had to be brave and good; he had to help the poor and those who were sick. When knights grew less powerful, some of them became robber knights.

Imagine you are standing inside a castle sometime during the Dark Ages. How busy it all is. People are walking up and down. They are all in festive dress. Some men are talking to one another.

'I wonder who will win the first prize in today's tournament?' says one of them. The tournament is almost ready to begin. Carpenters have built public galleries so that big audience can all see what happens.

Here comes a herald. How magnificenthisclothesare!Heblows a fanfare on his trumpet. At once the first two opponents ride sternly into the arena on fine strong horses. How their armour glitters! Their visors are drawn down to protect their faces. The plumes dance on their helmets. Each knight has a shield in his left hand. On each shield is painted a coat of arms. In his right hand, each grasps a lance.

Now both knights are standing at opposite ends of the arena. The combat begins. Again and again, they rush forward straight at one another. Each tries to hurl the other off his saddle by a blow from his long lance. Soon, one knight succeeds. His opponent tumbles with a clang of armour to the ground. The herald proclaims the winner; the winner claims his prize.

Today, this sort of tournament no longer happens. But we still use the word 'tournament' to mean 'combat' in sport – for example, in 'tennis tournament' and 'chess tournament'.

L

Laboratory. Mother does her cooking in a kitchen. The baker works in a bakery. Chemists, trying to discover new medicines, work in a room called a laboratory. This is a long name. But people often call 'laboratory' 'lab' for short.

Labyrinth. It was a palace on the Greek island of Crete. In this palace there were many rooms, yards and corridors. But there was only one way out. When people entered the palace they often lost their way.

Legends said that inside this labyrinth lived a minotaur – a monster. It looked half human, half like a bull. The Greek son of the king Theseus decided to kill this monster. He penetrated the labyrinth and unrolled a ball of wool as he walked in. When he had killed the beast he simply followed the wool back to the exit. So he easily found his way out. Nowadays 'labyrinth' means 'maze'. Have you ever been in a maze?

Ladybird. Can you see it? It has two big red wing-cases and six legs. And how shiny its wing-cases are! But they are not pure red. They have some black spots.

Do you know how high ladybirds can fly? Even higher than a church steeple. I expect you have caught one at some time or another to have a close look at it. Really, the ladybird is a sort of beetle that eats nothing but the harmful greenfly that feed on roses.

Lamps. Any device used for artificial lighting. The earliest forms of lamps were burning sticks or glowing coals held in braziers. Later, long-burning torches were used for illumination; these torches consisted of bundles of twigs or splinters of resinous wood that were bound together and dipped in fat or oil to improve their burning qualities. The precise origin of the oil lamp, the first true lamp, is obscure, but such lamps were in general use in Greece by the 4th century bc. The first such lamps were open vessels made of stone, clay, bone, or shell in which fat or oil was burned. Later lamps were partially enclosed reservoirs, containing fat or oil that were provided with a small hole into which a wick of flax or cotton was set. The fuel was drawn up the wick by capillary action and burned at the end of the wick. Large lamps of Greek and Roman times were equipped with a large number of wicks to give a brighter light. In northern Europe the most common form of lamp was an open pot of stone filled with grease, into which a wick was thrust. Lamps of this type are still used by the Inuit.

Land and sea. The earth's surface is not smooth. Its raised parts are called hills and mountains. In the earth's deepest valleys, water has collected to form the great oceans of the world. Where land and sea meet, run the coastlines of the world. A coastline runs straight. Sometimes the sea probes deep inland, and makes a big bay. Often, the land runs out into the sea until it is almost cut off. When a piece of land is almost an island we call it a peninsula. Have you ever heard of a cape? A cape is a mountains spit of land that runs far out into the sea.

In some places the sea is very narrow. Then we call it a strait. A narrow piece of land between two seas is an isthmus. And what is an island? Simply a piece of land surrounded by water.

Which is more plentiful on the earth's surface, land or water? Most of the earth is covered by water. Only about one-third is land. We call the biggest pieces of land 'continents'.

Language. Paras went to a big meeting of Boy Scouts. When he came back he said, 'I heard people speaking all sorts of languages as well as English at the camping ground. There were Italians, Germans, Dutch, Greeks and Arabs. Most people were speaking German or French.' Paras had listened carefully to all these languages.

Did you know that there are well over 200 million people on earth who speak English? English is spoken not only in Britain but also in North America, Australia, Africa and in large parts of India.

People speak French in France, southern Belgium, in parts of Switzerland, Canada, North Africa and Asia. Probably about 200 million speak Russian. And no less then 600 million people speak Chinese.

Lapwing. This morning I walked across a meadow. Suddenly a bird flew away. I had frightened it. It was lapwing. I recognized it straight away. A lapwing is as big as a pigeon but it has greenish feathers. On its heads stands a handsome feathered crest. It makes a crying sound like 'ki-wiet, ki-wiet'.

When I frightened the lapwing it kept flying and fluttering around my head. Why do you think it did this? It had been sitting on some eggs and it wanted to attract my attention away from its nest.

Larch. It is a needle-leaved tree. Its soft light-green needles grow in bunches and fall off all together in autumn. The larch is the only needle-leaved tree which is bare all winter. Its wood, which contains resin, is used by shipbuilders and cabinet makers.

Larvae. Every caterpillar is a larva. Where do caterpillars come from? A butterfly eggs. It is from these eggs that the caterpillars hatch. Caterpillars eat until they grow fat. Then they turn into pupae. In time a pupa splits open and out comes a butterfly. The butterfly lays eggs which hatch into larvae (caterpillars) and so it goes on.

Cockchafers come from grubs, which are another kind of larvae, and flies come from maggots, another kind of larvae. Almost all insects develop from larvae in this way.

Laurel. Laurels are glossy-leaved shrubs which you often see in our gardens. But their true home is the countries around the Mediterranean Sea. There, the summers are long, hot and dry. But the thick, shiny laurel leaves stay looking fresh and green, for they are specially made to hold moisture when there is little rain.

In the athletic contests of ancient Greece, the winner was often crowned with a wreath of laurel leaves, or leaves from the bay tree which looks much like the laurel.

Leaf. Any flattened, green outgrowth from the stem of a vascular plant.

Leaves manufacture oxygen and glucose, which nourishes and sustains both plants and animals. Leaves and stem tissue grow from the same apical bud. A typical leaf has abroad, expanded blade (lamina), attached to the stem by a stalk like petiole. The leaf may be simple (a single blade), compound (separate leaflets), or reduced to a spine or scale. The edge (margin) maybe smooth or jagged. Veins transport materials to and from the leaf tissues, radiating from the petiole through the blade. They are arranged in a netlike pattern in dicot leaves and are parallel in monocot leaves. The leaf's outer layer (epidermis) protects the interior (mesophyll), whose soft-walled, unspecialized green cells (parenchyma) produce carbohydrate food by photosynthesis. In autumn the green chlorophyll pigments of deciduous leaves break down, revealing other pigment colours (yellow to red), and the leaves drop off the tree. Leaf scars that form during wound healing after the leaves drop are useful for identifying winter twigs. In conifers, evergreen needles, which are a type of leaf, persist for two or three years.

Legends. They tell us about times long ago, about gods and heroes, witches and dragons, buried treasures and princesses kept in prison.

Do you know the German legends written down by the Grimm brothers? You really must read these; they are splendid.

Lemon. The weather is very hot. Let's make some nice cool lemonade from real lemons. Ugh! How sour it tastes. We must add some sugar.

Lemons aren't nearly as sweet as oranges though they belong to the same family. Lemon trees grow in the countries around the Mediterranean Sea. These trees sometimes have leaves, flowers and fruit all the year round.

Lens. A lens is a piece of glass which has been specially cut and shaped. Lenses are made for spectacles, magnifying glasses, opera-glasses, telescopes and cameras. There is also a lens in your eye, but this is not made of glass.

Lentil. A lentil is a pulse, just as beans and peas are pulses. Its seed is inside a pod. You can eat lentils. They taste delicious, in dal and soup. In the Bible we read that Esau sold his birthright to his brother Jacob for a saucer of lentils.

Leopard. Our tame pussy-cat belongs to a dangerous family. The powerful leopard is a member of this family. It lives in Africa and Asia. It has a yellow skin mottled with dark spots. Sometimes its skin is black. Black-skinned leopards are called panthers. Panthers lie along a branch waiting for their prey. Look out! A panther is a dangerous animal.

Library. Do you like reading? Do you care of all the books you are given? If you do, put them neatly next to each other on a shelf. It won't be long before you have a small library. And even a small library can give you a lot of pleasure.

Light. Sitting by a camp-fire at night under an open sky can be an unforgettable experience. How the wood crackles as the flames leap up, higher and higher. The wind soon carried off the smoke.

Just imagine what fun it would be to have a camp-fire indoors. But wait a moment! Long ago, people did build camp-fires on the open floors of their cave dwellings. They cooked food on their open hearths and the heat of their fires warmed the cave. The flickering flames gave them light, too. But the smoke was a great nuisance. Sometimes it must have been so thick that the people could not see each other. It was no pleasure living in a smoky cave or hut.

Every time someone wanted light at night he had to make fire. In time, people saw how clumsy this was. 'Why should we make a whole camp-fire?' they said. And they lit a long chip of wood. Fir-wood full of sticky, easy to burn resin, was the best wood for this purpose.

In other lands, people found that oil burnt well. They made stone dishes and poured oil into them. Later, they made metal dishes. So the first lamps came to be invented-oil lamps. But these lamps still filled a room with soot and smoke. In time people found some thing to prevent this. They put a wick in the oil and lit that. The wick slowly sucked up the oil in the same way as blotting paper sucks up ink. As wick and oil were the most important things in a lamp, people had to go on using a big, flat dish to keep the oil in.

Then, again, someone had a new and better idea. He dipped a wick in melted beef fat, and let the fat cool down. The fat stuck to the wick and he had invented the first candle. Wax candles were better than oil lamps but they were expensive.

Perhaps your think that this was a great improvement. But just you try reading by candlelight. Does a candle really give much light? Today, we are used to switching on an electric light as strong as 40 or more candles all burning together. In the past, only kings and very rich people could afford to burn candles on that scale.

'Goodness, how hot it is,' complained the ladies of those days, and they had to fan themselves to keep cool. Worst of all was the smoke from the candles. In next to no time a room became hazy just as it does in your kitchen when Mother is doing the washing. People were not satisfied with the light or the smoke of their candles. In time they improved on their old oil lamps by putting glass 'chimney' over them. In towns people could carry these lamps about the streets at night.

Nowadays of course you don't need a torch-bearer or a lantern-bearer to show you the way home through the darkness. Nowadays, all the streets, squares and roads are beautifully lit. Farmers and country-dwellers say that towns people have turned the night into day.

When town-lighting began, it helped to drive away the robbers who had made city streets unsafe by night.

People began to fill the lamps in their homes with paraffin oil, which burned very well. Paraffin lamps gave a bright, clear, friendly light. But people complained that they often had to clean their lamps and fill them with fuel.

Then an Englishman discovered that oil in itself does not burn. What actually burns is the gas which oil produces when it is heated.

'If I could manufacture lots of this gas,' thought the inventor, 'I could send it through pipes to houses all over a city!'

His invention was successful. So the first gasworks came into being. In almost every house in a big town, people began using gas-lamps to give them light.

Coal-gas is made from coal. We still use it for cooking and heating, and in some places for street-lighting. But even gaslight is not very convenient. First you have to find the lamp in the dark. Then you have to turn on a gas tap and light it with a match.

Electric light is much handier. When you come home in the evening you just switch it on and the electric-light bulb gives light and seems to burn. Does the bulb really burn? No. The thin filament of wire inside the lamp glows.

In many shops and streets you will see neon lighting. A neon lamp is a glass tube filled with a gas called neon, or treated on the inside with luminous substances. An electric current makes the lamp shine. Those lamps that are treated with luminous substance do not grow hot. Their light looks like daylight. People use this kind of light for hospitals and schools, workshops and factories. When you walk through the streets of a large town at night, you really can believe that night has become day!

Lighthouse. At night a lighthouse stands as a sign-post for ships. People build lighthouses at the entrance to harbours, at river mouths along the coast and on islands. At regular intervals of time, a lighthouse flashes its light signal. Every lighthouse has its own light signal so that a ship's captain, navigator or pilot who may see it will know just where his ship is.

Lighthouses help to prevent ships coming too near to dangerous sandbanks, rocks and wrecks.

There are even light-ships anchored out at sea. They stay there in all weathers, in storms in the midst of towering waves. The life of a lighthouse-keeper is a lonely one. He has a responsible job.

Lightning. Lightning struck our church tower during the last thunderstorm. There was a brilliant flash and a deafening bang. Luckily, nothing happened, for there is a lightning conductor on top of the church tower. Lightning is a giant electric spark. It jumps from cloud to cloud and sometimes down to earth. Then it often strikes high buildings or trees.

Lightning conductors. On some houses, towers and factories, you will see a vertical rod. This is a lightning conductor. A copper wire links it to the earth below. Then the lightning that strikes it runs harmlessly into the ground and does no damage. Nowadays people are using wire instead of rods more and more. Wire lightning conductors may run the whole length of a roof. They usually have two earthed wires.

Lily. Lilies flower in May and June. The big white lilies have a strong perfume, especially in the evening. The red golden lily does not have a scent. The mauve, dark-spotted Turkish lily has hanging blossoms which look just like a turban.

Lily of the valley. Chetan went for a walk through the woods. 'Hurray!' he cheered. 'There are some lilies of the valley.'

Lilies of the valley grow together in quite big clumps in some woods. How nice they smell! Their small white flowers hang from either side of each stem. In time, the white blossoms develop into berries. But don't eat them, for they are poisonous. But you can pick a few of the lovely flowers as an indoor decoration.

Lime. 'What is that? It looks like thick white porridge,' said Manish as he watched the bricklayer.

'That's mortar,' said the bricklayer. 'I've just slaked some quicklime to make it.'

'What does "slaked" mean?' asked Manish. The bricklayer explained. He said that people dig lime from quarries. Then they heat it in special ovens and the result is quicklime, which can make nasty chemical burns.

'I have just put some water on this quicklime,' said the bricklayer. 'Now it is turned into slaked lime. Next I mix it with sand. This mixture is mortar and I can stick bricks together with it. In air, mortar sets very hard. That's why the bricks of houses stay firmly fixed together.'

Lime tree. In the middle of the village stands a lime tree. What pretty pale-green leaves it has. When the tree flowers in June, bees are attracted to its yellow-green blossoms. Last winter our school-teacher carved little wooden figures for Diwali. For this work, he used wood from a lime tree.

Linoleum. It is a strong floor-covering. It is made from a jute fabric which has been treated with a mixture of linseed oil, cork powder and resin. Linoleum is waterproof. Mother polishes it properly with wax. 'Then it will last longer,' she says.

Lion. The lion is often called the king of beasts. Male lions have a long mane on their neck and breast. At night time, the lion goes out hunting. He seizes his prey in his enormous paws and carries it off in his mouth.

How big is a lion? About six feet long and just over a yard high. Lions can make huge leaps – they can jump up to 25 feet. Did you know that the cat belongs to the same family as the lion? Lions live on the veldt of Africa and in West Asia. Many countries have a lion on their coat of arms.

Literature. This includes all the works written by authors of poems, fairy stories, legends, novels and plays. Papers, magazines, encyclopaedias and the works of learned people all come under the heading of literature.

Lizard. In the old garden wall, which is full of holes, lives a little brown lizard. Anand ran after him and wanted to catch him. But Uncle shouted, 'Anand! Leave him alone!'

Lizards are very useful animals; they eat many insects that are harmful to our gardens. If you catch a lizard its tail may break right off. This is not very pleasant, though in time the lizard does grow a new tail. A lizard's legs don't seem long enough or strong enough to support its body, yet just watch a lizard dart away as you approach.

Some lizards don't have any legs. These are called slow-worms or blind-worms. All lizards belong to the reptile family.

Llama. You can see llamas in the zoo. They are rather like small camels with woolly hair and no hump. Llamas live in South America. There, the people use them to carry heavy loads; they also drink llama milk and eat llama meat. When llamas are teased they behave very badly, and start spitting.

Low tide and high tide. Have you ever been to the seaside? There, the waves are always lapping against the sandy shore. When the waves creep high up the beach we say that the tide is rising. Slowly but surely the water level rises until it has reached its highest point. Then it is high water or high tide. On our coasts it takes about six hours for the tide to reach high water. And it takes the same time for the tide to ebb back to its lowest level. Then we say it is low tide.

On many shores, at low tide, the sea leaves a wide strip of sandy beach where we can run about without getting our feet wet. During low tide at some seaside places you can walk dry-footed from the real coast-line across mudflats to islands that are quite cut off at high tide. But watch out! The tide is never still. When it rises again, the tide may catch you. Sea mists come up suddenly at times. You might discover that you can't find your way back. Sometimes people get drowned because they get lost in mist or caught by the rising tide.

In autumn and spring there are extra-high tides which bring great waves crashing high up on the beaches. Spring tides completely cover some tiny islands. In Holland they burst through dikes at weak spots and flood meadows. Sometimes these floods destroy farms. People and animals are drowned before they have time to escape.

Now you are familiar with the idea of high and low tides. But what makes them? Why does the sea rise and fall? There are tides because the sun and moon keep pulling the earth rather as magnets attract a piece of iron. The waters on the face of the earth are pulled to and fro and thus create high and low tides.

Lynx. People say of someone with sharp eyes that he has 'eyes like a lynx'. The lynx is a beast of prey and it belongs to the same family as the cat, the leopard and the tiger. It has long legs, long whiskers round its mouth, and bunches of hair on its ears. The lynx lives in northern Europe, America, Asia and Africa.

M

Machine. Device that amplifies or replaces human or animal effort to accomplish a physical task.

A machine may be further defined as a device consisting of two or more parts that transmit or modify force and motion in order to do work. The five simple machines are the lever, the wedge, the wheel and axle, the pulley, and the screw; all complex machines are combinations of these basic devices. The operation of a machine may involve the transformation of chemical, thermal, electrical, or nuclear energy into mechanical energy, or vice versa. All machines have an input, an output, and a transforming or modifying and transmitting device. Machines that receive their input energy from a natural source (such as air currents, moving water, coal, petroleum, or uranium) and transform it into mechanical energy are known as prime movers; examples include windmills, waterwheels, turbines, steam engines, and internal-combustion engines.

Magnet. Father has just upset his box of nails, and nails lie strewn all over the floor. Now we must start picking them up. But no! Father has a magnet. It looks like a horseshoe made of steel. When the magnet comes near a nail: hop! The nail leaps to the magnet and sticks to it as if held by glue.

The earth itself is an enormous magnet. That is the reason why the North Pole and the South Pole attract the needles of magnetic compasses.

Maize. Mother has bought some corn cobs.

'I shall boil them in salt water,' she says. 'Then they will taste delicious.'

Maize is an important cereal in many countries. Each grain of maize contains a lot of starch. Your body can turn this starch into energy. In Italy and Spain, people eat a great deal of maize. They feed coarse-grained maize to animals.

Mammoth. Of course you have all seen an elephant. What a huge animal it is. Imagine an even bigger elephant with long hair all over its body and tusks 14 feet long. That's what mammoths looked like. They used to roam wild in Europe and Middle East. But mammoths all died out many centuries ago. Despite this, scientists have found dead mammoths in Siberia which looked as good as alive. They were frozen deep in the ground. That's how they had kept in good condition.

Maple. The maple is a broad-leaved tree. People have introduced several kinds of maple into our country. When the maple seeds fall from their parent tree in autumn, they spin to earth, looking just like the propeller of a 'plane.

People use maple wood for carving toys and souvenirs. And people make violins and guitars from maple wood.

Marmot. If you ever go into the Alps, high among the mountain peaks, take a pair of field-glasses. Look at the distant alpine meadows. You may see some plump animals as big as a cat. They often sit bolt upright.

When danger approaches, each one warns its brothers and sisters with a piercing whistle. These animals are marmots. They live in deep holes which they dig themselves. They are shy animals, and sleepy-heads too. They spend the coldest months of the year dozing underground. See also **'Alpine animals'**.

Metals: Have you even been inside a factory? Many factories are full of powerful metal machines. If these machines were made of wood, their levers would soon break and their wheels would fall to pieces.

How lucky we are to have such things as metals like iron, copper, zinc and silver. People dig these metals from the earth. Usually they are mixed with all kinds of rock there.The rock in which we find a metal is called an ore.

In great heat, metals will become liquid. Then people can mix them with each other. People combine molten copper and zinc, and so make brass. Most metals are good conductors of electricity. Special sorts of called precious metals do not rust. They include platinum and gold.

Microphone. When there is a big festival, a famous person often makes a speech. There may be thousands of people in the audience who want to hear him. So he speaks through a microphone attached to a loudspeaker. In radio broadcasts speakers and musicians must always use a microphone.

Microscope. This is a clever invention made of glass lenses. When you look through a microscope you can see pieces of dust and small living animals magnified so that they look enormous. A microscope is much more powerful than a magnifying glass. Have a drop of water under a microscope and you will be amazed to see many little creatures swimming about.

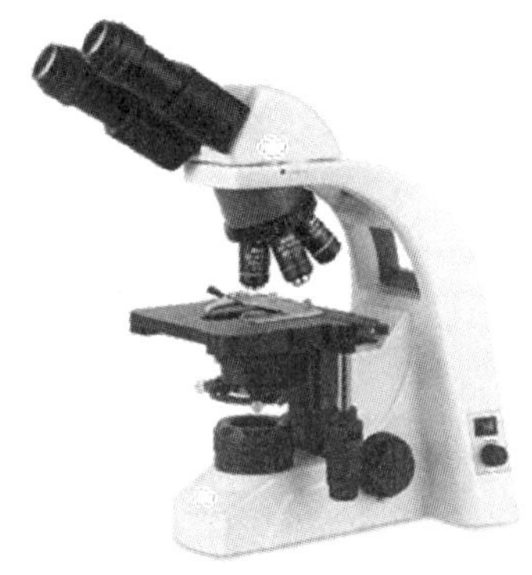

Migratory birds. Birds that live on insects do not find much food in our country in the winter. So they migrate, they fly to the sunny lands far south of our own. The chiff-chaff, willow warbler, nightingale, wheatear, cuckoo, whitethroat, turtle dove, swift and swallow are all migratory birds. They leave us in the autumn and return in the spring.

Milk. 'Would you like a glass of cold milk?' the farmer's wife asked Ritu and Chetan who were staying at her farm. She did not have to ask them twice. You soon get thirsty playing in the meadows. And milk is such a refreshing drink.

'If you like, you can come and watch me churn the milk,' the farmer's wife promised. It was nice and cool in the milk cellars. The children watched while the farmer's wife poured milk into a centrifuge. This machine separated the milk from the thick, yellow cream. Chetan and Ritu each ate a spoonful of cream. It tasted very good. Then they watched the milk go into a churner. The farmer's wife let Ritu turn its handle. It took quite a while, but at last the farmer's wife opened the box and took out the milk which had turned into lovely fresh butter.

She shaped the butter into a kind of loaf. She stamped some decorations on it with a wooden block; then the butter was ready. .

'Don't taste too much of it,' warned the farmer's wife. 'If you do, you will make yourself ill. You may drink the buttermilk that's left.'

The farmer's wife took the butter away into a store-room. She would feed the skim milk to her piglets. They soon grew fat on that. A farm-hand would take the milk cans full of milk, to the village. In the village was a special place where all the farmers around brought their milk every day. And every day a lorry came from a milk factory to collect the milk cans. The factory lay on the road to a big city.

Next day, Chetan had a ride to the factory, inside the milk lorry. At the factory he found things were very different from the little milk cellar back at the farm. The factory consisted of several huge halls. Inside the first hall Chetan saw people in white coats examining the milk. They were testing it to see if it contained enough fat and enough of many other substances. In the second hall stood rows of machines, one after another. They were heating the milk a little. Chetan found that this is called 'pasteurising'. Mother does not have to boil pasteurised milk because pasteurisation has killed any dangerous germs it might have contained. In the second hall Chetan also saw some big centrifliges and mechanical churners.

In the third hall a friendly gentleman showed Chetan how cheese and curdled milk are made. It was not so simple. It took a long time before sour milk turned into various sorts of cheese. Special bacteria and fungi had to help in the process.

Chetan liked the warehouse most of all. Here were rows of strangely painted boxes for storing cheeses. Next to these stood large round Dutch cheeses with red rinds, one after another. Outside, in the factory yard, many lorries stood waiting. People were loading them with milk, butter, cream and cheese. All these nice things were just off to the dairies in the city.

Before Chetan left, a gentleman gave him a booklet full of nicely coloured pictures. It told the story of milk. And it explained how nourishing and wholesome it is to drink milk. It said that milk contains many vitamins which we all need to keep fit. On the last page, Chetan read that people do not only use the milk of cows, goats, and sheep. In other countries, people drink the milk produced by horses, camels and reindeer.

Mills. Farmers come to the mill with large sacks of corn. The miller grinds dark- and light-coloured flour in his mill. There used to be many windmills in Holland and parts of our own country. Their huge sails were turned by the breeze. But today steam and electricity power most mills. Not all mills grind corn. There are many sorts of mill; at the edge of a wood you may see a saw-mill where people cut up tree trunks into planks.

Minerals. Minerals may be metals, precious stones or other substances found in the earth. For example, coal, iron ore, gold, oil and diamonds are all minerals. See also '**Mining**'.

Mining. People obtain coal, iron, lead and copper ore, precious stones, salt and many other things from deep inside the earth. Digging out these minerals is called mining. Miners take lamps with them and go down, deep into the earth, inside a big lift. Then they work in long underground tunnels. Their work is very hard and often very dangerous.

Moles. They tunnel under meadows and fields like little miners. They eat worms, grubs and many harmful animals. The mole is a quite useful animal. But the farmer does not like to see mole-hills in his meadows and gardeners dislike them on their lawns. But moles are hard to catch. They mostly only come out at night, to hunt snails and slugs.

Money. Yogesh took a rare African postage stamp out of his wallet.

'I have got two of these,' he said.

'Oh, I haven't got one of them,' said his friend Chetan. 'Shall we swop? I'll give you an airmail stamp.'

So the two boys exchanged their stamps and each got the one he wanted. Chetan got the African stamp and Yogesh got an airmail stamp. Neither had to pay money.

Of course when you have money you can go into a shop and buy the stamps there. You give your money to the shopkeeper and in return he gives you postage stamps. Isn't that a kind of exchange? Of course it is. Money is the most useful of all objects which we exchange. We can exchange money for a book, a pair of shoes, soap – everything, in fact.

Yet there are still people in the world who don't know what money is. They do just as Yogesh and Chetan did. They exchange objects. Some negroes pay each other with cowrie sea-shells which they thread on a cord and hang round their necks. The Congo negroes pay for things with pieces of material, while the Philippinos barter with grains of rice. In Mongolia, people even use small pressed pieces of tea. In these countries everyone accepts these objects as money. So everyone can use them, just as we use rupees and paises.

Before our ancestors had invented money, they exchanged goods as well. The commonest goods which they used for barter were salt, grain, cattle and skins. Some people travelled hundreds of miles to exchange cows for other goods. Later, people exchanged ornaments made of gold and silver. During this time perhaps some ornament went out of fashion and became less highly valued. Perhaps people no longer made gold and silver into ornaments. But small gold and silver pieces went on being passed from one merchant to another, just as our coins pass from hand to hand.

Of course people had to know the value of such and such a piece of gold or silver. So they weighed each piece. A merchant in the Middle Ages always carried a weighing machine around with him. This was a nuisance, especially when a piece of gold or silver was too large (when you had to cut a bit off) or too small (when you had to add another bit to it).

It was much simpler when kings and emperors had coins made for their countries. But even then, cheats cut pieces off the edges of the coins. But the master of one royal mint stopped this. He had fine grooves cut along the edge of each coin. We call this 'milling'. You can see at a glance if anyone has cut a bit off a milled coin.

On the front of each coin was stamped the image of the ruler of the country, and on the back his coat of arms.

If you bought a house in the days when people used gold coins, you needed a carriage to take all the money to the dealer. Just think of riding through a town with a carriage full of money! How people would stare at you.

Partly to help solve this problem, at last some one invented paper money. Then people could carry around large sums of money without having to hire a coach. Can a piece of paper be as valuable as a gold coin? Just go to a shop and see. Can you buy things with a rupee note? Of course you can. Each bank note has its value printed on it and our government sees that you get proper value for it.

Have you heard of forgers? These are people who copy coins or paper money. Of course this is against the law. When people copy money and try to spend it they are put in prison for years if they get caught.

When Manish receives his pocket money he goes straight to a sweet shop and spends it all on sweets. Harish is wiser. First he decides what he could buy with his pocket money. Once he saw a beautiful pocket-knife in the ironmonger's shop-window. Everytime he passed the shop he stopped and looked at it.

'It's very expensive,' sighed Harish. He calculated that the price of the knife was equal to six weeks' pocket money. But he saved hard and after the six weeks were up he bought the knife.

Manish was a bit jealous. But why hadn't he saved up? Manish had not been sensible, but Harish had. I'm sure you would like to be as sensible as Harish. Why don't you try saving up when you want to buy something special? Take your pocket money to a savings bank.

The people at the bank will write down in a book how much money you bring. After a few months the bank will pay you back your money and a little more, as a reward for lending them your money. We call the spare money that people put in the bank 'capital'. What the bank adds as a reward is called 'interest'.

Monkeys. You can spend hours in the zoo happily watching these agile climbers. See how quickly they leap from branch to branch, and how they use hands and feet to pull themselves up the bars of their cage. And what comic antics some of them perform. But don't tease the monkeys, and only throw them food they are allowed to eat.

The biggest monkeys are really called apes. There are several kinds of ape. The gorilla lives in Africa. It is the largest of all apes and weighs as much as two full-grown men. Some people think chimpanzees are the most intelligent apes. They also live in Africa. The Orangutan is the second largest ape. Orangutans live in the forests which clothe the Far Eastern islands of Sumatra and Borneo.

Besides the apes, there are many monkeys, including green monkeys, baboons and mandrills in Africa and Arabia, macaque monkeys and howler monkeys in Central and South America.

Moon. The moon is our earth's faithful friend. Year after year it circles around the earth. Each journey takes 29½ days. The moon always has the same side turned towards the earth so no one has seen the other side with his own eyes.

Why does the moon shine so brightly? Because the sun shines on the moon. At the 'dark' of the moon we don't see the moon at all because the sun is shining on the far side. But when it is 'new moon' we see a narrow sickle-shaped moon. The open sickle 'blade' is on the left. Each day we see more of the moon until we can say it is in its 'first quarter'. Each day as the sun shines on a bigger part of the moon the quarter grows until it is a half, and then a full moon. We can clearly see the mountains and valleys on the moon when it is full, and sometimes they seem to make the shape of a face. After a few more days, the moon gets smaller until again we can't see it at all.

An express train would take half a year to reach the moon. But you would be unable to live on it. There is no air or water on the moon. During the daytime it is very hot and, at night, very cold.

Moss. The ground in the wood is covered with soft carpets of moss. At least moss looks just like a soft carpet. What is moss? It is a tiny plant made up of very small stems with many leaves. These plants grow so close together that they do look more or less like a carpet.

If all mosses suddenly died there would be some tremendous floods. Moss sucks up water like a sponge, and releases it very slowly.

Motor-cycle. Bicycle or tricycle propelled by an internal combustion engine.

The first motor tricycle was built in 1884 in England, and the first gasoline-engine motor-cycle was built by Gottlieb Daimler in 1885. Motor-cycles were widely used after 1910, especially by the armed forces in World War I. After 1950 a larger, heavier motor-cycle was used mainly for touring and sport competitions. The moped, a light, low-speed motor bicycle that can also be pedaled, was developed mainly in Europe, and the sturdier Italian-made motor scooter also became popular for its economy.

Motors. They power the machines in factories. Ships and planes are propelled by motors too. A motor is a powerful machine. But it has a giant appetite. It must eat, otherwise it cannot work. What does a motor eat? Some motors eat steam, others eat hot air, petrol, diesel oil or electricity. The measure the strength of a motor in horse-power.

Motorways. Motorways are long, wide roads which cut through the countryside in straight lines. They are roads made specially for cars travelling fast over long distances. Bicycles, prams and horse-drawn carts may not move along these roads. They are meant only for cars and people on motor-cycles.

You might think that accidents happen often at the crossroads, because cars are driving so fast. But no. On a modern motorway there are no crossroads.

Mountain railways. Clever inventors have made it easy for us to climb the steepest mountains. They have invented several kinds of mountain railway. Of course, first they had to persuade wealthy people to pay for them to be built. Otherwise the inventors ideas would have been of no use.

On a rack-railway there is an extra rail between the two rails. On this rail there are notches called ratchets. A cog-wheel on the railway engine fits into these ratchets as it turns.

Mouse. 'Oh, a mouse!' screamed Ritu, and she ran away. But don't you be afraid of mice. They aren't dangerous. But they are harmful, for in the world's warehouses they eat millions of pounds worth of food each year.

Wolfgang Amadeus Mozart. One day, Mozart's father came home and was very angry. He found his little four-and-a-half-year-old son Wolfgang had discovered an ink well and had covered a music manuscript with lines and thick ink-blots.

'My dear boy,' cried his father. 'What are you doing?'

'I am writing a piece of music for the piano,' said Wolfgang, turning his inky face to his father.

'Writing music?' exclaimed his father in amazement. He was even more amazed when he looked at the paper. 'It really is a piece of music,' he said.

'If you want to play it you must practise hard,' said little Wolfgang.

This wonder-child became a famous composer. He wrote many operas, symphonies, songs and other pieces of music. People play them still. Have a look in this week's *Radio Times*. You are bound to find Mozart's name somewhere. Mozart was born at Salzburg in 1756 and died in Vienna in 1791.

Mummy. Father took Tom and Harish along to a museum. There, they saw a dirty-grey, painted body in a big glass case.

'What's that?' they asked, feeling a bit frightened.

'That's the mummy of an Egyptian king who died more than 4,000 years ago,' explained Father. 'His body was treated with resin and ointments and wrapped in linen bandages. Bodies preserved in this way cannot decay. Archaeologists digging up graves in Egypt's pyramids often find these mummies quite sound. Pyramids were the graves of Egypt's kings.'

Munchhausen. 'The most daring adventure was my journey on a cannon ball. We had just besieged a fortress and I wanted to spy out the land. So I jumped on a cannon ball which had just been fired by our soldiers. Near the walls of the fortress I became a bit frightened. But I did not hesitate. I jumped on a cannon ball which was just on the way from the fortress to our camp, and so I came back safe and sound to our soldiers.'

Do you believe this story? I don't. This and many more untrue stories were told by the Baron von Munchhausen. Have you read the book about his adventures? Munchhausen really lived, about 250 years ago.

Musical instruments. Although vocal performance is common to practically all musical traditions, instrumental performance has a more varied history. Stringed and wind instruments are mentioned in the Bible, and they fulfilled important functions in the ceremonies and entertainments of the Greek and Roman civilizations. While central to the religious rituals of many non-Western cultures, instrumental music was considered distracting or inappropriate to worship by the church authorities of medieval Europe, who severely restricted its use. However, such instruments as the harp, lyre, psaltery, and various winds and drums – most of which were derived from Oriental models – were employed in small ensembles to accompany songs and to play single-line (monophonic) dance pieces. Because only a few instruments from the Middle Ages still exist, much of the present knowledge comes from pictorial and literary sources and from folk music that preserves these traditions.

During the 16th and early 17th centuries viols, recorders, and other winds and strings were constructed in various sizes to form homogeneous consorts, and a repertoire of polyphonic keyboard, lute, and consort music developed independently of vocal music. Rare in music before the mid-1500s, larger ensembles consisting primarily of strings became common at European courts, leading to the standardization of the basic orchestral instrumentation in the late 1700s. For the past 250 years the profusion of instrumental music, in various solo, chamber, and orchestral or large-ensemble genres, has been among the most prominent characteristics of European music.

The comparatively rapid evolution of Western musical genres and instruments (in marked contrast to the stability of many other musical cultures) was frequently accompanied by a disdain for those of previous generations. Older instruments were often altered, "improved", or simply discarded, sometimes surviving intact only in private collections. Renewed interest in the performance of early music, and the revival of such instruments as the harpsichord since World War II, however, have resulted in a growing appreciation for performances on restored instruments or authentic reconstructions of early instruments. Many soloists and ensembles now specialize in early music played on these instruments.

Music-making at home. Recorders, guitars, violins and pianos sound nice when people play them together. Maybe you have some friends who enjoy making music with you. There are lots of lovely, and quite simple, pieces of music written for this sort of music-making.

Must. As soon as a farmer has harvested his grapes, he presses the juice from the fresh fruit. This juice is sweet, refreshing must. People also make it from apples and pears. In time, must starts to ferment and turn into wine.

N

Nail. In construction and carpentry, a slender metal shaft, pointed at one end and flattened at the other end, used as a fastener.

Most often used to join pieces of wood, nails are also used with plastic, drywall, masonry, and concrete. They are usually made of steel but can also be made of stainless steel, iron, copper, aluminum, or bronze. The pointed end is called the point, the shaft is called the shank, and the flattened part is called the head.

Natural catastrophes. Event of nature that takes human lives or destroys property.

Natural Catastrophes can be very dangerous to human lives and properties. For example.

Sometimes floods destroy some of Holland's dikes and large parts of the country disappear under water. People from all over the world have come to the aid of Dutchmen who lost all their possessions.

'The White Death' sometimes rages down a mountainside. Enormous avalanches, falls of snow, can bury people, houses, whole villages. Avalanches fall in springtime when snow begins to melt.

Terrific earthquakes sometimes make houses collapse in many villages and towns in Turkey. It takes a long time before they can be rebuilt and all the damage can be repaired.

Navy. A country's warships are called a fleet or a navy. Countries also have many peaceful ships which only carry people and goods from one continent to another. These ships are called a 'merchant navy'.

Needle-leaved trees. The spruce is a well-known tree of this kind. The 'needles' of course are really fine leaves. They stay green all the year round. Only the larch drops its needle leaves and is bare in winter.

The needle-leaved trees of different species look quite different from one another. You often see dark-green cypress trees in our churchyards, though their true home is around the warm Mediterranean.

Negroes. The negroes are the people who live in Africa. They have dark-brown or black skin, curly hair and thick lips. There are many different negro tribes and many negro languages.

There are also many negroes in America. Their ancestors were shipped to America long ago as slaves. Today, the negroes in America live just like the white people.

Nests. Many animals build a nest for their young. Birds often make their nests of plant fibres, feathers, moss, hairs and twigs. Swallows build their nests of mud and saliva. Squirrels make a nest from twigs, leaves and moss. Even some fishes build nests – sticklebacks, for example.

Nettle. How it stings when you touch a stinging nettle! If you put a nettle beneath a microscope you will see why. Its stem and leaves are covered with little hairs. These hairs are hollow. When your skin touches them their sharp-pointed ends break off and a burning liquid flows into the tiny wounds the points have made in your skin.

Neutral. Rohit and Ritu want to make a trip on Sunday, but they can't agree where to go.

'What do you think, Uncle Khatri?' they ask. But Uncle Khatri will not interfere with them. He is neutral.

Newts. A newt looks like a lizard. But he walks much more slowly on dry land, and has a damp, slimy skin. Newts live mostly in water. But they breathe air through their lungs. In summer, when they have laid their eggs in a pond, newts crawl out and hide under stones. They sleep under stones all through the winter.

Nightingale. Nightingales are birds that sing at night. They have plain, grey-brown feathers. Nightingales nest in bushes in woods.

Nomads. Nomads are wandering tribes. Often they travel about with big herds of sheep or cattle, moving always from one grassland to another. In Africa there are many nomads. The Bedouins are the best-known.

North Pole. It lies in the middle of the Arctic Sea. It is the most northern point on earth. In 1909 the American, Peary, became the first explorer to reach the Pole.

Northern lights. At the North Pole it is dark for six months of the year. But not always completely dark. Instead of the sun, people sometimes see the strange flickering of the northern lights. There are similar lights at the South Pole as well.

Numbers and counting. 'He can't even count up to three,' people say about someone who behaves in a silly, childish way. For tiny children often can only count up to two. And when they have to count many things, they do it in twos. In past times, everyone counted like that. Many native tribes still do.

There is a name which means two things: 'a pair'. Human beings have a pair of eyes, a pair of ears, a pair of arms and a pair of legs. Primitive man and modern children both count in pairs. But an old proverb says 'All good things come in threes.' This proverb comes from law and justice, from a time when an accused man was always brought to court three times.

Brahmi		—	=	≡	+	[illegible]	[illegible]	[illegible]	[illegible]	[illegible]
Hindu	०	१	२	३	४	५	६	७	८	९
Arabic	٠	١	٢	٣	٤	٥	٦	٧	٨	٩
Medieval	0	I	2	3	[illegible]	ς	6	ʌ	8	9
Modern	0	1	2	3	4	5	6	7	8	9

Many people have always thought three a mysterious number. Some have even called it a holy number. Magicians are often supposed to mutter their spells three times over.

Before people began using the figures we use today, many used Roman numbers. These came from the five fingers on a person's hand. A child learning to calculate, counts on its fingers. I don't suppose you still do that. But long ago everyone did it, and that's how the Romans got the signs they used for numbers. But after the number five (V) it was not so easy. So the Romans did it like this: V+I = VI .

To do this the Romans had to use their second hand: V and II = VII, V and 111 = VIII, V and IIII = VIIII and V and V = X. You got 'X' by turning the second 'V' upside down and putting its point against that of the first 'V'.

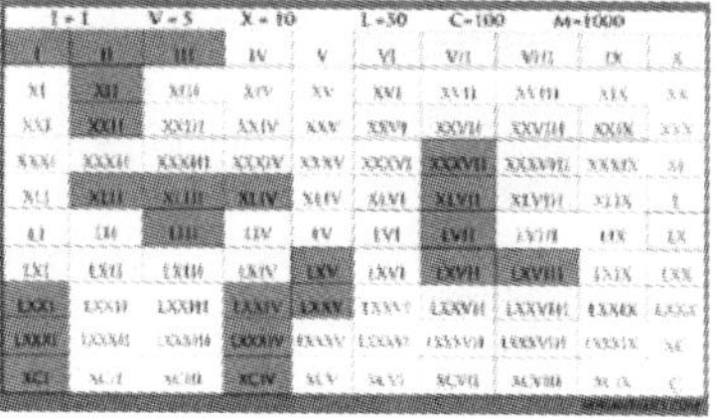

I = 1	V = 5	X = 10		L = 50	C = 100	M = 1000			
I	II	III	IV	V	VI	VII	VIII	IX	X
XI	XII	XIII	XIV	XV	XVI	XVII	XVIII	XIX	XX
XXI	XXII	XXIII	XXIV	XXV	XXVI	XXVII	XXVIII	XXIX	XXX
XXXI	XXXII	XXXIII	XXXIV	XXXV	XXXVI	XXXVII	XXXVIII	XXXIX	XL
XLI	XLII	XLIII	XLIV	XLV	XLVI	XLVII	XLVIII	XLIX	L
LI	LII	LIII	LIV	LV	LVI	LVII	LVIII	LIX	LX
LXI	LXII	LXIII	LXIV	LXV	LXVI	LXVII	LXVIII	LXIX	LXX
LXXI	LXXII	LXXIII	LXXIV	LXXV	LXXVI	LXXVII	LXXVIII	LXXIX	LXXX
LXXXI	LXXXII	LXXXIII	LXXXIV	LXXXV	LXXXVI	LXXXVII	LXXXVIII	LXXXIX	XC
XCI	XCII	XCIII	XCIV	XCV	XCVI	XCVII	XCVIII	XCIX	C

The Romans used a five-fold system of multiplying. They invented other multiple numbers: L = 50, C = 100, D = 500, M = 1000. For 1,000 times 1,000 (a million) they did not write MM because this would mean 1,000 plus 1,000, or 2,000. Instead, they wrote M/M or 1/M.

Anyone who wants to read Roman numbers must be able to add up: MDCLXVIII means 1,000 plus 500 plus 100 plus 50 plus 10 plus 5 plus 3 which all means 1,668. To make these long numbers a bit shorter, the Romans later subtracted some numbers instead of adding them. This was done, for example, with IIII = IV (5 less 1), VIIII = IX (10 less 1), XC (100 less 10) instead of LXXXX, DCCCC = CM (1,000 less 100),

MCM = 1,900. In this way people could read numbers more quickly.

Calculating with units, decimals, hundreds and thousands (the metric system) only became possible after people invented the number '0' to mean 'nothing'. The modern numbers that we use are the so-called Arabic numbers. In past centuries they looked quite different from the numbers in your arithmetic book. And people did not use them so often. But after an arithmetic book written 400 years ago by the German Adam Riese became well-known, everyone began using Arabic numbers. In Holland a man called Bartjes made Arabic numbers popular by writing a book. The Dutch still say, 'According to Bartjes, two times two are four,' when they mean 'Everyone knows that.'

In eastern countries the numbers 6 and 12 play an important part. You can find these numbers in some of our measurements. For example, a dozen is 12, a gross is 144 (12 times 12).

O

Oak tree. The oak tree is often called 'the monarch of the wood'. It has a stout wrinkled trunk, sometimes five or six feet thick. But in summer, dense foliage hides almost all the gnarled branches that grow from this trunk. An oak tree's leaves drop off each autumn and new ones sprout in April and May. In autumn, the oak tree's fruits ripen; we call them acorns. Pigs love to eat acorns. If people feed pigs lots of acorns they quickly grow round and plump.

Oak is a very hard sort of wood. People use it for making floorboards, sleepers on railways, and furniture. Do you know where cork comes from? It comes from the bark of a cork-oak tree. Many cork-oaks grow in the warm climate of Spain.

Oasis. A caravan is traveling through the desert. Both men and animals are hot and thirsty. Suddenly the camels begin to trot faster. Their drivers have seen some palm trees on the horizon. They are drawing near an oasis. An oasis is a green island in a dry, brown desert. At an oasis people can usually find fruit and fresh water. There are oases in the Sahara Desert and in Arabia.

Occupation. In our country, men and women work in fields, in factories and workshops, in offices, schools and shops. Every occupation has its difficulties, and some have drudgery, but work can be noble and important. Without working we could not live.

Olive tree. Olive trees grow in warm, European countries. People press out an oil from the blue-black olive fruits. This is called olive oil.

Olympic Games. In Greece, about 2,500 years ago, people held athletic contests every four years at the town of Olympia. In A.D. 1896 people began holding these competitions again. Nowadays the best sportsmen and women from all over the world meet once every four years and take part in many events. The most recent Olympic Games took place in 2010 at China.

On board. When you are in a ship, people say you are 'on board'. The cry 'Man overboard!' means someone has fallen from a ship into the sea.

Opera. Nisha is singing a gay little song. It comes from the fairy-tale opera called *Hansel and Gretel.* An opera is a stage play in which the actors sing their words, and seldom talk, like actors in an ordinary play. Usually a big orchestra accompanies their singing.

Many famous composers have written operas. Do you know the names of any operas by Mozart, or Wagner, or Verdi, or Richard Strauss?

A gay musical play where the actors sing, speak and dance is called an operetta. One of the best-known operettas is *The*

Merry Widow by Franz Lehar. It has some splendid tunes.

Operation. Bharti got a severe tummy-ache one day. The doctor examined her.

'Your appendix is inflamed,' said the doctor. 'But it won't hurt you much longer. We'll simply take it out.'

So our Bharti went to hospital for an operation. She was given something to breathe in, and then she fell asleep. 'That was because of the anaesthetic,' explained the nurse afterwards. 'Thanks to the anaesthetic, you didn't feel any pain at all while we operated on you. You will soon be quite well again.'

Optical illusion. A mistake in the perception of a sensory experience. Perception is the process by which organisms interpret and organize information received by the sense organs. An illusion occurs when what the brain perceives differs substantially from the actual qualities of an object or stimulus. Illusions may occur in any of the human senses, including vision, hearing, touch, smell, and taste. In general usage, however, the term is most often applied to visual illusions, also called optical illusions.

Illusions are common in normal perception and are natural consequences of the way our sensory systems work. Psychologists study illusions because they provide important clues about the functioning of perceptual systems. Magicians rely on illusions to trick and entertain their audiences. However, errors in perception are only considered illusions if they are experienced by a large number of people. For example, if you are the only person who misreads a word, that is not an illusion. But if a large number of people misread the word in exactly the same way, then it may be considered an illusion.

Optician. Father has dropped his glasses and broken their lenses. Harish went with his father to the optician and watched while the optician put new lenses in Father's glasses.

Orange. The orange is a berry. Yes, this may surprise you. But learned scientists are now agreed that it is so.

This juicy fruit grows in large quantities in our country. It also thrives in warmer countries like Spain, Italy and Africa. But you can buy several sorts of oranges in shops. They include sour oranges, which make good marmalade, and sweet oranges, which are good to eat raw. The big grapefruit, tiny mandarin and bitter lemon all belong to the same family as the orange.

Orchestra. Vinit said excitedly: 'We want to have an orchestra at school. We've already got four boys who can play the violin. Chetan plays the piano and Jim plays the cello. Now we need someone who can play the double bass, and we need a clarinettist, and a flautist to play the flute. We'll practise hard so that we can all play together at the school festival.'

In a really big orchestra there are many more than these six musical instruments. See also '**Musical Instruments'**.

Ore. Some sorts of rock contain metals. People call these rocks 'ores'. There are many kinds of ore; some contain iron, others copper, lead or many other metals.

Organ. 'They stand together like a row of organ pipes.' People sometimes say this to describe a family of children standing in a line, when each child is a bit taller than the one next to it. Organ pipes look just like this. They produce music when an organist presses his fingers on the organ's keys, and his feet on its pedals. Air is pressed into the organ pipes with bellows. Nowadays electricity works the bellows in most organs. Each pipe of a different length makes a different sound. Most churches have an organ. Sometimes you see a big organ in a concert hall.

Organisation. Rohit said: 'There was a terrible muddle on our last sports day. It started half an hour late and there was nobody to show the public to their seats. After waiting a long time, we walked on to the field in an orderly way. And what do you think happened then? Harish put on the wrong record. Instead of putting on marching music he played a waltz. We all got out of step.'

'We had been doing exercises a long time before Harish found the printed programmes. He had completely forgotten to give them out to all the parents who had come to watch. And so it went on until the end of the programme. As a finale, Harish announced that there would be a sack race. But no one could find the sacks anywhere.'

Rohit's sports day was not properly prepared. It was not properly *organised.* Harish ought to have organised everything first. He should have divided up the different jobs between his friends. If everything had been well organised the sports day would have gone without a hitch.

Ostrich. The ostrich is a bird that cannot fly; but it can run with huge steps across Africa's great plains.

Its strides are truly enormous. Each one may be seven or eight feet long! The fastest horse can barely keep up with a running ostrich. African ostriches sometimes grow eight feet high. The hen birds lay up to 15 eggs, which weigh about three pounds each. Each egg weighs about as much as 24 chicken's eggs. People breed ostriches on special farms. They do this for the birds valuable feathers. In South America and Australia live rheas and emus, which are smaller relatives of the African ostrich.

Owl. During daytime, owls live in holes in trees or sit silently high among the branches. Their dark feathers camouflage them and their enemies cannot see them. At night, owls fly silently low over the ground, seeking mice. Owls are useful animals. The long-eared owl eats mice and even bigger animals.

Oxygen. Oxygen is a gas which all people, all other animals, and all plants must breathe to keep alive. Air which lacks oxygen is unhealthy. That's why you should air rooms from time to time. When you are sitting indoors you are using up the oxygen in the air of your room.

P

Palms. They are trees which grow in hot countries. We know the fruits of various kinds of palm better than we know the trees they come from. Most of us have eaten dates and coconuts.

Palms have no branches. A tuft of huge leaves grows at the top of their slender trunks. Palm trunks are not smooth but covered with 'ribs' where the stems of leaves once sprouted when the trees were not so tall.

Parachute. If you hold a half-opened umbrella in the air above your head, then suddenly pull it down, it will open wide. In the same way a parachute flies open when a parachutist leaps from a 'plane'.

During floods or avalanches, aeroplanes drop food by parachute to towns and villages cut off by water or snow. When an aeroplane is damaged or on fire, its pilot often saves his life by jumping out with a parachute. His parachute rests on an air cushion and so breaks the pilot's fall. A parachute floats quite slowly down to the ground. Usually parachutes are made of silk.

Parliament. 'Let's stay on after school,' said Harish during the morning break. So at twelve o'clock the boys joined each other in the school grounds. Then they had to decide what to do. 'Let's buy a ball,' said one. 'Let's get some books,' said another. 'Let's go on an expedition,' said a third. Finally they put it to the vote.

It's the same in parliament. When members of parliament have to make important decisions for the whole country, they first have a discussion. Often they decide the discussion by voting on it afterwards. Every democratic country has a parliament that does this.

Parrot. 'Pretty Polly! Say Hallo,' cries a hoarse voice all day long from a bird cage. Can it really be a bird that makes such a noise? Can a bird speak? Listen! Now it's even singing a song. Only a parrot can do these things.

How brightly coloured are its feathers. And how jauntily it hops around its cage. Where do you think parrots come from? They live in the forests of hot countries like ours. In the zoo you will probably see parrots, cockatoos, parakeets, grey parrots, red parrots and blue and yellow parrots. They are all excellent climbers. To help them climb, they use their strong, curved beaks.

Passport. This is a document with a photograph attached to it. When a traveller goes abroad he has to show his passport to the customs officers.

Pasture. A pasture is a meadow where cattle graze. You will often see pastures on low ground near rivers and streams. Rivers sometimes overflow. This would damage corn crops. But flood water helps to make pasture grasses grow taller and more juicy.

Peacock. When people say: 'As proud as a peacock,' they are thinking of the big birds which walk gracefully up and down in the zoo or in our villages. A peacock is a beautiful bird. Its head is decorated with a feathered crest which it can raise. A peacock's feathers are red, blue and green.

Sometimes a peacock spreads its long tail feathers. They look like a huge, brilliantly coloured fan. Each feather has a big, colourful spot shaped like an eye.

The peacock's real home is among the mountainous woods of South Asia.

Pearl. 'Brrr!' A Malayan man shakes the water from his hair. He has just come out of the sea. Smiling, he shows what he has found: an oyster. He breaks its shell open. Ah! Inside lies a large, valuable pearl.

Pearls only grow when a foreign body – for example, a grain of sand – has got between the two shells of the living oyster. The oyster deposits a layer of slime around this object, and after a few years the slime turns into a pearl.

In Japan, people make artificial pearls by putting tiny objects inside the shells of living pearl oysters. They do this because pearls are one of the most valuable of all jewels. Real pearls cost a great deal of money.

Peat. Just watch our little Harish. He is helping his grandfather in the garden.

'Now let's mix some peat with the soil to loosen it up and give it some manure. Then we can plant the little seedlings,' explains Grandfather. And he shows Harish the big pieces of brown peat. 'Did you know that peat forms from plants which lived and died on swampy ground? People cut peat in slices, dry it and press it. Then it is called turf. You can use it to fertilise soil. And in Ireland people burn it as fuel. You can pack breakable goods safely in peat if they have to travel.'

Pedal. This is the name for all sorts of levers that we press down with our hands or feet. A bicycle has two pedals. All the time you press the keys of a piano its sound continues. The many keys of an organ are really big pedals. When an organist presses them down you hear the sound made by air whistling through the organ pipes.

Pencil. Pencils should really be called 'graphite sticks' because that is what the writing part is really made of. Pencils with hard graphite 'leads' contain more clay than the soft ones. A simple wooden pencil does its job just as well as its more important-looking brother the propelling pencil. When you write with a pencil on a piece of paper, very small pieces of lead stick to the paper. Thats why the lead of your pencil becomes shorter and needs sharpening. With the lead of one pencil you could draw a line about 40 miles long.

Penguin. What is the use of wings? To fly with. But the penguin's wings do not help it fly. It uses its wings as flappers to help it swim. The smart black-and-white penguins all live in the Southern Hemisphere, especially in the icy waters near the South Pole.

Peppermint. 'I like peppermint most of all,' says Vinisha. 'Peppermint smells nice and it has such a nice taste.'

People get peppermint-oil from the peppermint plant. This is the oil which gives peppermint sweets such a fresh taste and such a nice smell.

Perch. The perch is a greedy fish of prey. On its back you will see two fins. The front fin consists of two sharp prickles. With these, the perch defends itself against the fierce pike. The pike is its enemy. In some countries, people eat both these freshwater fish.

The pretty little coloured sun-perches come from North America. They are beautiful; people keep them in aquariums.

Petrol. About 100 years ago, the first cars drove, rattling, through the streets. How surprised many people were to learn that these vehicles were not pulled by horses, but driven by a few litres of yellow liquid: petrol.

Today, the whole world depends on petrol:

Cars, planes, factory machines, all need petrol. Father fills his lighter with it and Mother uses it to get stains out of clothes.

Where does petrol come from? People drill deep bore-holes into the earth where petroleum lies, trapped in great underground lakes. In America, one bore-hole is four miles deep. In North and South America, Russia and Iran there are enormous oil-fields where many drilling plants are set up close to each other.

People refine petroleum in huge factories. They can make many things from petroleum: petrol, paraffin oil, candles, waxes, colourings, tar, asphalt and medicines.

Pheasant. What a joke! Our Harish got a funny hat for Diwali with a long feather stuck in it. 'It's a pheasant's feather,' Harish's father told him.

'If pheasants have such long feathers they must be very striking to look at,' said Harish.

'Indeed they are,' replied his father. 'And the tail feathers of some sorts of pheasants grow even longer than this one. Much longer than you are tall. Cock pheasants have specially beautiful feathers.'

Photography. Rohit saved up his pocket money for a long time. At last he had saved enough to buy a camera. Rohit's camera is not a very big one, but Rohit can take very good pictures with it.

Making a photograph is not magic. When Rohit presses a button, a shutter inside the camera opens for a moment and lets a ray of light pass through the lens. Inside the camera is a film. On this film is a substance which is very sensitive to light. All the light and dark parts of the subject to be photographed are exactly copied on the film. Then Rohit takes the film to a photographic shop where people develop the film and make Rohit a print of each picture.

Pig. The pig is a domesticated animal. People eat its bacon and its fat. Pig skin is used to make leather and people use coarse pigs' bristles for making brushes. Brown-black wild pigs still roam free in the swampy woods of far-off lands. Young wild boars look very funny. They have light-brown skin and white stripes all over their body.

Pike. A pike is a fish of prey. It lives in our ponds, lakes and rivers. Pikes have wonderfully streamlined bodies which help them dart upon their victims. People sometimes say, 'He is like a pike let loose in a pond full of carp,' when someone turns everything upside down.

Pillory. 'Put her in the pillory,' shouted the people. Once, people would leave criminals in a pillory for days and mock them while they stood, helpless to move. This punishment lasted right into the Middle Ages. In some places a stone pillar still marks the spot where a pillory once stood.

Pine. The pine tree is a needle-leaved tree. It grows well in sandy soil, where oaks and other broad-leaved trees might perish. Its long, thin pine-needles grow in pairs from a central stem.

If you make a cut in a pine trunk, resin runs out until the wound closes up. People use resin to make turpentine and rosin. People rub rosin on the bows of violins, 'cellos and double basses.

Many children love to gather the cone-shaped seeds of the pine tree. See also 'Needle-leaved trees'.

Plague. 'The Black Death is in the next village!' Once, wherever anyone said this, everyone became very frightened. For the Black Death was a catching illness which spread swiftly from place to place, killing thousands of people. Victims of this plague suffered from pains and high fever and got ulcers and lumps on their skin.

Fleas which live on rats once spread this disease. But today we no longer need fear it. The plague no longer exists, thank goodness.

Plaice. It is a fish which makes a tasty meal. A young plaice looks exactly like many other fish. But soon it spends much of its time lying on one side. The eye on its underneath side and gradually moves to the upper side and its mouth becomes crooked. In this way a plaice becomes a flat fish, which lies with its light-coloured underside on the bottom of the sea. You can hardly see it because its upper side is the same colour as the sea bed.

Platinum. Platinum is a grey and white precious metal. People find it in East Africa, North America and the Ural Mountains of Russia. Platinum is three or four times as costly as gold. People often use it to make jewellery.

Poisonous plants. Did you know that only five belladonna cherries could kill the child that ate them? Did you know that thorn-apples, foxgloves, hemlock, henbane and daphne are all poisonous? The poison of the meadow saffron takes six hours before it begins to act. Some poisonous plants are very important medicines, but only when a doctor prescribes them to patients, and in small quantities.

Polar bears. These bear feel most at home on icy shores and at sea, on floating ice-floes. A polar bear's rough, thick fur and its thick layer of body fat protect it from the severe cold.

Polar bears attack seals and also eat the eggs of seabirds; and they catch fish when they can. A polar bear's white fur is very valuable.

Polar regions. These are the areas around the North Pole and the South Pole. The area around the North Pole is called the Arctic. It is covered by snow and ice. The northernmost parts of Europe, Asia, and North America all belong to the Arctic. At the South Pole lies a huge island continent. This is called Antarctica.

Polder. In Holland and Belgium, green meadows often run right up to the coast. They are called polders. Big herds of cattle graze on them for their grass grows lush and abundant. Dikes and sand dunes protect these polders against sea water.

Polders are specially interesting because once they were actually under the sea. Clever engineers shut the sea up in huge pools, then pumped out all the water. Where the sea was, the polders are today.

Pompeii. About 150 years ago, archaeologists dug up a town at the foot of the volcano Vesuvius, near Naples. More than 1,800 years ago, a tremendous volcanic eruption from Vesuvius had covered this town in lava and red-hot ashes. The town's name was Pompeii.

Pope. The Pope is the Roman Catholic bishop of Rome. He is the head of the Roman Catholic Church and Catholics say he is Christ's representative on earth. They call him 'Holy Father'. The Pope governs the Catholic Church. His advisers are called cardinals and his helpers are bishops. He lives in the Vatican.

Poplar. When Mabel was five years old her father planted a poplar tree in the garden. Now Maanu is 12 and the tree is as high as a house. Poplars grow very fast. Their small leaves quiver in the wind. Poplar wood is very soft. People use it to make delicate carvings and wooden clogs.

Poppy. Corn poppies are among the loveliest of all wild flowers. They are glowing red in the middle of a ripe, golden cornfield. Poppy seed vessels look like little beakers. When the seeds are ripe, they fall out of a special opening in their container.

Port and starboard. When you are on board a ship facing the way in which the ship is sailing, its port side is on your left hand and its starboard is on your right.

Post. All is quiet in the hail of the post office. Tick-tock, tick-tock, says the clock. All the counters are closed. For it is three o'clock in the morning.

The word 'Parcels' is written above the first counter. During the day, Mr. Soni stands behind this counter. He puts each parcel on a weighing machine and checks its weight, so that he can tell how much it will cost to post. Mr. Soni also accepts letters with valuable contents: specially sealed registered letters. When you send a registered letter you receive a receipt. On the receipt it says that the letter was handed in at such-and-such a post office.

The words 'Express letters' are written above the next counter. Express letters travel to their destinations by the very first train available.

At the next counter you can hand in cables and telegrams. Anyone who wants to send an important message in a hurry sends it by telegram. By telephone or 'telex' a post-office official tells someone at the receiving post office what is written on your telegram.

At the counter next to this hangs a letter-box. Above this counter are written the words 'Airmail letters'. When you want to send a letter to a far-off country you can pay extra postage and send it airmail. Airmail letters travel in planes and arrive far more quickly than letters sent by boat and train.

At the far end of the hall are many doors, each leading to a separate little glass room. In the middle of the hall at that end is a counter. The words 'Telephone calls' are written above the counter. If you have not a telephone at home and you want to speak to a friend in another town, you give the lady at the counter the name of your friend's town and his telephone number. When the lady has made contact with your friend by telephone you step into one of the telephone boxes and speak to your friend on the telephone inside it.

Next to the telephone boxes is a large cabinet full of closed compartments. These are special letterboxes. You may hire one of these and the postman will put your letters in it instead of taking them to your home, if you cannot wait to get there. The post-office people give you a special key so that only you can open your box.

At the next counter, you can send money to people far away. First you must fill in a postal order which says to whom the money has to be sent and how much it is. In exchange for this postal order the post-office person takes your money. You keep a torn-off bit of the postal order to prove you really did buy that postal order.

'Post Office Savings Bank' is written over the next counter. You can save money there and collect it by showing your savings bank book to a post-office official.

At the last counter you can buy postage stamps. Now we have been around the whole hall.

A bell rings. 'Here they are,' says a post-office worker, and he opens a gate. Outside he can see men bearing sacks on their backs. They are lit up by the headlamps of their post-office vans. These people have just collected mail from the railway station. The mail has just arrived by a night mail train.

'Good morning, Harish,' says one of the men. They carry their great bags of letters and parcels through the hall to the counters. Then they drive off again. The post-office worker stays at the gate and soon some more men arrive. They all say 'Good morning' as they walk into the post office. They are the post-office sorters. They take the letters and parcels out of their bags and sort them into streets and roads.

Outside it is slowly getting light. People are just beginning to go to work. But the sorters have already finished their first job of the day. And postmen have put the mail in their bags and begun to deliver it by seven o'clock in the morning.

Soon the post-office officials behind the counters will start their work: stamping letters, weighing parcels and giving information. And in between the telephone is always ringing.

Postage stamps. Rohit was in a hurry to get home today. In his pocket he clutched an envelope full of postage stamps. His uncle Yogesh had given them to him. When Rohit got home he opened his stamp album. Beside his album, Rohit keeps a stamp catalogue.

Carefully, he took the stamps from their envelope. Then he arranged them in order. He found out which country each stamp came from. He carefully looked at each stamp to see that it was not damaged. To be perfect, a stamp should have none of its perforations missing, and it should not be folded or torn.

Then Rohit opened his catalogue. First he looked up the dates when the stamps were issued. Then he stuck them carefully in his album. Rohit was very pleased with each new stamp. Each stamp told him something of the country it came from. The pictures on many stamps were very different from each other. On one stamp Rohit saw the picture of a famous man. On another was an important building.

Rohit likes many sorts of pictures: historical events, landscapes, sports festivals, means of transport, costumes and many other things.

Rohit is always specially pleased when he has completed a set. But look, he has two stamps alike. 'I will swop one with a friend,' thinks Rohit. In Rohit's class there are several boys who collect stamps.

Uncle Yogesh told Rohit that the first stamps were issued in England in 1840. In 1850, other European countries also began issuing stamps. Uncle Yogesh knows a lot about these things because he has been collecting stamps for many years. He has a fine collection. Uncle regularly reads a magazine about stamps and he is a member of a stamp collectors' club. Sometimes he takes Rohit along to exhibitions of postage stamps.

Potatoes. Sailors brought the first potatoes to Europe from South America about 400 years ago. At first, people did not know what to do with these strange vegetables. Many people grew them as ornamental plants. Some farmers cursed the potato and said it came from the devil. They had eaten the poisonous leaves and flowers, and as a result became terribly ill. Later, people discovered that you can eat potato tubers, the swellings in potato roots. Now, potatoes are grown everywhere in Europe and America. Even in Greenland people can grow potatoes. But there they grow no bigger than cherries.

Potter's wheel. The potter uses a round table with one leg. He can spin this table round. We call it a potter's wheel. The potter places a piece of damp clay on his wheel. Then he begins spinning the wheel, turning it by foot or by a motor. The potter shapes the clay with his hand until he has turned it into a vase, a saucer or a jar.

People have invented other useful kinds of turning table. Giant turntables on railways help railway engines to turn round quickly and easily.

Power station. Power stations generate electricity. The water from rivers or mountain torrents is held behind enormous dams. With terrific force, the water runs through pipes and falls on to the 'windmill' blades of turbines, to spin them round. These turbines power another machine which generates electricity, rather like the dynamo of a bicycle. Some power stations use steam pressure instead of water power. Water is heated to produce steam which spins the turbine blades.

Precious metal. Precious metals like gold, silver and platinum do not get rusty. A goldsmith can make many valuable ornaments from these precious metals. People often use gold and silver to make coins. The hard, valuable metal called platinum is hard to melt. So people use this precious metal to help them manufacture melting crucibles for softer metals.

Precious stones. How they shine and glitter in the jeweller's shop window. They are called precious stones. Precious stones are specially hard minerals with specially beautiful colours. Precious stones are rare, though there are many kinds of them. There are green emeralds, blue sapphires, red rubies and transparent diamonds which flash with all the colours of the rainbow.

People measure the weight of these gems in carats. When someone says that a gem is a five-carat stone he means that the stone weighs roughly one gram and a quarter, because a carat is about a quarter of a gram.

Primeval forest. Imagine a huge forest which human beings hardly ever enter. Its trees go on growing until they simply rot and fall down. The ground is a maze of interlacing vines and shrubs. This is a true description of a primeval forest. Perhaps you have already heard of the forests of South America, Africa and South Asia. But there are also primeval forests in Siberia and Canada. There, in colder climates, the trees are mainly needle-leaved. In Europe there were still big primeval forests about 1000 years ago.

Primitive people. Some people on earth live just as their ancestors lived thousands of years ago. They are usually hunters, fishermen or people who gather nuts and fruit. We call them primitive people. The pygmies and bushmen of Africa, the aborigines of Australia, and many Indians in South America are among the world's primitive peoples.

Programme. Vinisha and Margaret went to visit their friend Ritu. She received them with great dignity and said: 'I have arranged a programme for this afternoon. We shall eat at one o'clock. At two o'clock we shall go skating, at five we shall go to the puppet-show, and at eight o'clock to bed. Is that all right?'

'That's fine,' said Vinisha and Margaret. 'We think you have planned a splendid programme.'

You can buy a programme when you go to a theatre. This programme will tell you the name of the play to be performed and the names of its actors.

Prospectus. 'The fashion house, New Fashion, offers you silk shawls, shirts, trousers and coats of the best materials at the lowest prices. Visit us soon, and have a look around our big store.'

These words are written in a prospectus. A prospectus is a sort of advertisement. A bookshop may send you a prospectus describing all its books. In big cities, tourist information bureaus also issue a prospectus. It describes all the interesting sights of the town and tours which you can make nearby.

Pulse. When you have been walking fast, or when you run a temperature, your heart beats faster than usual and blood runs faster through the arteries of your body. You can feel the pulsing of blood best if you put one finger on the inside of the wrist of your other hand. We call this 'taking your pulse.'

Pumps. Pumps bring water up from wells, rivers and lakes. People who do not need much water often work a small pump by hand. But people who need a lot of water use a pumping engine. A powerful pump thrusts so much water through the hose of a fire-engine that firemen can easily put out most fires. To pump up the inner tube of a bicycle you need a bicycle pump.

Puppet-show. 'Are you all there?' cries Punch as he pops his head through the curtain. 'Yes,' answer the children. Then Punch pulls the curtain aside and the show begins.

All children love to watch Punch, though he is such a wicked character. He is always jolly and always manages to get away with his wicked deeds. But there are more puppets in the show beside Punch. There's a crocodile, a wizard, a king, a princess, a witch, a policeman and, of course, Punch's wife Judy.

A puppet-show is performed on a very small stage. Instead of people appearing on the stage, you see puppets. To work Punch and Judy puppets someone has to put his hand inside the puppet figure, as you would put your hand in a glove. So we call these glove puppets. Other sorts of puppet are worked by strings from above.

'I'd love to see a puppet-show,' says Dick. How about a puppet-show of your own, Dick? Well tell you how to make the puppets. Make small tubes of cardboard in which you can fit your first finger. Then cut wide strips of newspaper and put paste on both sides. Wrap the paper around the cardboard until you have built up a round ball. In this soft mass you can easily shape eyes, ears, nose, mouth and chin. Of course Punch's head must have the longest nose. Leave a bit of the tube clear so that it can become a neck to which you can fit a costume. When your heads are dry you can paint them. You can stick woollen hairs on the heads and add crowns and hats. Then you can dress them up. All puppets wear long clothes. Only

Punch has a pair of legs. This has always been so.

You can perform a play by yourself by holding a puppet in each hand. But that means there can only be two puppets on the stage because you have only two hands. Don't forget that each puppet must have a different voice. Perhaps you have a friend who will play with you. Then you might get up a little play with several puppet characters.

Of course you will need a stage. But this is very easy to make. Take a blanket and stretch it across the corner of the room, or across a doorway, so that the audience can't see the people behind it who are working the puppets. Stand behind the blanket and move the puppets about above it. It can be very tiring, keeping your arms raised all the time. Fix a plank a bit below the stage so that you can rest your elbows on it. Put a dark sheet of paper behind the puppets to close the gap left by the top half of the door. Perhaps you can also fix up a stage curtain. This will make your show look really professional.

Your father might help to put some finishing touches to the puppet-show. Switch off the room light when your audience is ready. Arrange it so that only the stage is lit up. At last the curtain opens, and here is Punch. Hurray!

Pyramid. Do you know what a pyramid is? Have a look in your box of bricks. If you have a square-sided brick pointed at one end, that is a pyramid. Thousands of years ago, the Egyptians built pyramids as tombs for their kings whom they called pharaohs. These pyramids were enormous stone tombs. The highest pyramid is the tomb of the pharaoh Cheops. This pyramid is 481 feet high.

Quicksilver. The thermometer has fallen on the floor and smashed. Little silvery balls are rolling all over the floor. They are hard to catch; they are called quicksilver, or mercury. Mercury is the only metal which is a liquid at normal temperatures. Heated, it expands. Cooled, it shrinks. So it is just right for measuring rising and falling temperatures. A column of mercury is put inside a hollow glass tube marked off in degrees As the temperature rises, so does the mercury in the tube.

Don't ever swallow mercury because it is a poison.

R

Rabbits. They belong to the same family as hares. Wild rabbits are grey-brown, much like a hare. They live in holes which they have dug for themselves. Tame rabbits are all sorts of colours – white, black and white, brown and white, or blue-grey.

Radar. When a plane flies through the dark night, how can its pilot know where he is when he cannot see the ground below? He has radar to help him. Radar sends radio waves to the earth. The earth reflects these waves back to the plane. These waves show as a picture of flashes and dots on a glass screen.

Airports and ships also have radar. This apparatus shows them just how far away a plane or a ship is, long before anyone can see it with his eyes. Even fishermen find radar a help. They catch large shoals of herring, guided by radar echoes.

Radio. Vinit turns a knob on his radio and a few seconds later music booms through its loudspeaker. The people playing this music may be hundreds of miles away.

For you to hear the music they make, two things are necessary: first a transmitter that turns the musical sounds into radio waves and sends them out into the sky. Secondly, you must have a radio receiver which catches the radio waves in the air and turns them into vibrations which you can hear.

Some years after the first radio sets, people invented television. A television set looks like a radio but it has a glass panel where pictures appear, rather as they do on the screen of a cinema. When there is a big procession in Delhi or when a play is performed, you can actually see it on your television screen as it happens. Your receiving set turns electric waves into light waves which make up a pattern on your screen. These electric waves may travel many miles through the air before they reach your home.

Radishes. Most of us only know the round red radish, which is good to eat raw in salads. But there are other sorts of radish. There is a turnip-white radish and a black-Spanish radish with a black skin which you have to remove before you can eat it.

Horse radishes belong to the same family as garden radishes, but they grow wild in parts of the country.

Radium. It is a rare white shiny metal which sends out radiation rays. In the dark, this metal glows with its own light. Doctors use radium radiation to help cure several illnesses.

Railway. Ritu is looking forward to going on a train journey with her parents tomorrow. Yes the good old railways will take us on our holidays. They bring our friends and relatives to see us. They make sure that all the things we want, like coal, foodstuffs, wood, iron and many other things reach us safely.

The coal which goes into one railway wagon would be enough to keep your family's fires alight for years. A goods train often consists of 50-60 wagons. So we should have to live for 500 years to use up all this coal. In a passenger train there are about 700 seats, so one train could transport 20 school classes in one go.

The carriages of the first railways were not pulled by a railway engine, but by horses. A horse can pull four times as much on a railway track as it can on a road. But imagine people's surprise when they first read in their newspapers that a steam engine, not a horse, had pulled wagons on rails in an English coal mine. 'The devil must be pulling it,' people said when they first saw this happening. 'People will never survive the speed and noise of a railway,' said others. But passengers enjoyed their first rides over the shiny new rails.

In the year 1829, Britain's Liverpool and Manchester Railway opened. It was the first passenger railway in the world to run a regular service. Soon other countries had their railways too. In Belgium people began to travel between Brussels and Mechelen by rail in 1835. In Holland the first train traveled between Haarlem and Amsterdam in 1839.

For nearly 100 years steam engines pulled trains. How does a steam engine work? You can read about it if you look up 'Steam engine'. But steam and smoke are a nuisance to passengers. They hang about big railway stations and inside tunnels.

Electric railway locomotives are much cleaner than steam

locomotives. They don't have to carry their fuel with them either. They get their electric current from an electrified rail or from wires which hang above the rails. The electric current runs through a contact bow, on the roof of the electric locomotive, to its motors. These motors power the locomotive's wheels.

For the last 50 years, diesel-powered railway locomotives have been running on many lines. Just like a diesel lorry, this sort of diesel locomotive has a diesel motor. This diesel motor generates electric power by means of a special turbine. This electric current powers the electric motors and these turn the wheels. So you see that diesel engines carry their own electric power station with them.

Many thousand railway workers keep watch day and night to see that no accidents happen. The signals along a railway track show each engine driver if the track ahead is clear or if he must stop, perhaps because another train is just in front.

Other workers are busy night and day at goods-stations, or working in the shunting yards. These people couple together all the wagons to go to one particular destination until a whole goods train stands ready to move off. The biggest stations are as busy at night time as during the day.

Our modern goods trains are very different from the days when horses pulled all heavy loads on rails. Our passenger trains are much cleaner to travel in, and much faster moving, than the first steam trains. And today, electricity has made it possible for people to build underground railways beneath big cities. The trains travel through tunnels deep underground. And with no other traffic in the way, they can travel very fast. In some towns there are viaducts. Trains run along the viaducts high above streets and houses.

Railway engine. Vinit was standing on the platform waiting for a train. Suddenly a huge locomotive came roaring past, pulling 10 long carriages behind it. In a few seconds the whole train had flashed by.

'That was a big engine,' said Vinit to his father.

Father nodded and said: 'When we go on holiday our train will be pulled by an express engine like that. Express engines only run over long distances, from one big city to aother. Ordinary passenger trains stop at some stations in between. Slow trains stop at every station.

'Do you see that long goods train? A specially powerful engine is pulling it. That kind of engine has to work very hard and does not go very fast. Many electric locomotives can pull heavy loads and still go very fast. There are also two kinds of diesel engine. One is powered by a diesel engine alone, the other by a generator. A generator is a machine (itself powered by a diesel engine) which produces electricity. It's an engine that carries its own power station.'

Vinit wanted to hear some more about the railway engines they could see in the station, but their train arrived and they had to get into a carriage.

'Next week we'll go to the railway museum,' promised Father. 'There you will find all kinds of railway engines.'

Rainbow. Red, orange, yellow, green, blue, violet and indigo. These are the colours of the rainbow which you see sometimes spanning the sky like a great dome or a huge, curved bridge.

If you like, you can make the sun build a rainbow for you. Do you know how? Stand in the garden so that the sun shines on your back. Then spray water into the air with a garden hose. Gleaming through the water splashes you will see a miniature rainbow - all your very own.

Raisins. 'I think raisins are the nicest parts of a cake,' says Vinisha, and she takes a raisin out of the cake mixture with her finger. That's rather naughty of her and Mother says: 'Can't you wait until I have cooked the cake?'

Raisins are dried grapes from countries near the Mediterranean Sea. The very large ones are Spanish raisins, the small black ones are called currants.

Rat. The rat belongs to the same family as the mouse. Most rats are grey or grey-brown and they are rather ugly animals. They grow up to eight inches long and they have bare, scaly, pink tails. Rats breed very quickly. They damage the foundations of buildings, eat up stored foodstuffs and they can carry dangerous illnesses. In many medieval towns, black rats were a great nuisance. I expect you know the story of the Pied Piper of Hamelin who charmed away a plague of rats.

Rattlesnake. The rattlesnake is the biggest poisonous snake of North America. All snakes cast their skin several times each year. Under the old skin is a shiny new one. The rattle at the end of a rattlesnake's tail consists partly of the remains of old skins. When the snake is frightened or angry its tail rattles.

Recipe. Anyone who wants to make a nice cake uses eggs and sugar, butter and salt, milk and flour. That is a good recipe for a cake. But it is not complete. Mother must know exactly how many eggs and how much milk and flour she needs. She needs an exact recipe to tell her these things.

Mother making cakes from a recipe is rather like a chemist making up medicine from a doctor's prescription. I expect you can read your mother's recipes. But could you read a prescription?

Record. Yesterday, Dinesh jumped three feet six inches high. He jumped higher than any of the other boys. Yes, all the boys from his class jumped. Dinesh set up a high-jump record because no boy had jumped so high before.

But today, Tarun jumped three feet seven inches. He has broken Dinesh's record. So Tarun is the holder of the class record. If Tarun should become the highest jumper in the world he would become the world record holder.

Recorder. This is an old musical instrument. But today, many young children are learning to play it, and it's not very difficult. This small wooden flute has a soft sound. When two or three recorders play together we say they are playing 'in consort'. That's how we get our word 'concert'. Once it meant 'together'.

Red Cross. You must often have seen this sign, perhaps on ambulances taking sick or injured people to hospital. There is a Red Cross organisation in nearly every country of the world. In Turkey, Egypt and other Mohammedan countries this society is called the 'Red Half-Moon'. In Japan it is called the 'Red Sun'. In Iran (Persia) it is the 'Red Lion'.

These societies set up hospitals in times of need. In wartime they help to nurse the wounded and they send doctors and nurses to the front lines. In peacetime they look after nurses' training and they teach people first aid. They also help at big accidents or natural catastrophes – for example, in floods or earthquakes.

We owe the founding of the Red Cross to a Swiss merchant called Henry Dunant. In 1859 he saw the terrible sufferings of wounded soldiers on battlefields. He decided to start an organisation to help suffering people in war and peace.

Today children and young people can join the Junior Red Cross and give a lot of help in their own way. Are you a member of the Junior Red Cross?

See also **'Junior Red Cross'.**

Redwood. Redwood trees grow to over 360 feet high. You would have to be a good climber to reach the top of a giant redwood tree. These mammoth trees grow in California, a state in North America. The trunks are sometimes so thick that people have cut tunnels through them, and driven cars through the tunnels.

Reindeer. The reindeer is a sort of deer that lives in the far north of Europe. In winter these animals live in forests. At the end of May, the reindeer travel north in huge herds. Reindeer have antlers which they shed each year in winter.

The food these animals like best is the moss which grows in the tundra – a huge area of land where little more than grass and mosses grow. Laplanders and Eskimos who live in the far north travel about, driving huge herds of domesticated reindeer. Reindeer supply these people with milk, meat and skins. They also serve as mounts and to pull loads.

Rembrandt. You probably know this name well. You will certainly read about it often. Rembrandt was a famous painter. He lived 300 years ago, in Holland.

Rembrandt's paintings are known all over the world. Perhaps you have seen his painting called '*The Night Watch*' or the painting of his mother, or one of his self-portraits.

Reynard the fox. It was a cold day on which Reynard the fox walked hungrily over a snow-covered field. Then he saw a crow sitting on the branch of a tree. The crow held a big piece of cheese in his beak. He had stolen it from somewhere or other.

'Hello, beautiful singer,' said the fox. 'I would be so grateful if you would sing me a song. You have such a lovely voice.'

The crow looked suspiciously at the fox, and kept his beak closed on the cheese.

'Just one song,' pleaded the fox. 'Just one little song.' Then the crow could no longer restrain himself. He began to think he really could sing well.

'Caw, caw,' he began to croak. But, oh dear, the piece of cheese fell from his beak. Reynard had been waiting for this. At once he picked up the cheese and ran away.

Reynard the fox is the most sly and most cunning of all the animals in the fables. He tricks all the other beasts and is too crafty for the strongest ones. There are many stories which tell about his tricks.

Reporters and **commentators.** 'Listeners, the score in the match, Scotland versus England, is two all. The excitement is intense. Now England is on the attack. The English centre-forward has the ball. He kicks across to his outside-right. He sends a beautiful pass. The ball curves across, in front of the goalkeeper. And there's the inside-left ready waiting. He shoots ... It's a goal! It's a goal!'

This is how a commentator describes a football match on the radio. Film reporters at the match will be recording it for cinema newsreels and television, newspaper reporters will be writing up the match for their newspapers, photo reporters will be taking snapshots to publish in their newspapers and magazines. Reporters and commentators describe the news of the day, political events, and news from other countries, as well a sport.

Reserve. Uncle Harish was driving through the country when the engine of his car spluttered and stopped. It had run out of petrol.

'Never mind,' said Uncle. 'I'll switch over to the reserve tank.'

A reserve is a store. Make sure you always have a reserve of money, food and clothes. It's sensible always to have something in store.

At city water boards there is always a reserve of water, stored in huge reservoirs.

Rhinoceros. This animal has a horn on its nose. The Indian rhinoceros has one horn and the African two horns, on its nose. Most species of the rhinoceros are dying out.

Rice. We can eat many kinds of meal made with the help of rice: rice porridge, steamed rice and rice with dal. Rice is the most important of all foods in India, China, and Japan. People plant young rice plants in the fields when they are about six weeks old. First, the rice fields are flooded. After four months the rice is ready to be harvested. People clean and often polish rice, though this removes much of its nourishment. People use the straw of rice plants for making strong, soft paper.

Roadstead. 'No room in harbour – stop – Come to anchor in roadstead – stop.' When a ship receives this radio message it does not steam into port. It drops anchor in the bay or river mouth outside the port. There it is still safe against storms.

Sailors call this place a 'roadstead'. Ships often anchor in roadsteads because they are too deep to enter port.

Robin Redbreast. Vinisha looks after the wild birds well in winter. Father has made a bird table on a tree in the garden. One of the birds is Vinisha's favourite. It is a small bird with a bright red breast. It is a robin. It whistles a happy song, even amid snow and ice.

Robinson Crusoe. He is every child's friend, or soon will be. Robinson Crusoe is the hero of a book written by Daniel Defoe. Crusoe was a sailor shipwrecked on an uninhabited island. There, he had to make every article that he needed.

Rocket. The world's fastest 'planes are driven by rockets. But is the rocket a new invention? No. Hundreds of years ago the Chinese were already building rockets. A simple rocket consists of a cylinder with one opening. An explosive is packed into the cylinder. Someone sets light to the explosive by a fuse. As the explosive burns, red-hot gases rush from the opening in the rocket cylinder. The gases kick backwards and this reaction drives the rocket through the air.

Perhaps your father has set off rockets for you on Diwali. People fire rather bigger rockets as distress signals from ships when they are in trouble. Today, scientists are making huge rockets, weighing many tons, and firing them right off the earth and into space.

Why do scientists do this? Because people want to find out what the moon is really like. And they want to examine the planets. To do this, scientists must first build little artificial moons which will revolve around the earth, just like its real moon. People could live on these little moons and use them as base stations for space rockets.

Rodents. Hares, mice, rats, squirrels, rabbits and beavers all belong to the rodent family. Rodents have very long incisors (upper and lower front teeth). These are just made for gnawing. They keep on growing, but rodents do so much gnawing that their teeth never get longer.

Roe and spawn. These are names used for the eggs of some fish, frogs and toads. When fish lay eggs (called roe) people say they are 'spawning'. Frogs lay their eggs together in big clumps of frogspawn. Toads lay their spawn in strings like strings of pearls.

Roe deer. In some parts of hilly reign, in the evening, you may see a graceful little roe deer appear at the edge of a wood. During daytime these animals stay safely among the trees.

Each year the roe deer sheds its antlers and grows a new pair. Sometimes these antlers have three branches. Young roe deer are born in May. They have light spots on their reddish-brown skin. A female roe deer is called a hind. Roe deer usually live in small herds of up to 10 animals.

Roller-skates. 'Hurray, we have been given some roller-skates,' shout Yogesh and Chetan. 'We are going to try them out straight away.' Learning to roller-skate is difficult, but it slowly becomes easier, like learning to skate on ice. There is a strip, of iron beneath an ice-skate, but little wheels under a roller-skate.

Roofing. When builders have raised the walls of a house, they prepare the roofing truss. This is really the roof's framework. It is made of thick beams and rafters. Builders skilfully lay roofing tiles on top of the rafters. Sometimes they nail slates on the rafters instead.

In past centuries, people covered many roofs with straw thatch, wooden planks or stone slabs. In northern countries, which have cold winters, people build steep roofs to stop the snow piling up and making the roofs cave in. In hot southern countries, where there is no snow, the houses usually have fiat roofs.

Rose hip. Rose hips are the red fruits of the wild rose. Each grows up from a green stalk. The dried dead rose blossom leaves a black cap on each rose hip. People use rose hips for making jam and rose-hip syrup. Rose hips contain a lot of nourishing vitamin C. In winter, when wild birds find little food, thrushes often make a tasty meal of rose hips.

Rowing. There are crowds of happy people beside the river. Harish and Rohit are there too. Like everyone else, they are watching the boat-races. Here come the racing shells. There are eight oarsmen in each shell, and one coxswain to steer them. Their oars flash through the water in regular strokes.

Along the towpath some men are cycling to keep up with the boats. They shout instructions to the oarsmen through a megaphone. 'Look,' says Harish. 'There are four oarsmen in that boat with a coxswain, and here come two oarsmen with no coxswain.'

Rubber. It is useful as a liquid, and as elastic, as well as in its solid form. Rubber has important properties. It is waterproof it does not conduct electric current and it is flexible and elastic.

Where do we get rubber from? Rubber trees grow in hot climates. Workers on Malaya's rubber plantations make cuts in the rubber trees. Then the crude rubber, a milky liquid called latex, runs out of the trees. But as soon as latex comes into contact with air it sets hard, just like resin from needle-leaved trees.

Nowadays people can make some sorts of rubber artificially, with chemicals.

Ruminating. At about midday, cattle lie down in the fields. They are going to ruminate – to chew over their food for a second time. Sheep, goats, deer, giraffes, antelopes, camels and gazelles all belong to the ruminants.

S

The **Sahara.** The Sahara is the biggest desert in the world. It has no woods, no rivers, no brooks, no fields. There are only rocks, stones and sand. Sometimes no rain falls on the desert for several years. During the day it is burning hot, and at night temperatures drop below freezing.

Scattered across the desert's surface are water wells and oases of palm trees which grow around them. People can grow fruit and corn around some oases.

The Bedouins travel through parts of the desert with their sheep and camels. But nowadays buses also cross parts of the Sahara.

St. Peter's, Rome. This is perhaps the most famous, and certainly the biggest, church in the world. It stands in Rome, on a huge square which is surrounded by an arcade. There is room for thousands of people to worship inside this church. St. Peter's was built by famous artist-architects more than 400 years ago. Long before the present St. Peter's was erected, another St. Peter's stood upon the same ground.

The **Salmon.** The Salmon is a fish which makes several tremendous journeys during its lifetime. Full-grown salmon live in the northern seas. Every year, in the autumn, full-grown salmon swim up rivers in large shoals. This is very tiring for them. They have to jump up waterfalls and rapids. People help them to do this. They even build 'salmon-ladders' to help these fish climb over high dams and waterfalls. When they get near a river's source, the salmon spawn.

After about two years of growing up in the river, the young salmon make their way out to sea. When a salmon is ready to swim upstream and spawn, its flesh is coloured pink. Salmon is delicious to eat.

Franz **Schubert.** *The Trout* and *The Erl-King* are two of the many famous songs written by the Austrian composer Franz Schubert. Sometimes people call him the king of all song-writers. But Schubert wrote many other pieces of music. Schubert lived in Vienna and died in 1828 when he was only 31 years old. All the music-lovers of Vienna mourned him because Schubert was not only a great artist but a good man.

Seals. Manish looks in the mirror and twitches his nose. Then he shakes his head and says:

'I can't do it. Only seals can do it.'

Manish has been to the zoo where he saw the seals close their nostrils when they swam underwater, and he wanted to try it too. But why do that, Manish? You don't live in the water like the seals.

Seals are specially built to be good swimmers. A thick layer of fat keeps their body warm in the coldest water. And they are streamlined to glide easily through the roughest sea. Seals have legs as well, but they look more like fins. A seal's toes are webbed. He uses his teeth for catching and holding fish.

There are several kinds of seal. They include the fur seal, the sea-lion and the sea-elephant, which may grow twice as long as a man. Then there is the walrus which has enormous ivory tusks.

Seasons. People who live in large towns often do not notice the changing seasons. They just see the horse-chestnut trees in flower, and fresh vegetables when they appear at the greengrocer's, and in the late summer they notice that there is more fruit for sale. When it snows or is cold they say:

'Winter has come.'

But it's the people who live in the country who can best see nature as it changes throughout the year. They see spring changing into summer day by day; and they know when autumn has arrived, for the trees turn to beautiful russet colours. Farmers who work amongst nature every day, know all its changing moods.

Sewing-machine. A sewing-machine can sew pieces of leather and bits of material together in no time. It is much quicker than sewing by hand. Mother has a treadle sewing-machine. She works a plate with her foot and machinery moves her sewing-machine needle up and down. Nowadays you can also buy electric sewing-machines. Most of the sewing-machines used by tailors and shoe-menders are worked by electricity. An electric sewing-machine can make 2,000 to 3,000 stitches a minute.

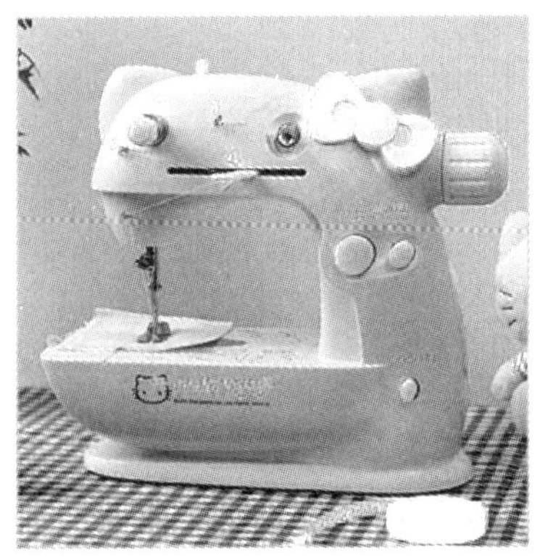

Shark. The shark is a ravenous beast of prey; a great fish which lives in warm oceans. The shark's mouth is on the underside of its head. Some sorts of shark attack people swimming in the sea. These are man-eating sharks. People use thick, rough shark-skin for making leather shoes and handbags.

Sheep. They are among the most useful animals. Sheep supply us with wool and meat, and some people drink their milk. The rams the male sheep – have horns which grow curled inwards.

Sheep-dogs. 'He is my best friend,' says the old shepherd, stroking his dog's head. 'He drives the flock when I tell him, and keeps them all together. When a few sheep stay behind he runs to them. Then he barks at them until they join the flock. My dog never bites the sheep. He only frightens them.'

There are several kinds of sheep-dog. In Britain shepherds use small Welsh sheep-dogs. In Germany shepherds use big Alsatians.

Shell-fish. A snail lives in a single shell. A shell-fish lives between two shells. Shell-fish live in the sea as well as in rivers. Some shellfish are long in shape, others are round and smooth. Still others are ribbed.

The insides of some of the shells glitter with all the colours of the rainbow. We call this lining 'mother-of-pearl'. People make shiny buttons from this substance. In the Pacific and Indian Oceans, and even in Scottish rivers, people find shells which sometimes contain valuable pearls.

Shipping. Thousands of years ago people knew how to sail up and down rivers and how to cross seas. First, someone must have noticed that wood floated on water. Perhaps the earliest boats were several tree trunks bound together with plant fibres to make a simple raft. On a raft, people could easily cross the widest rivers. Later, perhaps, they built canoes. To do this they hollowed out a thick tree trunk and made it pointed at both ends. The result was a boat – a dugout canoe that you could move about by paddling with your hands or with bits of wood. Other people learned to make coracles – frames of wood covered with waterproof animal skins. The Eskimos still use a sort of coracle. The Eskimos' boats are called kayaks. The Red Indians' canoes have also developed from coracles.

The Greeks and the Romans built much bigger ships, rowed by many slaves. These ships could cover huge distances. People had invented sails by the times of the Greeks and Romans. But they only worked well in a following wind. Most of the important work was done by the oarsmen.

By the Middle Ages people had learned how to build sailing ships that could travel far without oarsmen, and even sail into a headwind. Soon after these ships were first built, the great journeys of discovery began. Sailing ships went out from Europe in every direction and found great new lands. We all know about Columbus and his adventurous crossing of the Atlantic Ocean. Some daring sailors succeeded in encircling the world in their small vessels.

Thanks to sailing ships, a busy trade grew up between Europe and far countries. For centuries sailing ships plied across the oceans. Then the steam-engine was invented. By 1800 the first steamboats were sailing slowly up and down rivers. In 1807 the American Robert Fulton made a ship powered by a built-in steam-engine which turned two paddle wheels, one attached to each side of the ship.

Steamships soon traveled much faster than sailing ships. They plied up and down calm rivers; but on a stormy sea, with high waves, paddle wheels were often useless. People could only use them in calm weather. Then the ship's screw, invented by an Austrian called Josef Ressel in 1829, made it possible for steamships to cross the oceans in all weathers. The engines on most modern ships do not power paddle wheels but screws (or propellers) attached to the stern of a ship below its water-line. But nowadays people use oil-powered turbines and motor vessels more, and piston-engine steamships less.

Some passenger ships are very large; some weigh 80,000 tons and are over 900 feet long. Ships like these can carry more than 2,000 passengers. But they need a crew numbering several hundred. On some of these ships there are swimming pools, tennis courts, shops and cinemas. There is even sometimes a printing office so that passengers can buy newspapers with thc latcst news (which has been radioed to the ship). In this way even a voyage lasting several weeks does not seem very long to the passengers, though they may see nothing but sea for days and days. There is always plenty of entertainment on board a big liner.

Cargo ships may be less showy than liners but they are no less important. Cargo ships only have a small crew. They collect goods from all parts of the world and often make voyages which last for months. To carry petroleum from oil wells to the world's big cities there are special ships called oil-tankers. These ships have a hold divided into several parts, and these are filled with oil. When an oil-tanker reaches its destination the petroleum is pumped out again.

There are also ships which can transport whole trains over wide rivers or estuaries. These are railway ferryboats. When rivers or parts of the sea are frozen in winter, ice-breakers help to keep the way open for other ships. Ice-breakers are strong ships with specially tough, reinforced hulls. There are also lightships. These are ships which show the way to other ships at night. They are usually anchored outside ports and harbours.

Skating. All children love to skate. Perhaps you yourself can skate. Manish puts on his skates and undoes them himself. They are fixed to big boots by screws.

Ski-ing. Geeta has just come home. She has been on a ski-ing course.

'It was very good,' she says. 'I can ski quite well already. First we learned how to walk on skis up a practice slope. The first time we came down the slope it was a bit frightening. On the last day of the course we saw an expert who could do it easily. He could even jump on skis and he came down the mountain like a bird.'

People living in Norway and Sweden knew how to ski thousands of years ago, even before the birth of Christ.

Sky-jump. A ski-jump is nothing more than a big drop in the ground. Ski-jumpers slide down a steep slope to pick up speed before they reach the drop. Then they leap into the air and lean forward gracefully. A leaping skier waves his arms once or twice to keep his balance, then he floats down like a huge swallow. He lands softly in the snow and glides to a halt. To achieve such leaps you have to be quite unafraid. Big crowds watch the amazing leaps of ski-jumpers who compete in the Olympic Games.

Skin. We breathe air with our lungs. But our skin helps us to 'breathe out' impurities in our body through perspiration. Look at your skin with a magnifying glass. You will clearly see the tiny pores which perspire. Now you see why it is so important always to wash yourself properly to keep your pores clean and your body healthy.

Chetan and his friend lie in the sun, at first only for a few minutes. Each day they can safely lie out longer. Soon they are burned brown.

'We look just like negroes,' says Chetan. But really negroes have even darker skins and they don't have to sit in the sun to get their 'tan'. Chinese people have a yellowish skin and Red Indians a reddish skin.

Skylark. The children were walking over a meadow when they heard a bird singing somewhere nearby. Where could it be? There wasn't a bush in sight where it could hide. Ah, there it was, high above the children's heads, singing in the sky. They watched it climb even higher. Then the skylark suddenly stopped singing. It closed its wings and dived into the meadow. Somewhere among the long grasses was its nest.

Sledge. As soon as the first snow has fallen, we collect our sledge from the attic and go dashing down the snow-covered slopes of the meadows. In Russia, in winter, people even travel through city streets on sleighs, pulled by horses. Sledges are not just for fun. Farmers who live in mountains often bring hay and tree trunks down to the valleys on big sledges. In the Polar regions, sledges are often the only means of transport.

Sloth. A sloth is an animal which can hang motionless for days by its sickle-shaped claws. It lives in South America's virgin forests. At night it stretches and moves slowly about. In the rainy season sloths become camouflaged by a green fungus which grows amongst the hairs of their body.

When Indians want to catch a sloth they grab it by its neck-hairs, for it can turn its head almost right round and give a nasty bite.

Slow-worm. The slow-worm is a lizard without legs. It looks very much like a small snake.

Snail. This morning, Mother collected some lettuces from the garden. She was not very pleased to find several grey-green snails on one lettuce.

You often see big brown snails crawling over the roads on wet days, leaving a trail of slime. This trail glitters in the sun. Among the shrubs you will find the smaller, more brightly coloured snails. Their shells are yellow or pink or marked with dark stripes.

In fresh water you will find ramshorn snails and several other sorts. Some sea snails have very big shells decorated with lumps and sharp points. Like most other water animals, water snails breathe through gills.

Snake. Suddenly Anita stood stock-still with fear. Her eyes were fixed on the path which ran through the wood. A small grey snake was lying in the middle of the path. At first it made Anita jump, but she was sensible. She knew that snakes do not attack people without reason. But you should not disturb them. Most snakes are useful animals. They eat many harmful rodents.

Somersault. Everyone can go head-over-heels on the ground. But can you do it in the air? Vinit can. He can swim splendidly and he often practises somersaults from a diving board.

'Watch out,' he cries. 'I'm going to do a backward somersault.' Vinit takes a long run, leaps up and twirls head over heels backwards in the air. Plop! He has disappeared neatly into the water.

Circus artists can also turn clever somersaults as they fly from one trapeze to another.

Sparrow-hawk. The sparrow-hawk is the greatest enemy of many of our song-birds. This bird of prey has a dark grey back. Its breast is marked with a wave-shaped pattern of grey-brown feathers.

Speed. You can easily compare the speeds of different machines or animals. You time them over a short distance, then work out how far each would travel in an hour if each could keep up that speed. Pigeons can probably fly at 100 miles an hour, cheetahs can run at over 80 miles an hour, swordfish can swim at about 35 miles an hour.

Sport. Vinit can ski very well. Once he even won a prize for ski-ing. But his brother Chetan prefers swimming. Vinisha and Anita both play in their school basket-ball team. Manish likes athletics best. He goes in for running, long-jumping and javelin throwing. There are lots of gymnastic clubs which boys and girls can join, and where they can train with proper apparatus.

Which sport do you take part in? What's that you say? No sport at all? I can hardly believe it. Sports make you fit and strong. You should go in for some sport; but don't overdo it. Don't over-exert yourself. You should not cover long distances on your bicycle at first, and walking too far is bad for your body. For your body is still growing.

Spring flowers. When spring comes and the sun starts shining brightly, the snow-drops and crocuses begin to bloom. Their underground bulbs collected lots of food during the past summer. So they have stored up enough nourishment to produce their spring blooms. But primroses, cowslips, violets, daisies, wood-anemones and agrimonies take their food from ordinary rootstocks.

Spruce fir. Have you ever been in a big spruce-fir wood? Spruce trees grow best in damp mountain air. You can easily recognize these trees by their sharp, square needles. The long fruits, which you often find lying under the trees, are called fir cones. People use the light, soft wood of this fir tree for many purposes: for furniture and doors, and even for making artificial silk, and wood-sugar. See also **'Needle-leaved trees'**.

Squirrel. You can often see grey squirrels in our parks and woods. But in most of this country people seldom see handsome red squirrels. Both sorts of squirrel are nimble tree-climbers and leap fearlessly from bough to bough. As a squirrel bounds from one tree to another he uses his tail to help keep his balance. You will often see squirrels high above in the branches of fir trees, for they love to eat fir cones. They are also fond of all kinds of nuts. Just see how cleverly our red squirrel holds a nut between his paws. With his sharp teeth he gnaws the hard shell open and gets at the sweet kernel inside.

But squirrels do not eat all the nuts they gather. They carry lots of them to hole in trees. There, the squirrels keep their nuts in 'larders' for the coming winter (though they usually forget all about them).

On the coldest winter days, squirrels stay asleep inside their leafy nests, or 'dreys', high in the trees.

No bird's nest is safe from the squirrels. Squirrels drink the eggs empty and eat baby birds. Gamekeepers are always waging war on the common grey squirrel.

Stadium. A stadium is a huge sports ground with thousands of seats and standing places for the public. Inside a stadium, football teams pay off their matches and athletes run, jump and throw their javelins.

Stag. People call the **stag** the king of the forest. How proud a stag looks, complete with his fine, branching antlers. He uses these antlers as a dangerous weapon in battle against other deer. Antlers make a very good weapon of defence against other enemies too.

The reindeer and the elk both belong to the same family as the stags you see in our parks and zoos.

Stag-beetle. This is a very large beetle. Its upper jaw reminds you of antlers of a stag: that's why people call it 'stag-beetle'. The larvae of the stag-beetle live for five to six years in mouldering oak wood.

Starling. There is a nesting box in our garden. A starling has made it his home. Starlings mostly stay with us all the year round. But did you know that many starlings migrate? Many of the starlings you see on our lawns in winter have flown here from Sweden and even Russia.

Stars. Just look skyward, one clear night. Try and count the stars – there are millions of them: big stars and small stars. So many that you can count only a fraction of them.

When you are out at night the stars can tell you where north, south, east and west lie. How is that possible? Simple! You only have to remember that the Pole Star is in the north.

How can you find the Pole Star among so many others? That isn't difficult at all. Many stars are arranged in groups near each other. If you join them up with an imaginary line, they sometimes seem to form the outline of a figure. These are known as constellations.

Some constellations look like snakes, others like wagons. Perhaps you have heard of the Plough constellation. It's also called the Great Bear. It is a constellation you can easily find.

When you have located the Great Bear, measure the distance from the top to the bottom of the Plough five times over. When you have done this you have reached a star. This is not specially bright but it stands alone. It is the Pole Star.

The Pole Star is always in the north. When you are looking at that star, south is behind you, west is on your left and east on your right. Though the Pole Star looks just like many other stars it is rather special. To us, this star seems never to move, and the other stars seem to turn slowly around it. This turning is only an illusion; it happens because the earth spins round on its own axis.

Near the Pole Star you will also see some other stars. When you join them up with imaginary lines, you get another plough, smaller than the first. So people call it the Little Plough or the Little Bear. The Pole Star is near the end of the handle of this Little Plough.

There are many more constellations in the night sky. You can see lots of them with your naked eye.

Steam. A big cooking pot stood hissing on the hot stove. Its lid flapped up and down as puffs of steam forced their way out of the pot. Inside, boiling water was all the time turning into steam. Steam takes up much more room than water. That's why steam pressure kept lifting the lid. But large drops of water were running down the cold window pane, where the steam had cooled and turned back into water.

Steam-engine. Steam in a cooking pot is strong enough to raise its lid. But the steam which develops in a big boiler (in the boiler of a locomotive, for instance), is much, much stronger.

Inside the driver's cab glows the red-hot mouth of the stoke-hold. A fireman keeps it fed with coal. Soon the water in the locomotive boiler starts to boil and send off steam. The steam passes through narrow pipes to the engine's cylinder. Steam presses on a piston inside the cylinder; the piston moves a long rod, which in turn moves a huge driving wheel. Then the railway engine moves.

People also use this kind of steam piston engine in factories and many ships. In some power stations, electric current is generated by means of enormous steam turbines. The escaping steam powers large 'windmills' which we call turbines.

Stomach. Yes, our Dinesh is complaining again. But then, anyone who eats too many chocolates is bound to get stomach ache. I am sure that Dinesh does not know how hard his stomach has to work to digest everything he puts in it.

If Dinesh would only chew his food more thoroughly, to break it up and mix it with saliva. This would help the hydrochloric acid made inside his stomach. This acid is necessary to help him digest his food. Dinesh certainly treats his stomach unfairly: first he drinks hot soup, then at once he drinks cold water. Dinesh's stomach finds it hard work trying to keep him healthy.

Stork. It is spring and the children in many European countries cry: 'The storks have come!' The big white storks have flown all the way from Africa to nest on Europe's rooftops. Farmers often put an old wagon-wheel on their roof and storks build their nest of branches on top of it. For farmers believe that storks will bring them luck.

Storks find their food beside ditches and lakes and in meadows. They are very fond of frogs, mice, fishes and insects, and they will even eat a snake, tossing it down with their long beak.

Submarines. Submarines are ships that can travel on the surface of the sea and beneath it. Submarines are made of watertight steel plates. You might well ask how they can sink if they are watertight. Inside each submarine are big water tanks. When the submarine commander wants to dive he gradually fills the tanks with water. Then his submarine sinks slowly beneath the waves. When the commander wants to come up he pumps the water out of the tanks. The underwater explorer Piccard built a special submarine. In it, he could dive down thousands of feet below the surface of the ocean.

The **Sun.** How nice – the sun is shining today. Everyone looks pleased to see it. Soon all the fruit trees will be in bloom. In summer, the sun ripens our corn, vegetables and fruit. If the sun stopped rising, all plants, animals and people would die. The earth would be empty and desolate.

We say the sun rises in the east and sets in the west. But this is not really true. The sun does not move round the earth: the earth moves round the sun, and spins as it travels. So the sun only seems to rise and set.

The earth is not the only planet that goes round our sun. The earth has eight brother planets. These are Mercury, Venus, Mars, Saturn, Jupiter, Uranus, Pluto and Neptune.

How big is the sun? Imagine that the earth is a ball which you can enclose with both your hands. The sun in comparison would be a ball 35 feet in diameter (cut through the middle). The distance between the earth and the sun is about 100 million miles. You would have to travel for 111 years in a nonstop express train to reach the sun. It is lucky for us that the sun is so far off. If it moved only one and a half million miles nearer we' should all be shrivelled up with its heat.

Sunflower. Sunflowers grow so tall that you can see one from several gardens away. Inside each flower are hundreds of dark-coloured seeds. The flowers have yellow, tongue-shaped petals. The seeds contain oil, and birds are very fond of eating them. People press the seeds and use the oil for cooking.

Sunflowers sometimes reach a height of 10 feet. The flower; themselves always face the sun. That's how they get their name.

Swallow. One million flies and gnats: that is the number of insects a swallow family may eat during the six months of the year that swallows spend with us. Swallows have a red breast and deeply forked tail. They usually nest on houses or farm buildings. So do house martins (which have white stomachs and less deeply forked tails). But sand martins nest in holes which they tunnel in sandy cliffs and quarries.

T

Tadpoles. Frogs and toads lay eggs in water. A mass of frogs' eggs and a string of toads' eggs are both called 'spawn'. The animals that hatch from frogspawn and toadspawn are like little fishes. They breathe through gills and have a long tail, which helps them wriggle through the water in any direction. These tiny 'fishes' are really tadpoles. Tadpoles are the larvae of frogs and toads.

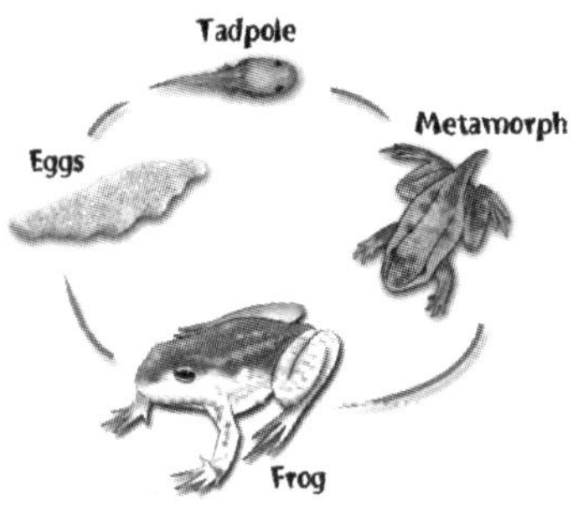

Tape-recorder. We have a tape-recorder at school. It is very useful. When we perform a play or sing a song at the school festival, we can record it. We switch on our recorder by turning its first knob; then the tape runs front one spool to another. We sing or speak into a microphone. Before we can play back the tape we must turn a second knob and let the tape run back to the first spool. If anyone makes a mistake in reciting a poem or playing a piece of music, we can 'rub it out' by turning a third knob, and record a new bit in its place.

Then we can store our tape in a box and bring it out whenever we want to hear our play or our song again.

Tea. In India, China, and on the islands of Ceylon and Java, there are thousands of big fields. In just one field there may be thousands of tea shrubs. When their leaves have grown big enough, men, women and children come and pick the tea leaves. They put these into white bags. People even wear gloves to pick leaves from the best shrubs. This is to make sure the pickers do not damage the leaves. Afterwards, the leaves are dried and roasted.

Telephone. Harish's parents have just had a new telephone put in their home. Harish had a good look at the new apparatus. The receiver lay in place on its hook. Suddenly… brring, brring! The phone actually began to ring.

Harish was a bit frightened at first, then he picked up the receiver. 'Hello Harish here,' he said in a clear voice, but not too loud. 'Good morning, Harish. This is your Uncle Khatri,' said a voice in Harish's ear. 'I wanted to be the first to ring you. A telephone is a fine thing to have, don't you think?' 'Yes, Uncle,' said Harish. 'If I wanted to speak to you before I had to travel by bus for an hour. Now I just dial your number and I can tell you all the news.'

Harish wanted to telephone someone for his mother, so first he looked up the number in a telephone directory. Then he dialled it. He heard a voice speaking to him. It was the greengrocer – just the person Harish wanted to speak to.

Telescope. There is a fairy tale about a telescope. It says you can look through this telescope and see everything that happens in the world, Of course, wonderful telescopes like that do not exist. But a good telescope shows you far more than you could see with your naked eye alone.

The field glasses used by hunters are also a kind of telescope, rather like the opera glasses that people take to the theatre. Telescopes have glass lenses made and arranged to enlarge all the objects you look at. In astronomical observatories there are enormous telescopes. With their aid you can see stars many million miles from earth.

Tennis. Of course you have watched lawn tennis sometime or another. Many boys and girls also play table tennis, which is an indoor sport. There is another tennis-type game which you can play in a hall or a big room. It is called badminton, People play this game with a small ball which has feathers on it.

Teutons. The Teutons were people who lived in northern Europe long before the birth of Christ. Gradually they spread all over Europe, from the Rhine in the

West to the Weichsel in the east.

The Teutons lived in wooden houses. They cleared forests, cultivated the land and kept domestic animals.

During the time of the great migration of nations (in about the year A.D. 400) the Teutons traveled as far as Italy and Spain, and even to North Africa. Dutchmen, Flemings, Germans, Swiss, Danes and Swedes, Norwegians and Englishmen are all partly descended from the Teutons. If you read the heroic legends of the Teutons you will learn how they lived, what their customs were, and who were their heroes and gods.

Theatre. What a treat! Tomorrow our whole class is going to the theatre. We shall have a lovely afternoon. And before the holidays begin we shall put on our own play. Rohit has written it. We have made the scenery and costumes ourselves. We have already performed fairytales in our own theatre.

Thermometer. We have four thermometers at home. One of them hangs outside the house, on a window. That one tells you just how hot or cold it is outside. The second one hangs in our living room. A living room must not be too cold or too warm; about 65 degrees Fahrenheit is a comfortable temperature. The third thermometer has a wooden handle. We use this in the bath to test the temperature of the water.

And the fourth thermometer? This one should be in every home. It is a clinical thermometer. A thermometer usually consists of a thin glass tube with quicksilver inside. On the outside of the tube is a graduated scale of numbers. You can see what the temperature is by reading the number level with the top of the column of quicksilver. In our country the Fahrenheit scale is the one we most often use. We write 98.4 degrees Fahrenheit (normal temperature) as 98.4° F. for short. An 'R' above the thermometer scale means it is measured as a 'Réaumur' scale. 'C' means it is 'Celsius' or 'Centigrade'.

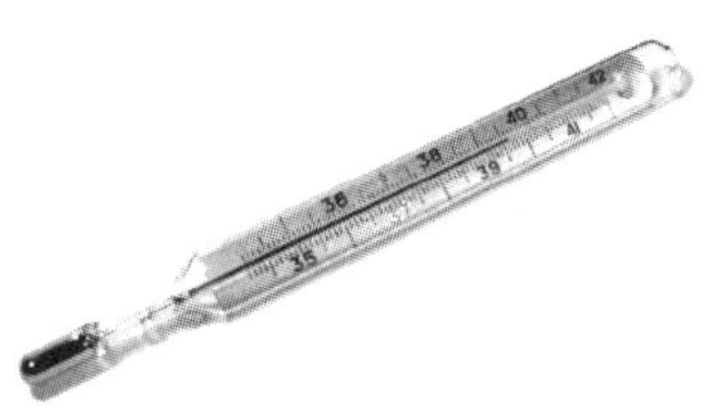

Thick-skinned animals. If you wanted to make a journey through a tropical forest, you might have to cut your way through its dense undergrowth with a chopper. But an elephant just walks straight through. This enormous animal has a skin nearly an inch thick. The horny skin of the rhinoceros is even tougher. Rhinos can walk unharmed through the dense thorn scrub which covers parts of Africa. If they do get a scratch it is seldom deep enough for them to feel it.

What about the fat, hippopotamus? He lives nearly all the time in water. But even if the water gets cold he does not worry. His thick skin and the layer of fat beneath it protect the hippo against sudden changes in temperature. Yes, nature seems to look after every sort of animal.

Thornback. 'Thornback' is another name for the fishes called rays. They are fiat fish with long tails. Biggest of all thornbacks is the manta. In warm oceans, mantas grow to giant size. They look weird and frightening as they swim by, flapping their fins up and down, like great under-water bats. But mantas are really quite harmless.

Tiger. The children were at the zoo, standing in front of the tiger's cage.

'What a fine animal,' said Harish. 'He must be at least 10 feet long.'

Manish looked a bit frightened 'I shouldn't like to meet him in the jungle,' he said.

The tiger is feared by almost every other wild animal. He can be dangerous to people too. Tigers live mainly in the forests of India and Malaya. Usually, tigers go hunting at night.

Titmice. They are graceful little birds with a pleasant little song. In winter we put out breadcrumbs for the tits and hang a bit of bacon rind on a branch, so these birds won't go hungry. For titmice stay with us all the year round – in winter as well as summer. They do not fly to warmer countries as the weather gets colder. Even in January we can hear them happily singing a see-saw 'zizibi-zizibi' song.

Toad. Many children are afraid of toads. But they are really quite attractive little animals. They are not at all dangerous, and are really quite useful. For at night, toads catch snails, caterpillars and many other harmful animals. The gardener is very pleased to see toads in his garden. Some toads grow quite tame and come to be fed at the same spot at the same time each day.

Tobacco. The first white men to explore North America found that the Indians had a strange habit. When the Indians met at a pow-wow they rolled the dried leaves of a plant, put the leaves in their mouth, and lit them. They sucked in the smoke. The Indians were smoking cigars. The Spaniards soon copied this habit, and in this way the habit of smoking tobacco spread all over Europe.

The tobacco plant belongs to the same family as the potato. People treat the leaves of the tobacco plant in a special way to make them into cigarettes, cigars and pipe tobacco. Nowadays tobacco is grown in all the warm countries. But the leaves of the tobacco plant contain a poison called nicotine. So smoking is not really good for your health.

Tool box. In the tool box something has happened. All the tools are talking at the same time.

'It's always the same,' they say. 'The boys do not know how to use us. They do not know what to use us for.'

Just hear what the chisel has to say. He is crying in a loud voice: 'I am made to pare off little pieces of wood. But what do these naughty boys do to me? They use me as a screwdriver. Look how blunt I've become!'

Over there a pair of pincers cry: 'Do we look like a hammer? The boys always use us to hit nails into wood.'

'It's very bad,' says the hammer. 'What am I for? I am the simplest tool in the world to understand and they even treat me in the wrong way. I have a long handle but they hold me near the head.'

'But listen to me,' cry a pair of pliers. 'I even have to open tins of sardines.'

'Well,' says the screwdriver, 'at least you are working with thin metal. But they heat me up to burn patterns on their wood. Now my end is so soft that I cannot possibly tighten or loosen a screw.'

The plane also has something to say. But you can hardly understand him. 'I cannot open my mouth,' he says. 'It is full of wood shavings. They never clean me properly. On top of that I have become blunt, and I'm just smothered in scratches. I like work but I can only tackle it when I'm fit. Oh, I feel so unhappy.'

Next, the saw starts to complain. '0h dear, oh dear, my teeth hurt so much. While I was sawing a plank I hit a nail. I screamed and gnashed my teeth, but they made me go on sawing. And look at me now. Three teeth are broken and the others are quite blunt.'

'And the things I have to suffer,' shouts the fret-saw. 'They never loosen me when they have finished with me.'

Suddenly all grow silent. Someone is opening the tool box. Father looks at his tools and says very angrily: 'A few days ago I put everything neatly in order, sharpened everything and polished all the tools. Just look at them now! Of course those naughty boys have been using them. They are always wanting to make something, but they use the tools the wrong way. I will teach them!'

Tracks. Anyone who wants to become a hunter or a forester must practice recognizing tracks when he is quite young. A track is usually made by the imprints of an animal's feet. Deer, wild boars, rabbits – all these animals leave tracks of different kinds.

Tractor. The farmer has bought a tractor. With this machine he can pull heavy ploughs, harrows and mowing machines over all his fields. A tractor will also tow heavily-laden wagons.

Tropics. Hoous-pocus! We twirl our magic ring, and presto, here we are, flying through the air. It is a long journey to the south, to a country near the equator. How hot it is here. The sun simply burns. But what is happening? We arrived beneath a blue sky. But black clouds have suddenly appeared in the sky and it has begun to pour with rain. It is raining cats and dogs. Now it has suddenly stopped again and the sun is shining as brightly as ever. In a moment, the puddles have dried up.

How hot and damp the air is. Much damper than in a greenhouse at home. It is little wonder that plants grow so well here. You can hardly make your way through the dense undergrowth. You would need a good sharp knife.

The tropics include many countries near the equator. They have unhealthy climates. It is hard for people to live in them and keep fit. But we obtain many useful things from tropical countries. They include cane-sugar, cocoa, rubber and coffee.

Tulip. The colourful tulip is one of many plants which flower early in the year. Three leaves and one flower grow from each bulb.

Tunnel. Joy and Vinit were traveling through Switzerland by train. They were enjoying the mountain scenery when, suddenly, everything became dark.

'Are you still there?' asked Joy, a bit frightened. Then the train came out into daylight again.

'That was a tunnel,' explained Vinit. 'We went right through a mountain.'

There are many kinds of tunnel: railway and road tunnels which cut through mountains and under rivers. The Simplon Tunnel in Switzerland is about 13 miles long.

Turbine. You have probably seen windmills and mill-wheels. These are two very simple kinds of turbine. In power stations, where water is used to spin the wheels, the turbine wheels are made of steel. These are much bigger than any water-wheel. They turn water-power into energy to power electric dynamos. There are also turbines which are driven by gas or steam.

U

University. When anyone wants to become a doctor, a lawyer or a teacher, he must first study at a university. Today there are universities all over the world. The universities of Oxford and Cambridge are many hundred years old. Each university contains many colleges.

V

Vacuum flask. Rohit was curious to know what would happen. This morning, while he was getting ready for his school outing, Mother put a hot chocolate drink in his vacuum flask.

'You will be glad to have a hot drink at midday,' she said. But Rohit wondered if his drink would really stay hot all that time.

At last the lunch break arrived and Rohit unpacked his sandwiches. His vacuum flask certainly did not feel warm on the outside. But when Rohit opened it, he found his chocolate drink was still hot – very hot.

The outside of a vacuum flask only protects the glass flask inside. This glass flask has two walls. Between them there is no air, so the heat cannot travel between them and escape. That is why the hot liquid in a vacuum flask does not get cold quickly, and why cold liquid does not become warm.

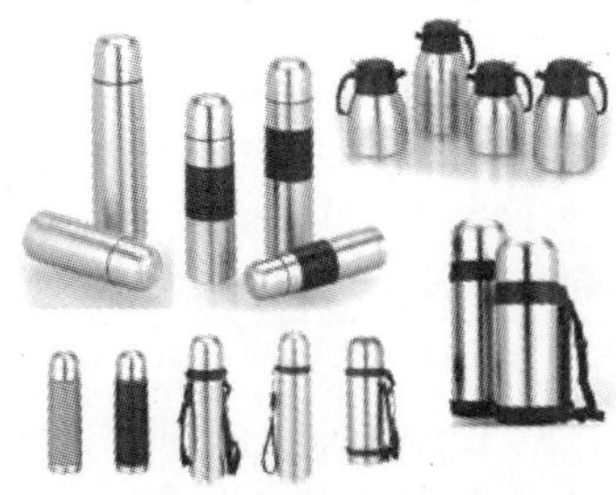

Valve. The purpose of a valve is to shut something off. Every tap has a valve. When you turn on a tap, the valve opens. Then the water can run through. When you turn the tap off, the valve closes.

Every steam locomotive must have a safety-valve. When there is too much steam in its boiler, a valve opens automatically and the Steam escapes.

Ventilator. Rohit was in a concert hall. It was very hot there. Suddenly he felt a cooling breeze. Someone had switched on a ventilator, driven by an electric current. Its small propeller spun very fast and sucked out the warm, stale air.

Veterinary surgeon. Poor Moti, our dog, has an injured leg. He can hardly walk on it. All right, old boy, I'll take you to see the vet. The vet looks at the sick animal, puts some iodine on the wound and bandages it up. Moti will soon be better.

An animal doctor's work is not at all easy. Animals cannot talk and tell the vet what is wrong with them. And vets have to know the illnesses of many kinds of animal. When dangerous diseases break out among chickens or sheep or cows, veterinary surgeons have a specially busy time.

Vinegar. If you leave a bottle of wine open in the summer, it will turn sour. The wine becomes vinegar. Pure vinegar (acetic acid) is colourless and has a very sharp smell. If you want to use it for seasoning food, you must first dilute it with water. You should never put food preserved with vinegar in brass or copper dishes, for the vinegar will form verdigris, which is a strong poison.

Vitamins. Harish always looked tired and pale. So his mother took him to the doctor. The doctor examined him and said, 'Give Harish lots of fruit and vegetables, milk, butter and cheese. These all contain important vitamins. And let him play a lot in the fresh air. In winter you must give him cod-liver oil. I will write out a prescription for him. With this you will be able to buy him vitamin tablets at the chemist. Vitamins only occur in tiny amounts in our food. But they are very important to keep us fit.'

Volcano. Mountains which erupt are called volcanoes. Active volcanoes have funnel-like craters which pour out smoke, steam, ashes and hot, liquid rock called lava. Two well-known volcanoes are Vesuvius in Italy and Etna in Sicily. There are many dead volcanoes in France and Germany. We say they are 'extinct' volcanoes.

W

Wagtail. A graceful bird perches beside a brook. It flies from one stone to another, walking quickly up and down and wagging its tail all the time. This bird is a wagtail.

Weeds. In summer, cornflowers, poppies, corn-cockles and daisies all flower in the corn fields. They look very pretty, but farmers do not like these flowers. They are weeds. They grow on places which are really meant for wheat and other crops, and they take nourishment from the soil which farmers want their wheat to have.

Of course these are only a few weeds; there are many other kinds, growing in fields and meadows. Weeds grow quickly, and that is why we often have to weed our gardens.

Whale. The whale is not a fish. In past centuries, people thought it was a fish, but now we know it is a warm-blooded mammal. A whale must also come to the surface of the sea to breathe.

These enormous animals live in the cold seas around the North Pole and the South Pole. They are the biggest creatures ever to have lived on this earth. A big blue whale weighs as much as 25 elephants! Yet it lives on tiny shrimp – like animals. People go to the polar seas in ships to hunt whales.

How the WHEEL developed. You can pull a piece of stone on a heavy sledge much more easily if you put tree trunks beneath the sledge. These tree trunks serve as rollers. Wheels may have developed from this sort of roller. At first, people had to move them forward all the time.

What do you think man first used as a draught animal? You will be surprised to learn it was – man himself.

Wild Ox. The wild ox is a horned beast which lives wild.

Woodpecker. The laughing call of a woodpecker echoes through the wood. He flies toward the trunk of a tall beech tree. You can see him clearly. He has green feathers and the top of his head is bright red. He climbs up the trunk in wide spirals. As he does this, he knocks all the time against the bark of the tree with his strong beak. He is searching for small insects. Ah, he finds something. His long sticky tongue flashes out and flicks an insect off the bark into his beak. He is a green woodpecker.

In our country there are other woodpeckers beside the green woodpecker. There are great spotted woodpeckers and lesser spotted woodpeckers. They are black and white with bits of red on their heads.

X

X-rays. About 100 years ago, the German Wilhelm Konrad Röntgen discovered invisible, mysterious rays. He called them 'X-rays'. He found that these rays can be made visible on a screen and on photographic plates. The rays penetrate wood, aluminium and the soft parts of our body.

Doctors are very grateful for X-rays. With X-rays, doctors can see if a person has a broken bone, or a metal splinter, or a bullet inside him, without having to cut the patient open.

Engineers use X-rays to examine the materials they work with. Scientists have invented X-ray machines for examining the iron girders of bridges, to make sure that there are no air-bubbles inside them, formed perhaps while the metal was molten.

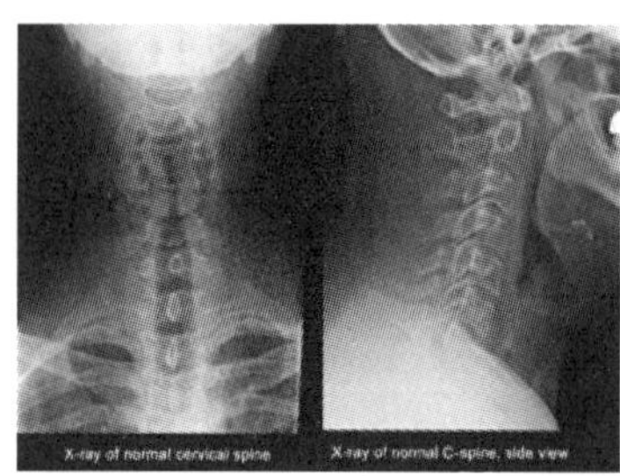

X-ray of normal cervical spine   X-ray of normal C-spine, side view

Xylem. Xylem is one of the two types of transport tissue in vascular plants the other being Phloem. The best-known xylem tissue is wood, though it is found throughout the plant. Its basic function is to transport water, but it also transports some nutrients through the plant.

Xmas. A common abbreviation of the word "Christmas".

Y

Yaks. Yaks are long-haired, cow-like animals that live in the high mountains north of India and nepal. People use yaks as beasts of burden. They also make ak-hair tents and drink yaks' milk.

Yeast. The word "yeast" comes to us from Old English gist, gyst, and from the Indo-European root yes-, meaning boil, foam, or bubble. Yeast microbes are probably one of the earliest domesticated organisms. People have used yeast for fermentation and baking throughout history. Archaeologists digging in Egyptian ruins found early grinding stones and baking chambers for yeasted bread, as well as drawings of 4,000-year-old bakeries and breweries. In 1680, the Dutch naturalist Anton van Leeuwenhoek first microscopically observed yeast, but at the time did not consider them to be living organisms, but rather globular structures. In 1857, French microbiologist Louis Pasteur proved that alcoholic fermentation was conducted by living yeasts and not by a chemical catalyst. Pasteur showed that by bubbling oxygen into the yeast broth, cell growth could be increased, but fermentation was inhibited – an observation later called the "Pasteur effect".

Egg **Yolk.** As a food, yolks are a major source of vitamins and minerals. They contain all of the egg's fat and cholesterol, and about one-fifth of the protein. Mixing the egg white and the yolk together before frying results in the pale yellow form found in omelettes and scrambled eggs.

Z

Zebra. A zebra is a sort of wild horse. Have a look at his white skin marked boldly with black-brown stripes. Zebras live in big herds, often with antelopes and sometimes with ostriches. They live on the great plains of Africa.

PERSONALITY DEVELOPMENT

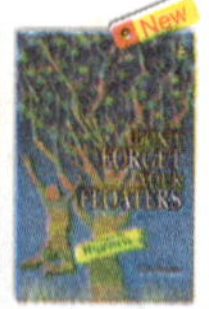

9487 E • Rs. 150/- 9490 H • Rs. 175/- 9450 B • Rs. 195/- 5642 A • Rs. 150/- 9447 C • Rs. 88/- 8966 E • Rs.100/- 9973 E • Rs. 110/- 5639 B • Rs. 80/-

Available in Tamil also.

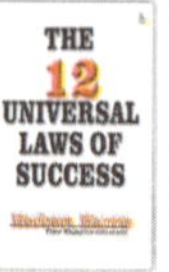

8868 D • Rs. 120/- 9028 D • Rs. 120/- 9981 B • Rs. 96/- 9088 C • Rs. 195/- 9070 B • Rs. 175/- 8997 B • Rs. 96/- 9430 B • Rs.150/-

STUDENT DEVELOPMENT

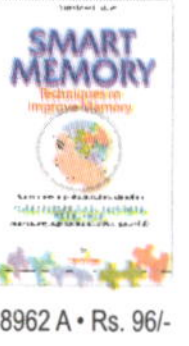

9457 E • Rs. 150/- 9455 C • Rs. 150/- 8962 A • Rs. 96/- 4016 D • Rs. 120/- 9089 D • Rs. 135/- 9967 C • Rs. 120/-

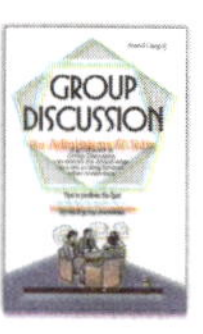

9071 D • Rs. 120/- 2244 D • Rs. 60/- 9441 S • Rs. 195/- 5622 A • Rs. 108/- 9090 A • Rs. 160/- 2241 J • Rs. 80/-

COMPUTERS

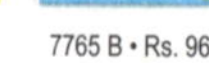

9478 K • Rs. 140/- 7765 B • Rs. 96/-

9471 C • Rs. 96/- 9460 J • Rs. 120/-

9462 M • Rs. 150/- 7766 A • Rs. 120/-

7712 K • Rs. 96/- 7711 J • Rs. 96/-

BODY/BEAUTY CARE

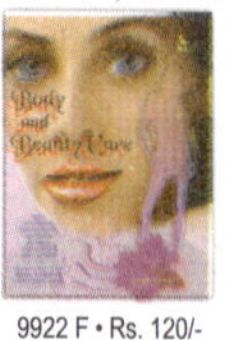

8093 D • Rs. 150/- 9986 B • Rs. 150/- 9922 F • Rs. 120/- 8865 F • Rs. 96/- 8971 B • Rs. 96/-

LOVE, SEX & ROMANCE

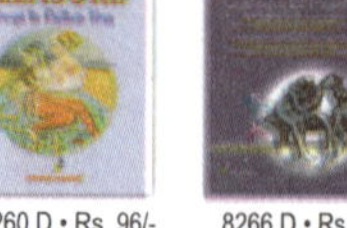

8260 D • Rs. 96/- 8266 D • Rs. 80/- 8278 C • Rs. 80/- 8916 D • Rs. 120/- 8268 C • Rs. 175/-

SAYINGS/QUOTATIONS/PROVERBS

8999 D • Rs. 80/- 9953 A • Rs. 68/- 5512 A • Rs. 120/-

8963 B • Rs. 80/- 9346 C • Rs. 60/- 9425 A • Rs. 60

SELF-IMPROVEMENT

9474 F • Rs. 150/-
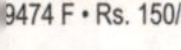

9464 R • Rs. 80/-

9096 B • Rs. 96/-

4008 J • Rs. 120/-

9027 D • Rs. 120-

8258 D • Rs. 120/-

9026 D • Rs. 175/-

9563 N • Rs. 125/-

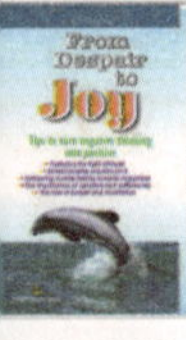

8928 D • Rs. 80/-

9066 B • Rs. 120/-

9081 D • Rs. 120/-

4010 L • Rs. 80/-

9091 B • Rs. 120/-

8885 D • Rs. 68/-

8947 E • Rs. 100/-

9449 A • Rs. 195/-

9466 T • Rs. 96/-

4009 K • Rs. 96/-

8943 C • Rs. 195/-

8935 D • Rs. 96/-

8990 C • Rs. 96/-

DIET & NUTRITION

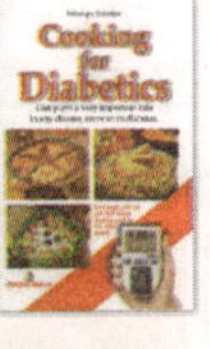

9941 D • Rs. 96/-

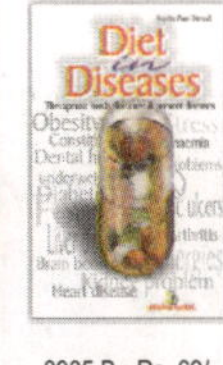

8985 B • Rs. 69/-

8904 D • Rs. 100/-

8276 A • Rs. 96/-

8968 G • Rs. 96/-

RELATIONSHIP

9458 G • Rs. 72/-

8998 C • Rs. 120/-

9438 B • Rs.150/-

9065 A • Rs. 80/-

9994 E • Rs. 120/-

JOB / CAREER

5623 B • Rs. 195/-

9404 D • Rs. 195/-

9439 C • Rs. 150/-

9431 C • Rs.175/-

4017 D • Rs. 120/-

4018 D • Rs. 80/-

9535 C • Rs. 150/-

PARENTING

9594 K • Rs. 80/-

8919 D • Rs. 96/-

8261 D • Rs. 150/-

ALTERNATIVE THERAPIES

8983 E • Rs. 100/- 8941 A • Rs. 80/- 8879 C • Rs. 60/- 5637 D • Rs. 96/-

8882 F • Rs. 150/- 8842 D • Rs. 100/- 8889 D • Rs. 80/- 8836 D • Rs. 135/-

8271 C • Rs. 96/- 2317 E • Rs. 60/- 9935 F • Rs. 120/- 9950 B • Rs. 120/-

GENERAL HEALTH

8877 A • Rs. 120/- 8870 D • Rs. 60/- 9029 D • Rs. 68/- 9075 C • Rs. 160/- 9940 D • Rs. 120/-

8938 D • Rs. 88/- 8948 A • Rs. 96/- 9025 D • Rs. 80/- 9038 D • Rs. 68/- 8859 G • Rs. 80/-

SLIMMING & FITNESS

9445 A • Rs. 150/- 8277 B • Rs. 80/- 8875 K • Rs. 80/- 8847 M • Rs. 60/-

COMMON AILMENTS & DISEASES

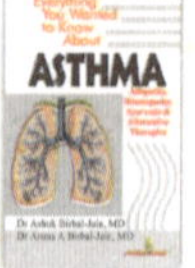

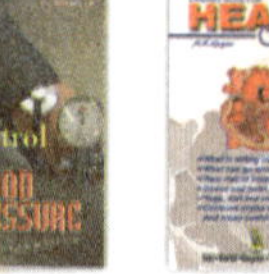

8281 A • Rs. 80/- 8094 D • Rs. 120/- 8888 D • Rs. 80/- 8908 D • Rs. 1

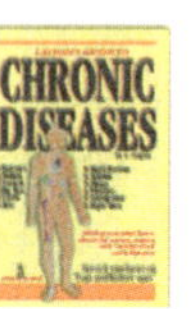
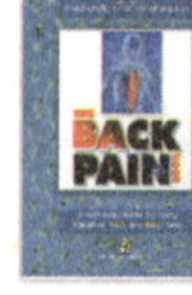

8964 C • Rs. 96/- 8848 D • Rs. 96/- 8878 B • Rs. 80/- 8891 D • Rs. 15

YOGA & MEDITATION

2118 F • Rs.120/- 8269 A • Rs.150/- 9087 B • Rs.120/- 9998 D • Rs.12(

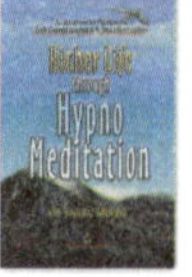

9080 C • Rs.24/- 8939 D • Rs.96/- 8099 D • Rs.80/- 8867 D • Rs.12

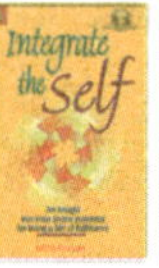

8901 D • Rs.120/- 9958 S • Rs.160/- (with CD) 2119 G • Rs.96/- 8892 D • Rs.120/- 9057 B • Rs. 9

HOMEOPATHY

9446 B • Rs.150/- 8887 D • Rs.175/- 8270 B • Rs.165

For buying online visit our *website:* www.pustakmahal.com • *E-mail:* orders@pustakmahal.com

HINDOOLOGY / RELIGION

Coffee Table Books

9453 A • Rs.340/- HB

4128 D • Rs. 250/- Colour (H.B.)

4177 C • Rs. 295/- (H.B.)

9987 E • Rs. 150/-

9812 R • Rs. 120/-

9983 D • Rs. 499/- Colour (H.B.)

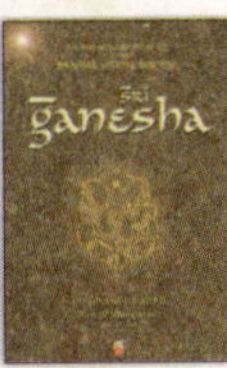
9508 D • Rs.95/-

4126 B • Rs. 96/-

9505 A • Rs.195/-

4183 A • Rs. 350/- (H.B.)

9585 A • Rs. 96/-

4151 A • Rs. 399/- Colour (H.B.)

4133 A • Rs. 60/-

8898 D • Rs. 80/-

4124 A • Rs. 80/-

9405 A • Rs. 195/-

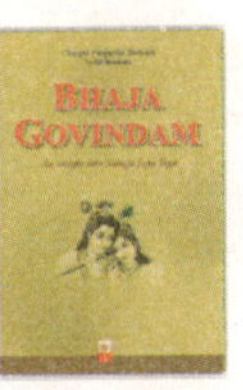
9514 B • Rs.60/-

9984 E • Rs. 399/- Colour (H.B.)

9513 A • Rs.175/-

4190 C • Rs. 160/-

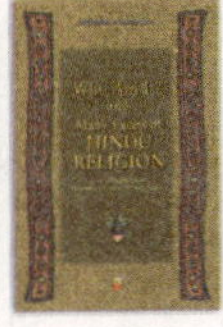
9520 D • Rs. 120/-

9510 B • Rs.120/-

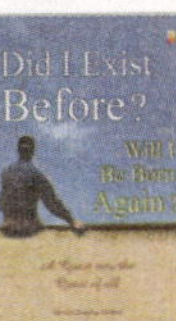
9542 B • Rs. 150/-

4182 D • Rs. 96/-

4130 B • Rs. 120/-

4152 B • Rs. 96/-

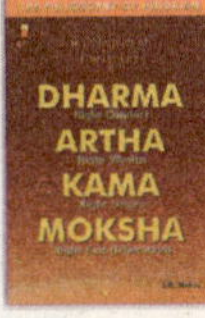
4134 B • Rs. 80/-

9509 A • Rs.150/-

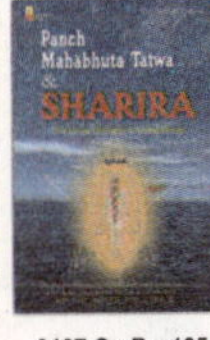
9407 C • Rs. 195/-

9525 A • Rs. 150/-

9504 D • Rs. 100/-

9989 D • Rs. 96/-

4181 C • Rs. 195/-

9540 D • Rs. 150/-

9069 A • Rs. 80/-

4179 A • Rs. 295/- (H.B.)

4132 D • Rs. 80/-

9063 D • Rs. 80/-

9997 C • Rs. 80/-

Commenteries on BHAGAVAD GITA

9959 D • Rs. 80/- 4113 D • Rs. 48/- 4188 A • Rs. 160/-

COOKERY BOOKS

9936 D • Rs. 120/- 9320 A • Rs. 125/- 9297 C • Rs. 125/- 9948 D • Rs. 80/- 9962 C • Rs. 125/-

9938 D • Rs. 100/- 9942 D • Rs. 80/- 9944 D • Rs. 80/- 9943 D • Rs. 80/-

HOMEMAKING / GRILLS & RAILINGS

3111 E • Rs. 175/- 3107 F • Rs. 88/- 3106 E • Rs. 88/- 3108 G • Rs. 90/-

3102 K • Rs. 195/-(H.B.) 3103 L • Rs. 88/- 3104 M • Rs. 88/- 3105 D • Rs. 88/-

JOKES

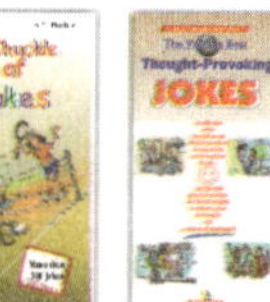

2319 B • Rs. 96/- 2341 B • Rs. 60/- 2318 A • Rs. 80/- 2330 B • Rs. 80/- 9226 A • Rs. 60/-

MYSTERIES / GHOSTS / ADVENTURE

9488 F • Rs. 100/- 9489 G • Rs. 100/- 9483 A • Rs. 100/- 5175 K • Rs. 10

2331 C • Rs. 60/- 9463 P • Rs. 100/- 9985 A • Rs. 80/- 9815 C • Rs. 100/- 5121 K • Rs. 10(

5164 E • Rs. 100/- 9977 B • Rs. 96/- 2337 C • Rs. 96/- 9465 S • Rs. 100/- 9472 D • Rs. 10C

5156 D • Rs. 72/- 5172 F • Rs. 72/- 5121 K • Rs. 72/- 2336 B • Rs. 80/- 51107 • Rs.100/-

5116 D • Rs. 72/- 2335 A • Rs. 80/-

Moral, Wisdom & Fairy Tales

8967 F • Rs. 80/- 9077 E • Rs. 120/-

9248 C • Rs. 60/- 2289 D • Rs. 72/-

QUIZ BOOKS

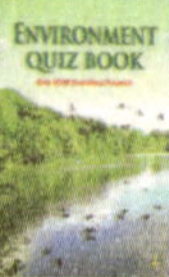

8965 D • Rs. 96/- 7727 L • Rs. 80/- 7723 F • Rs. 100/- 7726 K • Rs. 100/- 7753 G • Rs. 100/- 7722 E • Rs. 100/- 7725 J • Rs. 72/-

ASTROLOGY / VASTU / HYPNOTISM / PALMISTRY

25 D • Rs. 80/- | 8899 D • Rs. 110/- | 9432 D • Rs.150/- | 8259 D • Rs. 88/- | 2125 D • Rs. 80/- | 2133 B • Rs. 96/- | 2109 F • Rs. 120/- | 8902 D • Rs. 80/-

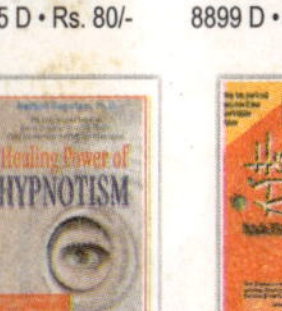

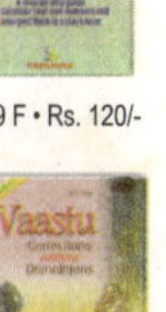

32 A • Rs. 150/- | 2127 D • Rs. 150/- | 9086 A • Rs. 295/- (H.B.) | 2112 D • Rs. 120/- | 2108 E • Rs. 80/- | 2116 D • Rs. 110/- | 3110 D • Rs. 96/- | 2120 D • Rs. 96/-

ENGLISH IMPROVEMENT

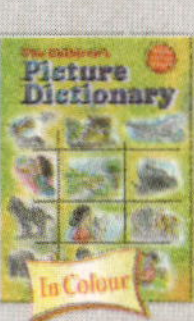
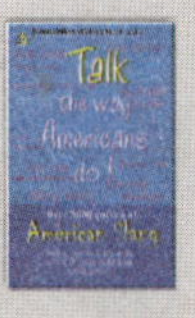

9448 D • Rs. 175/- | 5511 E • Rs. 72/- | 6651 E • Rs. 175/- | 5538 D • Rs. 80/- | 6607 L • Rs. 88/- | 5541 C • Rs. 196/- | 9040 D • Rs. 60/- | 9056 A • Rs. 96/-

GENERAL

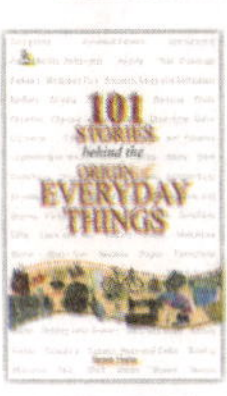

022 D • Rs. 80/-HB | 9041 A • Rs.195/- | 5114 B • Rs.68/- | 4175 A • Rs. 195/- | 9532 D • Rs. 250/- HB

FUN, FACTS

479 M • Rs. 120/- | 9816 D • Rs. 100/- | 9470 B • Rs. 100/- | 9326 B • Rs. 96/- | 6690 D • Rs. 60/- | 2328 G • Rs. 50/-

484 B • Rs. 150/- | 2275 D • Rs. 120/- | 2247 F • Rs. 60/- | 2327 F • Rs. 50/- | 2211 F • Rs. 60/- | 5110 A • Rs. 80/-

MAGIC

2250 A • Rs. 110/- | 2202 E • Rs. 80/-

2237 M • Rs. 60/- | 2242 K • Rs. 60/-

2208 M • Rs. 100/- | 2243 L • Rs. 60/-

3509/2/12

MANAGEMENT / BUSINESS & PROFESSION / STOCK MARKET

9461 K • Rs. 135/- | 5638 A • Rs. 110/- | 8979 A • Rs. 96/- | 9406 B • Rs. 150/-

5646 A • Rs. 225/- | 5643 B • Rs. 120/- | 8972 C • Rs. 80/- | 9402 B • Rs. 195/-

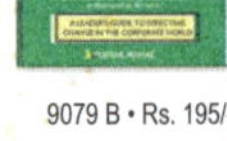

5614 E • Rs. 150/- | 9079 B • Rs. 195/- | 9403 C • Rs. 195/- | 5618 D • Rs. 88/-

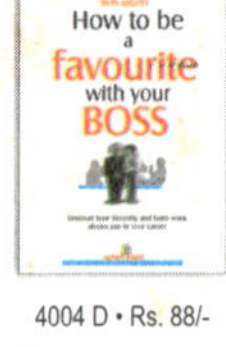

5615 D • Rs. 150/- | 4001 A • Rs. 150/- | 4004 D • Rs. 88/- | 5641 D • Rs. 195/- (H.B.)

5640 C • Rs. 120/- | 9313 D • Rs. 150/- | 8883 D • Rs. 120/- | 4005 E • Rs. 150/-

AYURVEDA

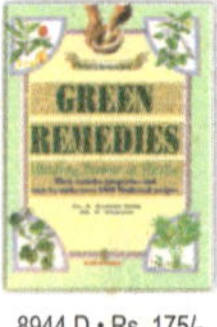
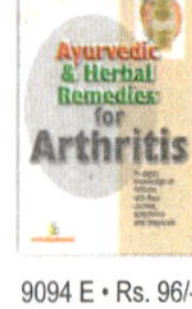

8923 D • Rs. 150/- | 8010 D • Rs. 88/- | 8944 D • Rs. 175/- | 9094 E • Rs. 96/-

TOP SELLING HINDI BOOKS

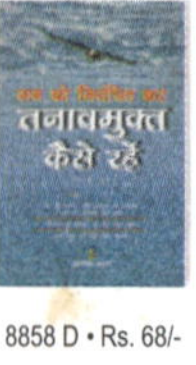

9913 G • Rs. 150/- | 9979 D • Rs. 80/- | 8858 D • Rs. 68/- | 8987 D • Rs. 80/-

9410 A • Rs. 72/- | 9975 H • Rs. 60/- | 8929 D • Rs. 100/- | 8880 D • Rs. 120/-

9471 K • Rs. 140/- | 9460 J • Rs. 120/- | 7765 B • Rs. 96/- | 9471 C • Rs. 96/-

9477 J • Rs. 100/- | 9454 B • Rs. 96/- | 8096 D • Rs. 150/- | 9990 A • Rs. 100/-

2260 D • Rs. 120/- | 9085 D • Rs. 120/- | 2214 S • Rs. 135/- | 8263 D • Rs. 80/-

9934 D • Rs. 80/- | 8011 A • Rs. 120/- | 9951 C • Rs. 72/- | 8993 B • Rs. 80/-